JET XI

✝

Forsaken

Russell Blake

First edition.

ISBN-13: 978-1540563156

Published by

Reprobatio Limited

CHAPTER 1

Baku, Azerbaijan

Martial music blared over a large crowd gathered at the Dede Gorgud Park plaza in the Baku city center. A pair of combat helicopters orbited in the cobalt sky above the paved expanse, where a grandstand had been erected near a wide pond, its black framework festooned with colorful streamers that shimmered like the tails of exotically plumed birds in the early fall breeze. Massive speakers framed the stage, where a band played with determination as the throng milled in front, killing time as it waited for the main event to begin, the mood festive as bottles made the rounds and laughter drifted from barrel-chested men with meaty faces.

Children ran through the freshly trimmed grass of a nearby field. The air was perfumed with rich wood smoke from food carts, where vendors grilled skewered delicacies. An old man tugged at a kite riding an updraft to the delight of three urchins, their faces upturned in amazement at the seeming miracle of the paper diamond's levitation. His gnarled but skilled fingers made it dance and spin as he played out a few yards of string to send it diving before it caught a gust and soared again.

Militarized police in riot gear stood on the sidewalk just beyond the carts, their bullpup machine guns and pump shotguns as menacing as their black helmets, Kevlar vests, and combat boots. The rally for the Nationalist Party's candidate was a controversial affair, and while the attendees were peaceful, the display of strength was to warn off any potential disruption by protestors who differed with the party's platform. An earlier rally in Ganja the prior month had been marred by violence as the incumbent party's adherents clashed with

1

nationalists, resulting in dozens injured and still more arrested.

Paddleboats meandered along the still surface of an emerald pond just beyond the shadows of the nearby Soviet-era apartment blocks that stretched toward the water like inky fingers. Clumps of inebriated spectators watched the watercraft while they waited for the main event to begin, the faint stench from the nearby zoo masked by the aroma of cooking treats.

Most had been there for hours, there being little else to do on a lazy Sunday. Some had been bused in by the organizers, others arrived by train; the party primarily appealed to the nation's large disenfranchised working class for whom personal cars were a luxury. The party's main support was in the country's slums, and it presented itself as the voice of the laborers who had been left behind as the nation's petroleum wealth disappeared into the pockets of connected administration cronies while the government stood by and did nothing.

A man in his early thirties, his dusting of beard flecked with premature gray, pushed a broom along one of the paths that led to an abandoned train station that had once served as the loading area for a children's railway that ringed the park in decades past. His blue coveralls were dusty and the knees stained, and he walked with a slight limp in scuffed boots worn from years of toil. A close inspection would have revealed eyes far above the intelligence level of the average laborer behind his cheap sunglasses, but nobody bothered, the security pass hanging around his neck sufficient to blunt any suspicion.

He paused and leaned on his broom as he killed time, taking in the security detail without seeming to, confirming their location at the perimeter, as well as the undercover cops stationed strategically around the plaza. While not lax, the security was mediocre at best, and the janitor had to stifle an urge to smile. Nobody had checked his rolling trash bin or the broom – not that they would have found anything unless they'd X-rayed them. Secreted in the broom handle was the barrel of an untraceable sniper rifle, and the false bottom of the bin concealed an Armalite stock, breech, and trigger mechanism, along with a commonly available commercial scope and a single round of .308 ammunition, preloaded. The entire assembly had been fashioned from a hodgepodge of Russian weapons, none of them traceable.

Yael was a seasoned professional with dozens of executions under his belt, and he'd already managed the trickiest part of the mission: getting within easy range of where the target would stand to deliver his speech. In less than an hour, the orator would shed his mortal coil while on stage, the victim of a lone assassin who would be shot before he could be arrested. Yael's handler had already set up a patsy – a drug-addled ex-soldier in the latter stages of terminal liver disease who would bolt from cover at the appropriate moment, pistol in hand, drawing the fire of the soldiers and cops in exchange for a handsome sum paid to his mother in an offshore account.

Like so many executions, appearances would be of a disgruntled militant rather than a highly trained operative of a foreign intelligence service, and the entire incident would be wrapped up neatly so there were no loose ends. Now, Yael simply had to find his way to the nearby sound booth, where he could conceal himself in the two-story platform and wait for the main event.

He returned to work, pushing the wide broom with the characteristic lack of enthusiasm of the other workers policing the area, and inched closer to the sound booth as he cleaned leaves and dust from the walkway. He was nearly to the booth when he felt a thrill of apprehension, and he slowed, searching to identify what had triggered his silent alarm.

There.

Two men in windbreakers, eyeing him, one of them with a radio in hand.

Yael remained outwardly relaxed and apparently uninterested in the scrutiny, but his heart rate increased by twenty beats per minute. He controlled his breathing, ignoring the undercover policemen, and offered a silent prayer that they would move on to more promising targets.

It wasn't to be.

The one with the radio raised it to his lips as the other began walking toward Yael, one hand in his pocket, the bulge of a weapon obvious to Yael's trained eye. Yael debated attempting to bluff his way through any questioning, but something about how they'd zeroed in on him gave him pause, and he swallowed hard.

Aborting the mission was a difficult option, but if it was a choice between that or being caught, there was nothing he could do but call it off. He continued sweeping as his mind churned, and then he whispered a few words that his concealed microphone would carry to his handler.

"Something's wrong. I'm pulling out."

He didn't wait for a response and instead picked up his pace slightly and altered his trajectory away from the sound booth, heading for a line of portable toilets that would offer cover. The cop was still at least fifty yards away, and the man hadn't broken into a run, which gave Yael pause – maybe he was overreacting, his nerves too close to the surface?

"You. With the broom," a voice called out, and Yael instantly knew he'd called it correctly. Somehow he'd been blown. How could be figured out later. For now, he needed to get clear of the plaza.

Yael pretended not to hear the warning shout, and then he was ducking behind the shelter of the toilets, all pretense of stealth abandoned as he made for the crowd lingering around the vendor carts on the opposite side. Nobody would shoot into a group of innocent bystanders – at least, that was his hope.

He was a fast runner, but he resisted the urge to bolt, keeping his pace to a fast walk, wary of drawing any further attention. But he knew he couldn't outrun the radio, and his options were diminishing with each passing second.

He reached the crowd and hunched down, continuing to walk quickly as he unzipped his overalls. Once in the press, he shrugged out of the sleeves and pulled the remainder of the outfit off, leaving him in nondescript jeans and a dun-colored sweater. He balled the overalls into a wad, dropped them into a trash bin, and slowed his pace so he blended in with the rest of the gathering.

Yael spotted the cop out of the corner of his eye as he neared the motorcycle he'd parked among several hundred others, and slouched lower. All he needed was a few more seconds…

"You! By the motorcycles. Stop! Police!"

Yael obeyed the order and waited as the cop came at a trot, his weapon now drawn. Any doubt that Yael was blown evaporated at the sight of the pistol. Nobody in their right mind would pull a gun and risk panicking the crowd unless they were sure there was a legitimate threat.

"What is it?" Yael demanded, his hands by his sides, keys to the motorcycle in his right, the fob in his palm.

"Put your hands up. Now," the cop warned as he approached.

Yael slowly obeyed, his expression puzzled. The cop spotted the keys and pointed at them with his gun. "Drop that," he ordered.

"What? These? It's just my keys," Yael said, estimating the distance to the officer at less than ten yards.

"I said drop them," the cop repeated as he drew closer.

"Why? What's going on here? And who are you?" Yael asked, stalling.

"I told you. Police. Now drop the keys. Final warning."

Yael shrugged and angled his hand, and then depressed one of the buttons. A blast of compressed gas coughed from it, and the cop grunted as the projectile Yael had fired struck him in the upper chest, easily penetrating his shirt. Yael threw himself to the side as the cop struggled to raise his weapon, and then the man crumpled as the weaponized toxin hit his system and paralysis set in.

Yael was back on his feet and lunging for the motorcycle even as the cop's gun hit the ground with a clatter, and barely heard the shriek of whistles over the sound of the big engine roaring to life. He slammed the gear shifter with his foot and twisted the throttle, leaning forward over the handlebars to present as small a target as possible, expecting gunfire at any moment as he leapt the curb and zigzagged toward one of the barricades that had been erected to block traffic. He picked up speed as he rushed toward it, aware of the soldiers nearby twisting toward him with their rifles in hand.

When the shots began, he was already zipping past the barricades in a blur, secure in the knowledge that hitting a fast-moving target, even with an assault rifle, was nearly impossible, especially if you wanted to avoid collateral casualties. His leg clipped one steel rod of a barricade as he blew past, sending a shriek of pain through him as he accelerated, his teeth clenched in determination.

A police car raced toward him, its roof lights flashing and siren klaxoning, and he swerved left and made for Koroglu Park, where the trees could provide cover. He jumped the curb as more shots rang out from behind him, and then he was streaking through the trees. Bullets snapped by him and ricochets whined off the pavement as he maneuvered. A startled family dove for cover at the sight of a madman tearing along the path amidst the barking of gunfire from the plaza, and he poured on the gas before exiting the other side of the park onto a busy street. He narrowly missed being crushed by a truck as he swerved onto the boulevard to a chorus of horns, and then he was speeding through gaps in traffic, urging the motorcycle to greater speed as he revved through the gears, the engine screaming into the redline.

A shadow passed over him, and he chanced a quick look skyward. A helicopter hovered above, shadowing him. Yael could almost feel the crosshairs of a police sniper on his back and understood that it was only a matter of moments before a high-velocity round tore through him, ending his flight. He wended back and forth, slowing and speeding up as his mind raced, piloting the motorcycle erratically. He needed to lose the aircraft or at least find a way to ditch the bike out of sight of the helo and buy himself enough time to evade it on foot.

A siren howled behind him and a police cruiser shot from a side street, forcing him forward at a suicidal pace. He darted through a tight opening between a bus and a car and cut hard right, drawing the bus's ire and a shriek of brakes. Yael gunned the engine and pointed the handlebars at the sidewalk, bumping onto the strip of cement and scattering pedestrians as he tore along the walkway. He rocketed past the entrance to a shopping area and twisted the front wheel back onto the street, sideswiping a vendor pushing a food cart in the process before darting between two trucks, leaving the squad car well behind.

Another glance overhead told him he wouldn't lose the helicopter so easily. If he didn't, it would radio his location, and it would be only a matter of minutes until his escape was blocked as the police organized. A horn warned him away from a van that had turned from an alley, and he cranked the handlebars hard left and entered the narrow passage between tall rows of buildings.

Yael slowed at an overflowing dumpster and stopped at a brick wall. The alley was a dead end and didn't let out on the next street. He looked around and spotted a set of steps that led to a maintenance walkway along the side of one of the buildings, and he coaxed the motorcycle up the stairs. The engine was deafening in the cramped passage.

He picked up speed once on the walkway and then nearly went over the handlebars when a steel access door swung open just ahead of him, and he was forced to clamp down on the brakes with all his might. A frightened man carrying a carton froze at the sight of a madman on a motorbike and then dropped the box and flattened himself against the wall as Yael sped past him in a blur.

The bike bounced out onto the sidewalk and into another busy street. Traffic streamed straight at him on the one-way thoroughfare. Yael ignored the oncoming cars and pointed the bike at the lane between the vehicles, determined to evade the helicopter while he still had a chance.

A traffic light ahead turned yellow, and he gave the throttle a brutal twist and downshifted to coax an additional burst of power as the onrushing cars honked and swerved to avoid hitting him. The grill of a large delivery truck loomed ahead, and he jumped the curb again to avoid being flattened, gunning the gas to make the light. He barely missed a lamppost on the corner and blew through the intersection – and then he was sailing through the air, weightless, the motorcycle somersaulting away from him as though in slow motion, the sky a blue so deep it resembled an endless sea, and the blinding pain that had shot through his body a moment before replaced by numbness as he stared at the heavens in wonder.

Traffic screeched to a standstill and a woman on the sidewalk screamed in horror, but Yael barely registered any of it as he completed his arc, strangely at peace for the first time in forever. When he hit the pavement like a rag doll, his skull and upper body were instantly liquefied by the force of the landing, and he was dead before the first bounce. Nearby, steam hissed from beneath the hood of the yellow delivery van that had ended his run, the front crumpled as though struck by a giant fist.

CHAPTER 2

Subotica, Serbia

Matt stepped back from the second-story boardinghouse window and shook his head. Jet looked up from where she was reading to Hannah from a children's book and offered him a smile.

"Still a nightmare?" she asked.

"Streets are teeming," he replied.

"That's good. Nobody's going to be looking for us in this chaos."

They'd decided to make their way to the Hungarian border, where refugee camps had sprung up to accommodate the hundreds of thousands of refugees trying to enter the European Union, fleeing the destruction in their countries from nonstop wars in Syria and Iraq. The humanitarian crisis presented an opportunity for them to blend in with the masses, as all of the systems at the borders were overloaded from the endless tide of desperate humanity. Modern dangers to Jet and Matt such as facial recognition software and fingerprint databases had been overwhelmed by the crisis and abandoned early on in favor of processing the refugees as speedily as possible.

Of course, as in all conflicts, there were opportunities for unscrupulous operators, and they'd assumed this situation would be no different. After nosing around for a few days, they had learned that the city had a thriving underworld catering to the migrant trade, able and willing to supply anything one could want, assuming they could pay. Guns, paperwork, drugs – all were available for a price.

They'd decided to become Syrian refugees rather than attempting to cross into Hungary using their current passports upon learning that migrants were processed differently, with fewer safeguards and nonexistent checks. Most had no paperwork and thus would be issued the equivalent of a passport after a cursory check, making it relatively straightforward to acquire and use that documentation to enter the EU under the radar.

Many of the Syrians had European features, so Matt's and Hannah's appearances wouldn't stand out, making their story plausible as long as they kept silent; neither Matt nor Hannah spoke Arabic, so Jet was the only one who could withstand questioning. They'd agreed that Matt would claim to be mute and deaf if confronted, and Hannah was too young to have developed much in the way of language skills and could be claimed to be in shock from the war, if pushed.

But now they needed to source a reliable provider of papers so they could continue on their way, ultimately to Italy or Portugal, where many areas had little in the way of modern systems and were much as they had been for centuries, enabling them to remain incognito. Perhaps life in a hill town of Umbria or a village in Sicily would provide the tranquility and safety that had eluded them so far. At least, that was the hope.

"Much as I'm enjoying the charms of greater Subotica, we need to keep moving, Matt," Jet said.

"I know. I think the landlady will be able to help."

They'd already spoken with the innkeeper, a heavyset woman in her forties whose pores exuded the remnants of the prior evening's libation and whose flushed complexion left little doubt about how she spent her leisure hours. After some broad hints by Jet, she'd promised to touch base with her cousin, who had set up shop crafting travel documents for those who didn't want to spend months in the squalor of the camps, waiting for the real thing. That had been yesterday, but when they'd gone down for lunch, there had been no sign of the woman. Her replacement, a truculent younger version of herself, eyed them like they were lice.

They had deliberately chosen a boardinghouse filled with the more fortunate refugees – escapees from their region who had managed to land in Serbia with at least some money. The camps were grim, disease-infested hellholes, and anyone who was able to avoided them until their wherewithal ran out. Once in Serbia, Jet had adopted the modest attire of a Syrian woman and scarcely drew a second glance when out of the room, but even so she was keeping to the boardinghouse as much as possible, reluctant to risk any altercations with locals who were clearly fed up with the never-ending procession of misery.

A rap at the door startled them, and Jet handed Hannah's book to Matt before rising and moving to the door.

"Yes?" she asked, her Serbian deliberately rusty sounding.

A muffled voice answered through the door. "It's Elena. I have news."

Jet slipped the bolt free and opened the door to the innkeeper. Elena hesitated and then stepped inside. "My cousin agreed to help you. I can take you to him now."

Jet nodded. "Great. Let me get my things, and I'll meet you downstairs. How far away is he?"

"Not very. We can walk."

Jet waited until Elena left and then gathered some of her cash and slipped it into the pocket of her cargo pants. She covered her clothes with a dark abaya, pulled a hijab over her head, and turned to leave.

"You think this is legit?" Matt asked, his brow creased.

"She's got no reason to con us. I mean, besides the usual, I suppose. Only one way to find out."

"Be careful."

Jet bent down to Hannah and smoothed her hair. "Mama will be back in a little while. Don't give Matt any trouble."

Hannah nodded, her face angelic.

Jet swallowed hard and left her loved ones in the room. She heard the bolt snap back into place behind her and walked down the seedy hallway to the stairs. The building was easily a century old, half of it spent without any maintenance or cleaning that she could see. Music from one of the rooms echoed off the walls, a caterwaul that sounded like two cats fighting while someone pounded on a barrel. Jet's nose wrinkled at the stink of food seeping from beneath the doors, a clear violation of Elena's rule against cooking in the room that she seemed oblivious to as long as the boarders paid their rent on time.

The innkeeper was waiting in the squalid lobby and set off at a march down the cracking sidewalk before Jet's feet had left the stairs, leaving Jet to catch up as best she could. They walked three blocks down a main street, turned onto a smaller tributary, and continued toward the town center, past distinctly Turkish-influenced architecture, all columns and arches and spires.

Elena stopped at a run-down building where several toughs were lounging on the stoop, smoking and commenting on the passersby. One nodded to her and looked Jet over with eyes the color of lead. Jet averted her gaze, ignoring the obvious distaste in the young man's expression. His barely concealed hatred wasn't her problem as long as he didn't start trouble.

"Got another rat, eh?" the man said. The other laughed harshly, his voice ravaged by alcohol, cigarettes, and probably drugs, judging from his junkie pallor.

"She speaks some Serbian," Elena snapped, her tone hard.

The punk shrugged. "I don't care if she understands or not." He nodded to the entry. "He's inside."

Elena pushed past them and Jet mounted the steps, determined not to retaliate if one of the toughs made a grab at her. Fortunately, nobody did, and moments later they were in a run-down tenement that was only slightly better than the inn. Elena powered toward the worn stairs and mounted them with surprising energy for a big woman, trailing a faint scent of alcohol from her afternoon bracer. Jet accompanied her to the second level, and they stopped at the third door from the landing. Elena glanced at Jet and rapped on it twice with knuckles the size of walnuts.

"Yeah?" a male voice yelled from inside.

"It's me. Open up," Elena called.

Ten seconds later the door swung wide, and a rail-thin man in his early thirties, his hair greasy and a smoldering cigarette hanging from his lips, stared at them for a long beat. Elena brushed past him and he stepped back for Jet to step inside, his eyes roving over the hallway as though expecting to be attacked at any moment.

He locked the door behind them and joined them in a postage stamp-sized living area with the world's saddest sofa against one wall and a dingy area rug on the hardwood floor. The sunlight filtering through filthy gauze curtains seemed somehow tainted by the atmosphere. The man took a seat on a rickety chair while Elena and Jet sat opposite him on the sofa's stained fabric.

"I'm Eric. You need papers?" he said, the cigarette never leaving his lips.

Jet nodded. "That's right. We want into the EU."

Eric named a relatively reasonable price, which instantly put Jet on guard. If the forger sensed her caution, he didn't show it, his air disinterested but his body language anxious. "Half now, half when you pick up the documents."

"How long will it take?" she asked.

"Two days. You have the money?"

"Barely. What about photos?"

"You need to get some taken at one of the shops. Bring them to me when you come to pick up the papers. It only takes a few minutes to attach them." Eric offered an oily smile devoid of humor. "Everyone knows what size. It's a big business these days."

"Can I see a sample of the work?" Jet asked.

Eric's eyes hardened. "I don't hand out samples. You want me to make the docs or not? If no, you know where the door is."

"No offense, but I want to make sure they'll hold up."

Eric gestured impatiently to Elena. "Where do you find these people? Why are you wasting my time?"

Elena rose, her expression angry. "She said she needed help. How was I to know?"

Jet softened her tone. "Everybody calm down. If you guarantee the work, that's good enough for me."

Eric smirked. "This isn't my first time. Now you have the money, or are we done? I've got things to do."

Jet looked at the overflowing ashtray and the half-full bottle of beer on the coffee table, but kept her expression neutral. "I have it," she said, and removed the pre-counted wad from her pocket and slid it across to Eric, who counted it carefully before nodding once.

"What do you want on the documents?" he asked.

Elena walked to the door.

"I'll leave you to it. You can find your way to the boardinghouse without me?" she asked Jet.

"Yes. I remember the way."

Ten minutes later Jet was back on the street, taking in the surroundings, an uneasy feeling in her stomach. She ignored the leers from the toughs and made her way down the sidewalk toward the main boulevard, where the streets were crowded with refugees wandering with the aimless shuffle of the hopeless. Jet paused at the corner, aware that she was being watched from several of the windows, the frowning women's faces behind the glass damning her wordlessly for being there.

"Only a little while longer," she muttered to herself. While her situation was temporary, a cover she could discard whenever she liked, for the rest this state of purgatory was their constant reality, and she again felt in her gut the anxiety that had troubled her since their arrival. The locals and the refugees had established a cautious truce, but nobody was fooled that the migrants were welcome. Her hope was that they could get their documents and make it across the border without incident, and once en route, leave the enmity behind. While she could appreciate how the Serbians felt, she recognized a powder keg when she saw one, and would exhale in relief when they were in Hungary and free to travel to their ultimate destination without the constant stigma and barely contained hostility at every turn.

She picked up her pace, rounded the corner, and melted into the crowd, unremarkable in the wave of humanity and grateful for the anonymity her disguise afforded. After a week on the run from Romania, being just another faceless cypher carried with it a freedom she hadn't felt since Bosnia – a freedom that had proved to be as illusory as it was seductive.

CHAPTER 3

Baku, Azerbaijan

Moonlight silvered the surface of a puddle in the middle of an alley only footsteps from the waterfront. The distinctive smell of the Caspian Sea drifted along the narrow street, carried by a light wind that whistled through the beams of a construction site at one end of the block. Fog had begun rolling in from the water, and its ghostly tendrils seeped across the pavement, its timeworn cobblestones slick from condensation. The area was deserted at the late hour except for the slinking form of a half-starved feline nosing through sacks of refuse on the sidewalk in search of a midnight meal.

A black Mercedes sedan pulled to a stop at the back door of a closed nightclub, and a pair of overfed men in their fifties emerged from the rear of the vehicle and strode to where a guard was waiting in the shadows, the bulge of a shoulder holster wrinkling his suit jacket. The men nodded to the sentry, and he looked them up and down before stepping aside and returning his attention to the darkened street.

Inside the club, another gunman with a pockmarked face directed the arrivals down a hall to a gray steel door, where still two more guards waited with submachine guns, their expressions those of experienced killers, their eyes slits in stony countenances. The taller of the gunmen regarded the pair and grunted.

"Inside," he said, his sandpaper voice gruff.

The second guard pushed the door open, and the new arrivals entered a storage room where a dozen men were seated around a battered oval conference table. A groaning ventilation system struggled to clear a haze of cigarette smoke that hung over the

15

gathering like a shroud. A hatchet-faced man at one end of the table looked up as they entered, his wire spectacles flashing in the light from the overhead fluorescent bulbs, and nodded.

"Gentlemen, good to see you. Have a seat, and we can get this show under way."

The speaker waited as the men settled in before continuing, taking the room's measure with a jaundiced eye. Yashar Bahador was an experienced politician who was playing a high stakes game for the future of the country. As the highly recognizable candidate of the Nationalist Party, he was hated by the status quo almost as much as he was feared by the cronies of the ruling Labor Party – a collection of elite billionaires and criminal oligarchs who ran the government from behind the throne.

He cleared his throat and sat back, allowing his gaze to settle on each of the group before speaking again.

"As I was just saying, we've reached a crisis point for our future. This is the election where the current regime must be overthrown. We cannot afford any more of the corruption that's typified the last decade. The economy is in shambles, and the disparity between the rich and poor grows wider with every hour. Most are no better off than they were under Soviet rule, living hand-to-mouth in near poverty. It's unconscionable, given the wealth of natural resources we hold, that most of the prosperity is so tightly concentrated in a few greedy hands."

A stern figure at the opposite end of the table, his face deeply lined and swarthy, his high forehead topped by silver hair slicked back like a cinema villain, raised an eyebrow at the pronouncement. "Yes, yes, Yashar, we are all aware of the situation. You don't need to carry on like we're at a fund-raising rally. Why have you called us together at this late hour in this…place?"

General Pasha Guliyev had the no-nonsense delivery of a man accustomed to command, and Bahador allowed the question to hang in the air for several seconds before responding. He sat forward and folded his hands in front of him on the table, checking the time on a cheap metal watch as he considered his words. Instead of lashing out at the general, he looked to his right, where a younger man in an impeccable foreign-tailored suit was slouched in his chair. "Sergei?"

"The president is not going to relinquish power voluntarily," Sergei said. "We're already receiving reports of preparations to rig the election. That cannot be allowed to happen."

Guliyev's frown deepened. "We've heard the same thing. But what can be done?"

Bahador matched his scowl. "We're protesting to international organizations chartered with ensuring the vote tallying is fair, but the administration seems unfazed. Their actions are increasingly bold, and coupled with the clampdown on dissidents, it's looking like they will succeed in their power grab."

"Will that be enough? Last time they turned out to be largely useless. They cited numerous irregularities, but so what?" Guliyev asked.

"Gentlemen, we're here to brainstorm," Bahador said. "With the elections only a few weeks away, nothing is off the table, no matter how outlandish. Among all of you, a tremendous amount of power is gathered in this room. We need to understand the depth of your commitment and what support we can expect in a variety of scenarios – some of them highly unpleasant."

Guliyev shook his head. "You talk like a gypsy, in riddles. If you have something to propose, spit it out or stop wasting our time."

Sergei cleared his throat. "It has come to our attention that there are factions we may be able to work with, who can counter much of the president's scheme," he began, and continued speaking for five minutes. When he finished, the men's faces were ashen.

The discussion continued well into the night, and by the time it broke up, fatigue was setting in. Calls were made and cars arrived to ferry the conspirators back to their homes, leaving Sergei and Bahador alone with their guards and their thoughts.

Sergei stood and moved to one of the cabinets, retrieved a bottle and two tumblers, and set them on the table as he sat beside the presidential hopeful. He poured each half full and then held his aloft in toast. Bahador clinked the rim of his glass upon Sergei's, and they tossed the liquor back, swallowing the liquid fire without changing their expressions, the only hint of the strength of the drinks the moisture that welled in their eyes.

"So where does this leave us? Can we trust them to act?" Bahador asked.

"As much as we can trust anyone."

"You sound unconvinced."

"They're loyal and brave, but they are men with hammers to whom everything looks like a nail. They seem resigned. My take is that in spite of everything we say, they don't understand how critical this election is." Sergei paused. "If Hovel continues to rule, the country is doomed."

Bahador nodded. "I don't disagree. But it was valuable to get a read on their reactions."

Sergei poured another dollop in their glasses and shook his head. "And we planted the seed. Funny thing about the unthinkable – once you speak it out loud, put it out there, it becomes just a little easier to consider."

Bahador offered a wan smile that looked like a wince. "You're a keen judge of human nature. You can be sure their minds are working overtime now."

"If they are, that's half the battle."

Bahador nodded again and raised his glass. "Then mission accomplished."

Sergei sat back, a pensive expression clouding his face. "At least the first part of it."

"All journeys start with a first step." Bahador paused, took a swallow of his drink, and set the tumbler back on the table. "Let's hope that we don't have to go down a road we'll all regret."

"Sometimes the only way to build is to first destroy."

The older man shook his head. "Maybe. But there's no point to winning if we do so without the full confidence of the people. Stealing the election, even if it were possible, isn't an option. We must be better than that, or we're equally unfit to lead as our adversaries."

Sergei nodded, having heard the rhetoric many times before. The Nationalist leader was an idealist – which was fine, as far as it went, but sometimes hindered him when faced with real world problems that required...moral elasticity.

Bahador tossed back the remainder of the fiery liquor and rose. "Come. It's late, and we have a big day tomorrow. We shall slay dragons then. Now, we rest."

Sergei watched as his master strode to the door and swung it wide, his shoulders squared like a prize fighter ready to step into the ring, and his chest swelled with pride that he was the great man's most trusted confidant. Sergei finished his drink and rubbed a tired hand across his face before joining Bahador and the guards, keenly aware that as the clock counted down to the election, they were on borrowed time.

CHAPTER 4

Jet adjusted her hijab and checked her watch a final time before planting a kiss on Matt's cheek and moving to the door. Two days had crawled by, but in twenty minutes she was to pick up their paperwork. Photos of herself, Matt, and Hannah were secreted in a small envelope in her pocket along with the second half of the payment in cash.

"You sure you don't want me to go with you?" Matt asked.

"Absolutely. It's best if you aren't seen. Just in case."

"You think something's off about the forger?"

"I don't know what to think. I just know that it's getting more tense out there by the day as more refugees arrive, and eventually something's going to trigger blowback. I don't want you and Hannah on the street any more than necessary."

They'd remained in the room most of the time, taking their meals, barely edible slop at egregious prices, downstairs in the communal dining area, where they were safely insulated behind locked doors. When they'd gone for their photographs, Jet had heard several insults hurled their way by young men as they'd walked past, and had squeezed Matt's hand so he wouldn't react. Best to pretend not to understand than to engage. They weren't there to change minds, and this wasn't their battle.

"You have your phone. Call mine if you run into trouble," Matt said. They'd bought burner cells when they'd arrived in town, and had only used them to confirm they worked.

"I will." She took in his pensive frown and kissed him again. "Don't worry. This is a cakewalk."

"I suppose it doesn't do any good to tell you I get more worried when you tell me not to worry, does it?"

"I can take care of myself."

Matt nodded. "I know."

After kissing Hannah, Jet let herself out and took the stairs two at a time, breathing slowly, her pulse barely above normal. Being cooped up in the small room was driving everyone stir-crazy, which accounted for Matt's uncharacteristic fretting. They both knew she was capable of taking on an army without breaking a sweat – so his concern, while touching, was unnecessary.

Because of its cheap shops and restaurants, the district attracted more refugees than the upscale areas, and the streets were clogged. The Syrians were easy to pick out from the Serbs, marked by their gaunt faces as well as the Arabic that drifted on the breeze as she pushed past clumps of men with the slack gaits and hunched shoulders of those with no place to go, no work to do, no money to spend.

When she arrived at the forger's block, she slowed and scrutinized the vehicles crammed together along the curb, checking for obvious signs of surveillance but seeing nothing. Her eyes roamed over the windows of the buildings lining both sides of the street, but it was impossible to be sure of anything, the national pastime of the elderly apparently watching the world go by from their perches like geriatric owls. She didn't pick out anything that triggered her internal alarms and so continued to the forger's stoop, which thankfully was empty, the thugs gone to greener pastures this afternoon.

She mounted the steps, entered the building, and waited for her eyes to adjust before making her way to the stairwell. A creak from one of the ground-floor tenements ahead stopped her, and she found herself staring at the wide eyes of a toddler scarcely older than Hannah, her black hair matted to her head, dressed in a stained pink top emblazoned with a faded Hello Kitty graphic. Jet smiled but the child was gone, replaced by a frowning woman in her forties clutching a wooden spoon.

"Get in here," the woman commanded, and then the door slammed, the sound as loud as an explosion in the hallway. Jet shrugged to herself and reached for the bannister railing, anxious to avoid any further encounters with the residents, already feeling too exposed and, worse, weaponless.

Eric answered her knock with a silent glare and stepped aside so she could enter. Jet made for the front room, and he followed her in. The ever-present cigarette trailed a noxious plume.

"You have the money?" he snapped, by way of greeting.

Jet nodded. "Assuming you have the documents. I pay when they pass muster, not before, remember?"

His eyes narrowed. "Your Serbian is better than the previous visit."

Jet held his stare. "I've had time to practice." She held out a hand, remaining standing by the sofa, uncomfortable with Eric's sudden tension. "Let's see what you've got."

"Show me the money."

Jet debated refusing, but saw nothing to be gained by doing so. If he was going to rob her, he likely wouldn't do so in his apartment. She extracted the wad of euros and waved it at him before slipping it back into the folds of her robe. "There. Now let's see your work."

Eric grunted and disappeared into the back of the apartment before returning with a file folder and placing it on the coffee table. "Have a seat. I just need to affix the photographs and laminate the pages, and you're done. You remembered to get them, right?"

Jet continued standing as she reached for the file. "Of course."

She reached down, slid a blue booklet from the file, and opened it. Her eyes roved over the pages as Eric stood by, waiting. When she looked up at him, her stare was cold. "This is junk," she said. "Garbage. I've seen real ones online. This is obviously fake."

Eric blustered indignantly. "Nonsense. It's perfect. You must not be familiar with the newer ones."

"The newer ones have machine-readable code along the bottom. Yours doesn't. And the font's all wrong. That, and the pages don't have the watermark the genuine article does. This wouldn't fool a two-year-old."

"Lady, I did the work. I expect to be paid," he snarled.

"I want my money back."

A switchblade materialized in one hand. "Hand it over, or you'll regret it."

Jet reflected on her vow to avoid trouble and then pivoted and drove her booted foot into his midsection. His eyes saucered and the cigarette blew from his mouth with a woof, and he dropped the knife to the floor as his knees buckled and he sank to the floor, struggling for breath. Jet calmly toed the switchblade aside and it skittered behind a chair. She held up the file. "What did you make these on? Where's the computer?"

Eric gasped, his face red, and pointed down the hall. "There…" he managed.

Jet nodded. "Show me."

The forger pulled himself up using the chair, and Jet caught the cunning in his sidelong glance, telling her he wasn't as badly winded as he appeared. She took a step back to give herself more maneuvering room, wary of another attempt, but the fight seemed to have gone out of him, and he stumbled down the hall toward the bedroom. Jet stayed on his tail and then pushed him hard in the middle of his back when he reached the door, keeping him off-balance. He staggered into the room, where she spotted a laptop computer on a small table beside a cheap printer.

She pointed at the bed. "Sit down. You move, I break your legs."

His eyes said he believed her, and when he was seated on the edge of the bed, she moved to the laptop and did a quick skim of the screen. Nodding to herself, she powered the device down. The forger glared hate at her.

"Now you're robbing me?" he snapped.

"Where's my money?" she demanded, ignoring his question.

"I…It's gone."

"Then I'm not robbing you. I just bought your laptop. I gave you enough for five of these, so it was a pretty good deal for you."

"You can't do that."

She disconnected the computer and regarded a rack on the closet door. "I'm going to bind your hands and feet and gag you. Try to fight me and you'll regret it."

"I can't believe this."

"You pulled a knife on me, and you tried to cheat me. You're lucky I don't use the blade to carve my initials into your face."

She moved to the belts hanging from the rack, selected a thin one, eyes on him the entire time, and then approached him. "Turn over on your stomach, hands behind your back. Try anything and you'll be pissing blood for weeks."

Eric grudgingly complied, and Jet made short work of his wrists and, after retrieving another belt, his feet. She finished by knotting a tie around his head, gagging him, and then stood back to inspect her work.

"I'll tell your cousin you need help when I get back to the inn. I'll also tell her you tried to rip me off," Jet said.

Eric grumbled something unintelligible from behind the tie, and she took a final look at the bindings and returned to the foyer, notebook and file in hand. She listened for a long moment and then eased the entry door open. The hall was empty as when she'd arrived. Jet pulled the door closed and crept toward the stairs.

At the first floor, she fished the cell phone from her pocket and called Matt. He answered on the fourth ring, and she summarized her meeting in a few clipped sentences.

"So dead end," Matt said.

"Right."

"Are you okay?"

"So far. Pack our things and get Hannah ready to go. We'll want to blow out of there when I arrive."

"It'll take me ten minutes to get back to the room," Matt said. "I took Hannah out for a snack. I can meet you somewhere if you want."

She considered it and frowned. "I need to pull the hard disk and wipe the cache on this computer, and it would be nice to have some privacy. Let's meet at the inn."

"We can be ready to go in a blink – it's not like we have a ton of stuff to pack." Matt paused. "Back to square one on the docs, though."

Jet eyed the entryway and nodded. "I know."

She signed off and slipped the phone back into her pocket, and then made for the stoop. The pair of thugs had returned and looked her over with exaggerated leers. She avoided eye contact and pushed past them, ignoring their obscene proposals as well as the impulse to break their jaws, and hurried down the sidewalk before it could occur to them to wonder why she was toting a laptop and a file.

The skin on the back of her neck prickled as she traversed the block, and she paused at the corner to check over her shoulder. The toughs were gone. Where, she didn't know, but she wasn't interested in pressing her luck. She ducked around the building and picked up her pace, anxious to be in and out of the inn before Eric could work himself free and sound the alarm, assuming he had sufficient network to do so. He wouldn't go to the police, she was sure – his work was so amateurish there was no way he'd been forging for long, so he was unlikely to have developed law enforcement contacts. But there was always the possibility a distant relative was on the force, and she wanted to take no chances. Jet hurried along, hoping that her feeling of being watched was just nerves and not something more substantial.

She stopped abruptly at a shop and eyeballed the street in the reflection of the display window, but there was nothing out of the ordinary – nobody making sudden moves, no cars inching along, no one darting into doorways or stopping for no reason; in other words, nothing to fear.

The thought brought her no comfort. A simple transaction had just gotten far more complicated, and now they would need to find a different place to stay and begin their hunt for a forger anew, this time with no leads. She resumed walking, picking up her pace as she reached the main boulevard, and swallowed back the resentment at having had two precious days wasted with nothing to show for it but unusable junk and a building sense of anxiety that soured her every breath.

CHAPTER 5

Elena looked up from her position behind the reception desk when Jet entered and offered an uncharacteristic smile. Jet returned it, faking as much warmth as she could muster, and hurried to the stairs. Elena called out as Jet neared the steps.

"So how did it go?" the older woman asked.

"Everything went smoothly," Jet lied.

Elena eyed the laptop under Jet's arm and her brow furrowed. "What's that?"

"Oh, my computer. I use it to read. I wasn't sure how long I'd have to wait." Jet glanced at her watch. "Anyhow, thanks a million, but we need to get going. Now that we have our papers, there's no point in delaying, you know?"

Elena frowned and checked the time. "Right now? It takes a good long while to get to the border, and you don't want to have to wait overnight. They only let a few people through every day."

"Thanks. We'll think about it."

Jet didn't want to continue the discussion and pretended not to hear when Elena said something else. She didn't trust the woman's sudden friendliness, and the knot of tension that had been twisting in her gut tightened as she climbed the stairs.

Once inside the room, she did a perfunctory inspection of their bags and the dresser, and her lips pressed into a thin line. Someone had gone through their things, which confirmed her suspicion that the innkeeper was in on the fraud. Elena wouldn't have found anything of interest – Jet always took her passports with her when she left the room and carried the diamonds in a satchel hanging from a lanyard around her neck – but it was clear they were in danger, her instinct to be rid of the miserable boardinghouse vindicated.

26

Matt entered with Hannah in tow a few moments after Jet had removed and pocketed the hard disk from the laptop, and Jet held a finger to her lips and leaned into him.

"They searched our bags. Pack your duffle and I'll deal with Hannah's stuff. I want to be out of here in two minutes," she whispered. "It's a matter of time until the forger gets loose, and I don't want to push our luck. Hurry up."

Matt nodded and wordlessly stuffed his few possessions into his bag while Jet did the same with her daughter's clothes and books and handed Hannah the small children's backpack before packing her own with her clothes. When she was done, she looked up at Matt, who was peering through the curtains at the street below.

"Anything?" Jet asked.

"No. It looks clear."

"Then let's get going," she said, sliding the laptop into her bag and zipping it closed.

"What are you going to tell the woman?"

Jet's expression darkened. "Good riddance."

Elena looked up as they descended to the lobby level and took in their bags with concern. Jet tossed the key onto the counter and fought to keep her voice even.

"We're checking out. Thanks for all the help."

"I really think you should stay the night and try in the morning. You have no idea what you're getting into. I've heard stories," Elena began.

"Thanks, but we'll take our chances. Oh, and your cousin Eric? He said to tell you that he wanted you to come by whenever you have a chance."

Puzzlement lined her face. "He did? That's odd. I wonder why he didn't call."

"He was kind of tied up, and he knew I'd be seeing you shortly."

Elena looked uncertain. "Oh. Well, okay then. Thank you."

"Give him my best."

Jet didn't wait for a response and moved to where Matt waited in the entryway with Hannah. They pushed through the door and Jet scanned the sidewalk, alert for signs of pursuit. Seeing nothing, she led Matt and Hannah down the street, made a right onto another large boulevard, and flagged down a taxi. The driver slowed and looked them over, and then sped up with a shake of his head and a two-finger gesture.

"Natives sure are friendly, aren't they?" Matt grumbled.

Jet smiled and eyed his dyed black hair and goatee. "Nothing worth doing's ever easy. We'll find one eventually."

"Where are we headed?"

"To find another fleabag hotel that won't ask questions." Jet gave him a more complete account of her altercation with the forger, and the corners of his mouth pulled down.

"You think he's going to retaliate?"

"We'll be long gone. He was small time. I've got the documents. They look like a ten-year-old made them. We need to find someone competent, and asking the hotel obviously isn't the way to go."

"Any ideas?"

"The usual. Once it gets dark, I'll hit the local watering holes until I find some criminal types. In a frontier town like this it shouldn't take too long. They'll be plugged into the local underworld – we know there's a thriving black market for documents, so there's no question there are competent forgers here. We just need to find one."

"I can go."

She waved at another taxi and this one pulled to a stop at the curb. "I'd rather handle it. They always underestimate a woman. Might as well use that to our advantage."

The driver climbed from behind the wheel and rounded the car to open the trunk. "Where you headed?" he asked, his tone distrustful.

"Somebody told us there was a reasonably priced rooming house over on the other side of town," Jet said, figuring that was vague enough to open the door for the man to make a recommendation for someplace that gave him a commission for directing travelers.

"Yeah? You remember the name?" he asked, wedging Matt's duffle into the trunk and extending a hand for Jet's.

"Something Magyar," Jet improvised. As close as they were to the

Hungarian border, there was bound to be something with Magyar in the name.

He eyed them skeptically. "You have money?"

"Yes. How much will it cost to take us there?"

The driver stated a price. "Show me the cash."

Jet withdrew a few dinar notes from her pocket and flashed them at the driver. His frown eased, and he motioned for them to load into the back of the car. When they were inside, Hannah between them, he slid into the driver's seat and craned his neck. "I know a better place, if you're interested. Cheap, and the owner's a decent sort. Takes in a lot of refugees."

"Is it far?" Matt asked.

"Closer than that other hellhole. You won't be sorry."

Jet delayed an appropriate amount of time before nodding. "Okay, then. As long as it's not expensive."

The driver grunted and jammed the shifter into gear, and the car lurched into traffic. Jet and Matt sat back against the cracked vinyl seat, bouncing as the dilapidated cab's nonexistent shocks rattled their teeth over every pothole. Jet turned occasionally to verify that they weren't being followed as they snaked through columns of plodding vehicles, the driver obviously anxious to deliver them to their destination before they could have second thoughts.

The neighborhood degraded as they wended their way east, and when they pulled up to an ancient three-story building near the end of a block where most surfaces were marred by graffiti, Jet scowled. "We need someplace safe," she warned.

"Oh, don't let that fool you. Local kids. This is a reasonable area," the driver countered.

"Doesn't look too good," Matt whispered.

"We're not going to be here very long, with any luck," Jet said, and nodded to the driver. "This is it?" she asked, regarding the blinking hotel sign with skepticism.

"That's right. The owner's name is Vaclav. Everybody knows him. He's an honest man. Tell him Arnost sent you. He's a friend of mine."

They collected their luggage and paid Arnost, who watched
through the windshield as they approached the scarred wooden doors
of the hotel and climbed the three steps to the entry. Jet leaned
against one of the doors and it groaned inward, accompanied by the
tinkling of a bell, and they stepped into a reception area that could
have doubled as a holding cell at the police station. A bald man in his
sixties tore his eyes from a geriatric television on one end of the
counter and looked them over.

"Yes?"

"Arnost the taxi driver recommended you. We need a room for a
couple of nights."

The man nodded and named a figure in the local currency. "Per
night, payable in advance. That's with a community bathroom. If you
want one with a private bathroom, it's an extra two thousand dinar."

The number was higher than they'd been paying at the inn, but
they were in no mood to negotiate and so agreed and paid for three
nights.

"You take euros?" Jet asked.

"Of course."

The clerk inspected each banknote as though they'd printed them
that morning, and only once he'd done so with each bill did he slide
them into a drawer and hand Matt a key. "Two D. Second floor.
Faces the street, so you'll want to keep your window closed at night.
It can get a little noisy. Meals are served from eight to eight in there,"
he said, indicating a doorway to their left. "Maid will check all the
towels are still there when you check out. Any missing, and they
come out of your deposit," he said, and then went back to watching
soccer.

Matt nudged Jet's arm and made for the stairs, pausing to whisper
to her at the bottom step.

"There goes the towel-theft ring idea," he said.

"Seems like a trusting soul. Arnost didn't mislead us," Jet agreed.

"Can't wait to see what the honeymoon suite looks like."

"Lead the way."

They found the room and it was everything they'd imagined from the exterior of the building – the bed older than Jet, the shower a series of wooden slats over a hole in the bathroom floor with a greasy plastic curtain for privacy. She set her bag down and offered Hannah a smile, ignoring the sounds of male voices in the next room, arguing in Arabic. "At least it's got a roof," Jet said, and Hannah returned the smile uncertainly.

Matt heaved his duffle onto the bed and walked to the window, through which wafted engine noise and the smell of raw exhaust. He slid the window shut and looked at the smudge of dirt on his hand before turning to Jet and shrugging.

"Maybe a tent in one of the camps wouldn't be so bad," he said, deadpan.

Jet's face was impassive, but her eyes sparkled mischievously. "Be careful what you wish for. That might be next."

CHAPTER 6

Tel Aviv, Israel

Amit Mendel reclined in his seat and stared at the other men in the room – a room that officially didn't exist, in a compound that wasn't on any map, four stories below ground in a hardened complex that housed the Mossad's field operations as well as a third of its data collection and mining division, and its European cyber-warfare group, a relatively new team known only as Group A.

Amit sighed, his face world-weary and creased by a decade of heading one of the clandestine organization's black ops groups as well as the Turkey-Armenia-Azerbaijan group, and toyed with a pencil as he considered the report he'd just received. "I want to better understand how our operative was blown, Fischel. We spent months planning this. It was a straightforward neutralization. We've performed countless like it without incident."

Ziv Fischel, three years Amit Mendel's junior, ran spiderlike fingers through a mane of thick curly hair above glasses thick as windowpanes. "Nearest his control officer can tell, something he did aroused the suspicion of the security detail. You know the rest. He took evasive action, we ran what interference we could, but it went bad." He shrugged. "I don't have to tell you that, while regrettable, it happens."

"Yael was the best. Seasoned. I find it difficult to reconcile his string of operational successes with him slipping up and drawing attention to himself," Amit said. "That part makes no sense."

"I'm as aware of his triumphs as anyone," Ziv agreed. "But we have to rely on the handler's assessment, subjective as it can be."

"What about a leak? Who else knew of the operation besides Yael and his control?"

Ziv frowned. "Nobody. We've been through this already. It was all compartmentalized. Not even the station chief had been informed."

"We drew our information on the event from somewhere."

"Local informant. He had no knowledge of what was planned."

"Perhaps not the specifics. But depending on how the information was gathered, it might have triggered something in Azerbaijani intelligence. That makes more sense to me than that one of our top people made a mistake."

"In the end, does it change anything?" Maor Lachman, a small, pudgy division head from the cyber-warfare group countered.

Amit nodded slowly. "Yes. We now have a problem. The Nationalists will be on high alert, so eliminating their candidate is no longer viable. Which means we need a new plan to achieve the same goal – but using a different approach."

It was Ziv's turn to sigh. "Anything happens to their candidate now, and it will be pinned on the administration. The whole point of Yael's mission was to make it look like the act of a lone gunman. If another attempt is made, that narrative falls apart. We don't need a JFK moment in Baku at this stage of the game. It will raise too many questions and undo years of work."

The men chuckled at the reference to the American assassination – the archetype of botched executions that required the relevant documentation to still be classified as top secret fifty years after it had occurred. No intelligence group wanted that sort of blemish on its record if it could help it.

Amit stared off into space for several moments. When he spoke, his voice was softer than earlier. "Maybe we've been coming at this the wrong way. If we can't eliminate the opposition party, then we need to strengthen the position of the incumbent."

Ziv shook his head. "Hovel's hated by much of the country. Hard to strengthen his popularity. He's a bully and a despot."

Amit allowed himself a small smile. "Since when did that ever matter?"

"In this case, it's a real issue."

"Then maybe instead of trying to figure a way across the angry sea, we part it."

Ziv appeared perplexed, and Amit placed his hands palm down on the table. "It's important we keep the ultimate objective in focus and not get lost in the details. We want Hovel to be reelected at all costs. What we tried didn't fly, so now we need a different solution. One that will result in the same outcome, even if it appears to be the polar opposite at first blush."

He outlined his thinking in a few terse sentences, and the men around him were speechless at the audacity of the gambit he proposed. They argued over tactical considerations for half an hour, but ultimately, Amit proved once again why he had retained a position of power in an organization that had a brutal rate of attrition.

When the meeting adjourned, everyone had action items, and they'd agreed to reconvene in twenty-four hours after studying the feasibility of Amit's proposal. Ziv had undertaken most of the heavy lifting, and his staff would be working around the clock, evaluating scenarios and attempting to predict the geopolitical ramifications of Amit's scheme.

That there were gaping holes in how they could deliver the needed result didn't trouble them – these were men who were accustomed to achieving the impossible, and if the analysts agreed that Amit's idea held water, they'd drill down and figure out how to execute the plan.

Amit's step quickened as he left the conference room; he lived for the challenge of developing a workable scenario. The world was a chessboard, and he had been gifted with the ability, like all grand masters, to think many moves ahead. If he was right and his people came back with findings that the reaction domestically would be positive, then they'd turned a devastating setback into a triumph.

If it got any better than that, he didn't know how.

CHAPTER 7

Jet clung to the shadows as she walked toward the area of town populated by countless bars and nightspots. She'd exchanged her robe for a dark top and her cargo pants – garb that working-class locals might wear on a night out. She moved without haste, aware of her surroundings and wary of being jumped. The threat of violent assault had been heightened with the influx of refugees, some of whom were criminals back in their home countries and had brought their predatory ways with them. Jet had heard plentiful accounts of rapes and assaults blamed on the new arrivals, and while she could attribute some of it to hysteria, there was a distinct pattern, and there was no question that a young Iraqi's or Syrian's view of women might be different from a European's.

She'd decided to forego her refugee outfit when trolling the bars for an introduction to the mafia rumored to run much of the city. Better to be viewed as neutral, even if it might mean paying more for the documents. She wouldn't have been welcome in the watering holes otherwise, and didn't want to risk the ire of the Serbs.

Music and laughter carried down the street as she approached a string of bars she'd been directed to by a taxi driver who'd dropped her three blocks away at her request; she didn't want to be seen coming or going in a cab. She had no real plan other than to pump the bartenders for information – some things didn't change anywhere in the world, and it was always a safe bet that those who served the drinks knew the players.

The first bar was a dive that featured a nautical theme wholly out of place in the landlocked city, whose patrons appeared to be end-stage alcoholics. She ordered a drink and probed the bartender for information, but the man was as forthcoming as a rock, and she gave up after a fight broke out between two vagrants who were so drunk they could barely stand up.

The next watering hole featured a neon outline of a goat dancing on its hind legs, hoisting a beer stein in celebration. Jet smiled at the image and entered. The interior was everything she'd expected: a series of small tables occupied by men with gloomy expressions, a long bar running the length of the far wall, and several pros seated with dresses hiked to afford better views of their wares between the odd patron nursing a drink and staring into space or at a sporting event on a flat-screen television above the bottles.

Jet counted two dozen customers and checked the time as she neared the bar – ten o'clock, so perhaps too early for the real crowd to show up. Then again, perhaps this was the crowd. Absent a band or any draw, the place was on the lower end of the scale, even by Serbian standards.

She took a seat, and a man shaped like a brick approached.

"What's your pleasure?" he asked.

She named a beer she'd recognized on one of the tables, and the man gave a curt nod and opened a refrigerated door under the bar. He popped the top and placed the bottle in front of her. "Paying now, or running a tab?" he asked.

"I'll pay now." She tossed a Serbian dinar note on the dull wooden surface. "That cover it?"

"Got some change coming."

"Keep it."

He appraised her. "Thanks." He paused. "You're not from around here, are you?"

She smiled. "What's the giveaway?"

"Your accent…and your looks."

"Can't do much about either."

He laughed. "You don't have to." The bartender studied her for a moment. "We don't see a lot of ladies in here, is all."

"Dancing goat doesn't draw them in?"

Another laugh. "Crowd's a little rougher than most."

She shrugged. "That's okay. Might work out better that way."

His eyes widened slightly. "Yeah?"

"Yeah," she answered. "I'm looking for someone who can help me with some business that might not be...strictly legal."

His expression hardened again. "We don't do any drug trade out of here. Sorry."

She shook her head. "Not that. Looking for an introduction to someone who can help me with papers."

He regarded her for a moment. "You a cop?"

"Do I look like one?"

"That's not an answer."

"No, I'm not a cop." She hesitated. "If you don't know anybody, that's fine. I don't want any trouble."

He shook his head. "I don't. Sorry."

She took a sip of her beer and shrugged. "Worth asking."

Ten minutes later, she'd drunk a quarter of her bottle and was preparing to leave when a dark-haired man wearing a leather jacket and black jeans sat on the stool next to her, his clothes rank with stale cigarette smoke and poor hygiene. He nodded to the bartender and leaned slightly toward Jet.

"You looking for anything special?"

She turned and appraised him: shaggy haircut, jaundiced skin, the sickly emaciation of an end-stage alcoholic, eyes as dark as coal that skittered from point to point like a frightened rodent's.

"That depends. I could use some help with documents."

"I might know some people."

"That's nice."

"Buy me a shot and I'll see if I can remember who's dealing with that sort of thing these days."

Jet sighed and pointed at the bar, and then held up a finger to the bartender, who nodded. He'd obviously put out the word to some of the local bottom feeders, as she'd hoped, and her bait had drawn the first bite of the night.

The drink arrived, a water glass with three fingers of clear liquid in it, and the man drained half in a thirsty swallow, belched loudly, and laughed, revealing a set of decaying teeth. Jet's expression remained unreadable, her emerald eyes regarding him evenly. He took another pull on the drink, and she slid a bill to the bartender before turning back to her new friend.

"Well?"

"What kind of docs you need?"

"Refugee."

His ferret eyes darted across her face, sizing her up. "Those are expensive."

"Nothing in life's free."

His gaze lingered on her breasts before meeting her stare. "You police?"

"No."

"Mind if I frisk you?"

"Good way to wind up with broken arms."

"I need to make sure you aren't wearing a wire. Follow me to the bathrooms."

The lowlife finished his drink and slid off the barstool. He cocked his head at her and walked to the back of the bar. Jet drew a deep breath and stood, and then trailed him into a darkened hallway with a door on either side and an exit sign over a steel slab at the end.

The man's hands roamed over her and she endured the groping, which went on far too long to be strictly business. When he stepped away from her, he was leering in the dark, and her stomach muscles tensed as she fought to keep her voice calm.

"All right. You had your fun. Now cough up or we're done."

"This way."

He led her to a booth near the bathroom, where a small mountain of a man sat, his shaved head glistening, a beard and blue knit turtleneck sweater doing nothing to hide his three chins. The drunk motioned to the bench seat opposite the man and then pulled up a chair and sat on the end.

"This is Milun," he said, indicating the big man.

Jet nodded and waited for the weasel to continue. He leaned in and murmured in Milun's ear. One corner of the big man's mouth twitched, and he studied Jet for a long beat.

"You have cash?"

Jet shook her head. "Not on me."

"It will be two thousand euros apiece."

"That's fine. I need three. But they have to be perfect. Otherwise I don't pay."

"The people I deal with only do perfect."

"I had a bad experience with someone making the same claim."

They stared at each other, and Milun nodded slowly. "Satisfaction guaranteed. Cash only."

"How do we do this?" Jet asked.

"I make a call. Bran here will introduce you to my man. You meet, tell him what you want, come back here and give me the first half of the payment."

"How late will you be here?"

"Till it closes." Milun removed a cell phone from his pocket and placed a call, his eyes locked on Jet the entire time. He had a short discussion in rapid-fire Serbian and then hung up and tilted his head at the weasel. "Bran will take you there now."

Bran pushed back from his chair, and Jet slid from the booth. "I'll be back before closing time with your money, assuming your man is competent."

"Oh, he's competent. Like I said, satisfaction guaranteed."

The forger turned out to be an elderly man who lived four blocks away, on the third floor of a brick walk-up whose stairway stank of urine. Jet sidestepped a used syringe in the hallway outside the forger's door and followed Bran inside as the older man locked the door behind them.

They sat in the kitchen at a cheap breakfast table, and the forger slid a blue refugee passport to her. "Made that yesterday. Indistinguishable from the genuine article," he said.

Jet studied it carefully and then nodded. "Nice work."

"Yours will be the same. Our friend says you want three?"

"Correct. Two adults and a child."

"You'll need to come tomorrow so I can take photos."

She shook her head and reached into her pant pocket for the small envelope containing the headshots. "I already have them."

Jet tossed the forger the pictures. He tapped them out onto the table and frowned. "No, these are wrong. I need black and white, not color. You can see that from the sample."

"I was told color."

"You were told wrong. For passports, yes. Not for the new refugee documents. They changed it last month." He paused for a moment, working out some schedule in his head. "Two o'clock tomorrow afternoon work for you?"

"How long will it take to create the docs?"

"Three days."

"I'd prefer to have the photos taken somewhere professional and bring them to you."

The forger shook his head. "That's not how I work. I'm a one-stop shop. Two o'clock tomorrow. Be on time."

The trip back to the bar passed in silence, and Jet left Bran outside. "I'll be back in a few hours. What time does this dump close?"

"Three."

"Plenty of time. Tell Milun he'll see me before then."

Jet hurried to the corner and flagged down a taxi, anxious to conclude the transaction. The passport had been high quality and the price reasonable, although something about the old man nagged at her.

She shared her misgivings with Matt, and he shook his head when she finished.

"Your instincts are good. If you think something's off, it probably is," he said.

"But the document was good. If there's a burn, that isn't it."

"Then what?"

She counted out three thousand euros, folded the wad in half, and slipped it into her back pocket. "I don't know. Let me think about it on the way back to the bar."

"If you aren't comfortable, keep looking for someone."

"I know. I'll figure it out."

She eyed Hannah, asleep in the center of the bed, and pecked Matt on the cheek before heading for the door.

"Call if you run into trouble," Matt said.

"It won't be tonight, I don't think. Milun seemed like the typical mob boss."

"Still. Don't take any chances."

She smiled at his concern. "Hard part's done," Jet said, and let herself out, mind racing as she made her way down the stairs, sure there was a catch but unclear on what it might be. For now, there was little to do other than fork over the money, and if she was right, that part of the transaction would go through smoothly. She was a fair judge of character and made Milun for a dependable criminal enabler rather than a cheat. Which meant that if the payment part of the deal went smoothly, if there was a scam, it would be either the forger or Bran who'd attempt it.

And get far more than they'd bargained for. She'd see to that.

CHAPTER 8

The following afternoon Jet arrived at the forger's district twenty-five minutes early to reconnoiter. She had the taxi drop her off three streets away and approached the man's block draped in her refugee robe, eyes hidden behind sunglasses. Unlike the area by the hotel, the neighborhood was quiet, with only a few pedestrians in evidence, and she felt conspicuous in her attire as she made her way down the sidewalk.

She paused at a corner market and pretended to study a magazine rack under the watchful gaze of a merchant who eyed her as though she was going to make off with it in a mad dash. Jet took in the buildings and studied the parked cars for signs of watchers. Seeing nothing, she continued along the street and slowed at the sight of an empty police car in an alley near the forger's building. She continued past it, senses on high alert, eyes roaming the area as she strode with deliberation past the building and proceeded to the corner.

Jet stopped and withdrew her cell phone, thumbing it as though texting as she scrutinized her surroundings. Halfway down the block a vendor pushed an overloaded cart toward a shop, but other than that, the area by the forger's entrance was empty. She shifted her focus across the street and spotted two men seated at a table near the display window of a small café, and swore under her breath. To her eye they looked like plainclothes police, their overfed faces and interest in the forger's building as obvious to her as a neon sign.

She rounded the corner and walked away at a measured pace, leaving the area before pressing speed dial on her phone and holding it to her ear. Matt was waiting for her go-ahead before catching a cab to the forger's, and she was glad she'd taken the precaution of arriving before the meet. She knew at a glance what would happen –

she would show up with her family, and then the police would burst in and shake her down for cash. It was a common scheme and one of the risks of dealing with unsavory types in Serbia, who were often in league with the police, preying on the desperate.

Matt answered on the first ring.

"No go." She filled him in as she walked.

"So now what?"

"I get our money back from Milun."

"It's not worth endangering yourself."

"I won't be in any danger. He's the one who'll have to worry."

She hung up and considered her next move. Matt was right that the money was incidental in the scheme of things, but that wasn't the issue. Jet wasn't going to let Milun sandbag her. If he'd arranged for the ambush, she'd be able to tell by his reaction; and given that they had no other options, it was worth the effort to confront him. At worst he was guilty and she was out the money, leaving her no poorer than if she did nothing at all.

Jet was beginning to regret their decision to pose as refugees. What had seemed viable before arriving in Serbia now seemed hardly worth the trouble, although their reasoning was no less valid: by joining the multitudes fleeing the war, they'd be effectively below the radar, since the tracking systems were inadequate to deal with the sheer numbers that threatened to overwhelm it.

Back at the hotel, Matt greeted her with Hannah by his side. Jet's heart melted at the sight of her daughter, radiant as the sun in her innocence, joyful at her mother's return. Jet knelt to hug her and looked up at Matt as she embraced the little girl.

"So much for that," she said.

"Nothing worth doing's ever easy."

She smoothed Hannah's hair. "What's gotten into you?" she asked.

"I love you, Mama."

Jet's voice cracked when she answered. "I love you too."

"I think somebody's tired of being cooped up," Matt said softly.

"Maybe we can go to a park? Not like we have anything more

productive to do." She paused. "At least until tonight."

Matt frowned. "There's no way to talk you out of it?"

She met his serious expression with a smile. "You can try."

Jet arrived at the nightclub district at dusk and took up position across the street from the bar in a darkened doorway. Several men mistook her for a prostitute and propositioned her, but she blew them off without escalating the interactions and continued to watch for Milun. Her vigil was rewarded just before nine o'clock, when his distinctive bulk stepped from a black SUV and lumbered into the bar, trailed by two heavily built men with ponytails and slab faces.

She waited ten minutes, and when Bran failed to appear, Jet crossed the street, pushed through the doors, and made straight for Milun's table. The big man looked up from his drink and frowned. One of the two hired musclemen bristled as she neared, but Milun held up a hand and waited for her to speak.

"Surprised to see me?" she asked, her tone neutral.

"I expected him to take longer. You have the second payment?"

Her eyes narrowed. "It was a setup. You double-crossed me."

Milun's frown deepened. "What are you talking about?"

Jet studied him and concluded that he either genuinely didn't know or deserved an academy award.

"There were a couple of undercover cops waiting for me and my family by his place today when I was supposed to show up."

Milun didn't blink. "How do you know they were cops and they were waiting for you?"

"I spotted their car. They were watching his building. Sloppy."

He sat back and motioned for her to take a seat across from him. The pair of goons got the message and moved away, leaving them to discuss their problem. She slid into the booth, her eyes locked on his, and waited for him to make the next move.

"You want your money back? I don't have it with me," he said, his voice low.

She sized him up. "I'd prefer you honor our deal."

"I had nothing to do with a shakedown."

"Which still leaves me needing papers, and you with my money."

He appraised her with interest. "You don't strike me as a refugee."

"What I am is someone who gave you what you asked for and got nothing in return."

"I can fix that. Ivan must have gotten greedy."

"How can you fix it?"

He frowned at his watch and exhaled heavily. "We'll pay him a visit."

"When?"

"Now."

Milun pushed his bulk from the booth and Jet trailed him to the door, where his men were standing like bookends. He growled instructions and one of them raised a cell phone to his ear and spoke a few words before nodding. Milun held out a hand the size of a ham and Jet opened the door, wary of a trick. The rumble of the SUV's engine approaching told her what the call had been for, and she waited as the crime boss joined her on the sidewalk while the vehicle rolled to a stop.

He opened the back door for her and she climbed into the car, keenly aware of her lack of a weapon. Then again, proximity could work in her favor if she were forced to engage – her training had taught her fifty ways to kill using her bare hands, and one of the easiest was in a car, neutralizing first her target and then the driver.

Milun wedged himself beside her and barked the forger's address. The driver nodded once and accelerated away from the curb. Milun turned to Jet with the trace of what might have been a smile on his face.

"Don't worry," he said. "I'm not taking you to a field to whack you."

Jet decided to play meek. "Is it that obvious?"

"I'd be nervous about getting into a car with strangers at night if I were you."

Her stare was unreadable. "What could go wrong?"

That drew a laugh. "Seems like Ivan picked the wrong woman to cross."

Jet saw no reason to respond, and they sat in silence until they reached the forger's building. Milun huffed like a water buffalo as they mounted the stairs, and when he pounded on the forger's door, his glare could have melted steel.

"Go away," the forger said, voice muffled by the door. "Don't want any."

"Ivan? Open up," Milun said.

The lock snapped and the door cracked open three inches. The forger's face appeared in the gap, wearing an expression of surprise. "Milun! What brings you–"

Milun pushed the door the rest of the way, and Ivan registered Jet behind the big man. The forger sputtered in bewilderment. "You! You were supposed to show up today. What's going on here, Milun?"

Jet followed Milun to the dining room, where his girth filled most of the cramped space, his glower fearsome to behold even though she wasn't the object of his wrath.

"My young friend here thought she saw a couple of police loitering when she came to get her picture taken. Know anything about that, Ivan?" Milun asked, his tone suddenly velvety.

The color drained from the forger's face, telling them her suspicion was correct. "N-no. She must be mistaken."

Milun held Ivan's stare. "That could be. But seeing as she's nervous about things, I'm thinking that you might want to give her the specifications for the photographs you need, and she'll get them taken and delivered to you. One of my men can bring them tomorrow."

"That's highly–"

"Doable," Milun finished, nodding as though they'd reached agreement, his expression conveying that it wasn't a request.

"Yes. Yes, of course it is. I prefer to take them so there are no problems, but if it's important to you…"

Milun continued nodding. "It is."

Ivan scratched out the size of the photos he needed on a pad of paper, underscoring that they had to be black and white against a neutral background, and handed Jet the note with a trembling hand. She took it and cocked her head as she read it, and then slipped it into her pocket.

"I'm hoping we won't have any more difficulties, Ivan," she said, her tone sweet.

"There was never any problem," he insisted, but his words rang hollow.

"Great. Glad we could settle things. Will you still have the documents for her in three days, as promised?" Milun asked.

"I'll do everything I can, Milun."

Milun slapped his thigh. "Then we'll leave you to your work." He turned to Jet. "See? I told you everything was fine. You have nothing to worry about. Ivan will treat you as though he were dealing directly with me." He narrowed his eyes at the forger. "Won't you?"

Ivan swallowed with difficulty and managed a nod, Milun's message received. "Of course."

"I'll send my man around one," Milun said, and trundled to the front door, Jet in tow.

Back in the car, Milun looked furious. "Sorry about that. He's the best, but he obviously stepped over the line. You won't have any more problems."

"My concern is that now we know he tried to set me up, he'll leak the information about our documents to the border guards out of spite."

Milun shook his leonine head. "Don't worry about that. I'll introduce you to one of the supervisors on the Hungarian side." He hesitated. "For an additional charge, of course."

Jet nodded her understanding. "That seems only fitting."

"From there, you're on your own. He sets his own prices for helping you. I'm paid for the conduit, nothing more."

"How much?"

Milun calculated quickly and smiled wolfishly. "Fifteen hundred."

Jet's eyes widened. "For an intro?"

"It's the difference between success and failure for many." He shrugged. "But you don't have to take me up on it. Maybe you'll get across without any problems. The paperwork will be good. It's more of an issue of whether someone's feeling particularly proactive or you draw their attention for some reason."

"Like Ivan whispers to the wrong person."

Milun brooded for a long moment. "I'd like to say he wouldn't dare, but the incident with the police gives me pause."

Jet understood the nature of the extortion, but she didn't mind paying the toll if it meant they got into Hungary unmolested. Truth was, she'd have gladly paid triple that for safe passage, and the refugee passports had cost less than half what high-quality counterfeit Spanish or Italian documents would have cost, so she was still ahead. She shifted on the seat beside the portly crime boss and nodded.

"As long as it buys a guarantee of no problems, consider it done."

CHAPTER 9

Jet delivered the photos to Milun the following afternoon at his office – a bakery that specialized in elaborate special-occasion cakes, advertised on signs that looked like they predated the fall of the U.S.S.R. A middle-aged woman showed her to the back of the shop, where Milun was seated behind a large metal desk, bickering into a phone handset, obviously unhappy.

He pointed to a chair in the corner of the room, and she sat while he finished berating someone on the other end of the call. After he slammed the phone down, he peered at her over a pair of tortoiseshell reading glasses.

"You have the shots?" he asked in greeting.

"Yes." She rose and set an envelope on his desk.

He didn't look inside, instead punching an intercom button on the phone and barking a name. An instant later one of the ponytailed guards entered, and he tossed the man the envelope.

"Take these to Ivan. Call if you have any problems."

The guard nodded and departed, and Milun eyed Jet. "You have the money for the introduction?"

"Yes. How is it going to work?"

Milun waved to a small refrigerator to the right of his desk. "You want a soda or water?"

"No, thanks."

Milun reclined in his oversized executive chair. "The Hungarians are only allowing one group of refugees across per day and limiting the size to a couple hundred, tops. Everybody in the EU gateway countries is overwhelmed, and the number trying to get in is increasing daily. They don't have the personnel to handle the volume. My contact is the one who decides who gets in. Every morning there are thousands trying to get over, so it's chaotic, but if he knows you're coming, he'll look for you and ensure you make it."

"How does he do that?"

"You'll fill out applications in the morning and submit them to an immigration official on this side, who'll hand it to his Hungarian counterpart. My contact will take it from there."

Jet withdrew a sheaf of euros and counted off the fifteen hundred. She rose again and handed it to Milun, who pocketed it with a smirk that chilled her blood. She hated having to depend on him for this part of the journey, but she saw no other option and was left with only the hope that he would perform his part as expected.

"Ivan should have the documents in two more days. Come by here at the same time then, and I'll have them here. You pay me, meet my people early the following morning, and they'll take you to the border." He paused. "Where to from there?"

"We haven't decided," Jet said. The less Milun knew about their plans, the more comfortable she would feel.

"Greece is a train wreck, I hear, so I'd avoid it. Portugal, especially the Algarve, is lovely this time of year, though, and I understand it's relaxed about checking bona fides if you're free with your cash. I know people in most of the southern countries – France, Spain, Portugal, Greece… Let me know if you decide on someplace specific, and I can hook you up."

It was Jet's turn to smirk. "For a price."

"Nothing in life is free. I have overhead. My products are information and access. Is it so distasteful that I charge for them?"

"I have no problem paying for your services."

The phone jangled, loud as a fire alarm. Milun scowled at it and his glance flitted back to Jet. "Back to work. You know the way out. See you in two days."

Jet retraced her steps to the shop and paused at the display case. One of the workers approached her. "Can I help you?"

"The Hello Kitty cake. Is it fresh?"

"We made it this morning. All of our cakes are same day."

"What flavor is it?"

"Chocolate cake with raspberry and chocolate icing inside. Raspberry and white chocolate outside."

A vision of Hannah floated through Jet's imagination and she blinked once. "I'll take it."

"Is it a special occasion?" the woman asked as she pulled the cake from the case and set it into a cardboard container.

"Is what?"

"The celebration. A birthday? Do you want something special on the cake?"

"Oh. Um, no, just as it is. Thank you."

Jet left the shop with her parcel in hand and ambled toward the larger street, pleased with her impulse to get Hannah a treat. Uprooting the little girl from her life in Bosnia and taking her on the road was unsettling, and her daughter deserved a reward for enduring everything that their survival had required. Jet felt terrible subjecting her to the ordeal of posing as refugees, but there was little choice, and what was done was done. Her daughter adored Matt and seemed well adjusted in spite of her experiences, so she would be fine, Jet believed. Children were resilient, and as long as Jet and Matt treated their latest escape as an adventure, it would seem more exciting than anything.

Of course she worried that her daughter had been scarred by the constant moving, but so far Hannah had shown no sign of it, for which Jet thanked Providence each day. Still, there were limits, and she wanted her daughter to grow up well adjusted, so the gypsy lifestyle had to stop. Soon Hannah would be an age where school and friends would be important, and Jet desperately wanted to settle someplace with a sense of permanence, where her daughter could just be a child and not have to be prepared to leave everything behind at a moment's notice.

Whether that was even possible, with a criminal CIA faction searching for Matt, and Jet's numerous enemies looking for her, was unknown; but she owed it to the little girl to at least try. It broke Jet's heart to consider a future of never-ending pursuit, not so much for herself, but for Hannah. It was times like this that she wondered whether she'd have been better off raised by the foster family David had arranged for, which in turn darkened her mood when she recalled how she'd been misled into believing her child had died at birth.

She forced herself to snap out of the funk she felt enveloping her and made for a taxi stand she'd spied on the way there, returning to scanning the street to ensure there was nobody following her, the automatic impulse as natural to her as breathing. When she was sure she was clean, she abruptly switched direction and hailed a cab that was preparing to pull to the rear of the line and jumped into the backseat, ignoring the driver's protest and handing him a high-denomination dinar note along with the address of a café a block from the hotel.

The young man's objections vanished at the sight of the money, and he nudged the taxi into the rush of traffic while Jet peered through the back window until she was convinced nobody was in pursuit.

"What's wrong, lady? Forgot someone?" the driver asked, noting her behavior.

Jet caught his stare in the rearview mirror and shook her head. "No. Got stood up for a meeting, that's all."

"Sorry to hear it."

He seemed about to say something else, but Jet looked away, not wanting to encourage any further conversation.

"It happens."

CHAPTER 10

Baku, Azerbaijan

Taymaz Hovel glared at the assembled advisors in the conference hall of the presidential palace from his position by one of the twelve-foot-tall louvered windows, where he was pacing nervously. The morning had brought a string of minor disasters: a food riot in one of the slums; a police shooting of an unarmed popular local activist during a traffic stop; a call from one of the powerful oligarchs who dictated terms to him in exchange for financial support for his campaign, as well as large donations to a numbered Austrian account whose owner was undocumented.

That was all the expected business of government to which he was accustomed, and none of it fazed him. It was a system of power brokering and pay-to-play as old as time, where those in power milked the rest out of as much as possible while delivering the least amount of value they could. Hovel certainly hadn't invented the game, but he'd refined the more unsavory aspects of it to a high art, and the possibility that he wouldn't get another term during which he could loot the treasury and dole out favors chilled him.

His chief of staff, Aydin Hasanov, was delivering a report on the unofficial polls, which had never looked worse. Of course, the results wouldn't be published – the administration saw to it that only polls that showed Hovel far ahead made it to print – but his ability to stage-manage perception was waning to the point where he'd called this crisis meeting to discuss the situation.

"In short," Hasanov finished, "our numbers have sunk from bad to abysmal, and there's a very real chance that no matter what we do, it will be obvious we didn't win."

Hovel swatted the observation away like an errant fly. "We'll stuff the ballot boxes, as usual. It won't matter what the vote is, only what those counting the votes say it is."

"That could be a problem," Hasanov countered. "The UN observers we've been forced to allow to monitor the election will be watching for it. Their presence changes everything in the precincts where they're active."

"We'll see to it that they're only present in the areas we deem prudent. Simple."

Hasanov shook his head. "That isn't how it works, unfortunately."

"It will be this time."

"They'll pronounce it a sham before we even begin. We can't afford the international scrutiny if they do."

"Then we bribe or blackmail them in the key polling places."

"Any whiff of impropriety will be reported. It will undermine our hold on power, even if we appear to win. We could expect widespread rioting and perhaps even civil war, with our numbers as bad as they are. Our strategists tell us that massive unrest is a very real possibility. We would have to use the army to quell it, but that would draw international condemnation and hamper our exports. Sanctions would be guaranteed."

"I'm not hearing cause for optimism," Hovel complained. "What's the solution?"

"The people are fed up. They want regime change, sir. That's the overwhelming majority sentiment."

"They're ingrates, and uneducated fools at that. They shouldn't be allowed to vote for dog catcher, much less president."

Hovel was voicing a common complaint whispered in the halls of power. The veneer of democracy and self-determination was a necessary charade to maintain order and evade sanctions for human rights abuses, but when the masses were allowed to voice their choice in a manner that resulted in an outcome that was different than the one desired by those with the necessary education and understanding of political realities, it was disastrous.

The alternative was totalitarianism, which was attractive to Hovel, but after decades as subjects of the Soviet Republic, the population wouldn't tolerate it. They'd tasted freedom and were unlikely to accept another yoke, no matter how much it might be in their best interests.

"We'll launch a more intensive public relations campaign," Hasanov said. "Position editorials that opine that the country will devolve into depression if the nationalists are elected. All the fanfare about a change is fine, but when the average person reads that they're going to suffer in the pocketbook, that might make a difference."

"The problem is that many who will vote against us are already poor and don't trust the media," Hovel griped.

Nobody in the room dared to point out that they had no reason to trust the official mouthpieces that masqueraded as impartial press in the nation. They had long been co-opted by the regime and merely parroted whatever the official narrative was, often taking orchestrated sides of an issue to create the illusion of serious division of opinion – an effective mechanism to keep the population divided and powerless to act in any unified fashion. The issue Hovel had was that even the dimmest peasants saw through the manipulation now that the media's portrayal of the state of the union differed so markedly from the reality with which the average person contended every day.

Hovel's administration had scored numbers so low as to rival those of the final days of the U.S.S.R., when everything from official sources was automatically assumed to be a lie. So a media blitzkrieg proclaiming the nationalists as a threat to the country's future was likely to have slim, if any, effect.

Still, they would go through the motions. Hovel was a keen student of human nature and understood that Lenin's aviso to repeat a lie until it was assumed to be the truth was sound advice and had worked miracles for the world's superpowers.

"What about a terrorist threat? Something existential? That did the trick for our Russian comrades with Chechens, I recall," suggested Surat Aliyev, Hovel's Minister of the Interior.

"I'm afraid the Americans have played that card too many times for it to be believable any longer," Hovel said, his tone rueful.

"How about anarchists? Hitler had the communists to blame. Why not anarchists? A series of seemingly pointless attacks on high-profile civilian targets for maximum outrage?"

Aliyev had a point. Populations tended to maintain the status quo when they believed they were threatened. Change, which was what the nationalists promised, was welcome when there was no obvious enemy; but if trains or restaurants started blowing up, Hovel's reputation as a stern master who could clamp down on the enemy might carry the day.

Hovel smiled at the thought, but ultimately shook his head as he returned to the table and sat heavily at its head.

"Not enough time. We have only three weeks to turn this around. That's not enough. For a false-flag campaign to work, we would need months. And there's always the chance the nationalists cry foul." Hovel paused. "Part of the problem is the damned Internet. Hard to control the message when so many can access unofficial sources."

"We've already covertly clamped down on the most critical bloggers and sites," Hasanov said. "Maybe we should knock out a major traffic hub so there's an effective online blackout?"

Hovel nodded. "It's worth considering. Do we have anyone who could pull it off and make it seem accidental?"

"Well, since we were discussing false flags…"

Hovel frowned at Hasanov. "We would need a plausible reason that anarchists would target a hub, for starters."

Hasanov's face fell, and then his expression brightened. "Because they're anarchists! They want to cause mayhem and chaos. Pandemonium. So they're attacking the infrastructure."

"The nationalists will claim it's us. No, that's too easy to counter. It could backfire on us." Hovel poured a glass half full with water from a pitcher on the table and took a sip before continuing. "I think we need to focus on controlling the vote counting. That's the surest way of swaying things. We must ensure our people control the transport of the boxes to the counting stations. It's the only way."

Aydin looked thoughtful. "We could always get voting machines for the critical precincts using the excuse we're modernizing. The

Americans pulled that off, and their population bought it. Everyone knows the code can be hacked or the memory cards fiddled, but we can just point to them as the model and insist everything's legitimate. Even with sworn testimony in their Congress that there are backdoors to fiddle the results, they still use them, and only a few complain."

"Great idea, but we should have done it months ago. Again, any last minute change like that will smack of corruption and be countered by the nationalists. They'd never allow it – they'd block it, at least for this cycle." Hovel absently tapped at his Patek Philippe watch and shook his head. "No, we do this the old-fashioned way. We buy off who we can and extort those we can't. This election is too important to trust to the people." Hovel pushed away from the table and stood. "We can get to the judges who will ultimately rule on the results. They all have families. If they won't accept bribes, we point out their grandchildren might not make it home from school one day soon. There are few who will stand up to power if it means their loved ones suffer."

Hasanov's brow creased. "It could get messy pretty quickly."

"I'm not saying play that card yet. But have it ready," Hovel countered.

"Then when do we approach them?" Aliyev asked, his expression puzzled.

"Let's see how the next week or so goes. We'll want to be ready two days before the election, no earlier. Don't give them time to think too much, or they'll find a way out of the box."

"If anyone talks…"

Hovel turned away, his interest in the meeting over. "See that they don't."

CHAPTER 11

Horgoš, Serbia

Jet held Hannah close to her in the backseat of the nondescript sedan that Milun's man, Bojan, had loaded them into in the predawn. The crime boss had made good on his promise to get them refugee passports, and it was now time to put them to their first serious test at the border. The sky had transitioned from plum to salmon on the drive north and glowed tangerine as the sun burned off the morning mist and the ground fog along the highway melted away.

Bojan had insisted on chain-smoking the entire way from Subotica, the cloud sucked from the cracked window each time he exhaled. Hannah's frown at the stench lasted the entire trip. When he'd first lit up, Jet had asked him to put it out, but he'd refused, insisting that he needed the nicotine to keep him awake. One look at his red eyes and hungover puffiness and she opted for conflict-avoidance – she didn't need to get into it with Milun's driver when they were this close to the home stretch. Matt had thankfully stayed out of it, deferring to Jet to decide how to handle things, and as the long field that was the refugee camp just before the Serbian border station at Horgoš came into view, she exhaled in relief and squeezed Hannah reassuringly.

"When I drop you off, you'll need to register with the guy who's collecting the day's names," Bojan said, his voice gravelly. "It should be Josif today. Tell him you're a friend of Milun's, and he'll do the rest. He's expecting you."

"Should be?" Jet repeated.

"Don't worry. He'll be there."

Jet was wearing her robe and headscarf and Matt the scruffy worn clothes of a migrant. Their belongings they'd stuffed into a pair of backpacks acquired at a flea market the day before, the high price of their travel bags a giveaway to anyone with a sharp eye, though they'd had to discard half their clothes, figuring they could buy more once out of the refugee camp in Hungary. They'd researched the logistics, and both sides of the border had camps with tens of thousands of refugees, mostly young men. Those on the Hungarian side sometimes waited weeks for their turn to board a train to Germany, France, Italy, or Spain, and they didn't want to stand out until they were well away from Hungary.

"And what about Olaf?" Matt asked. Milun had told them that the Hungarian immigration supervisor assigned to the Horgoš crossing was named Olaf, and it was with him that they would need to negotiate preferential treatment in order to get out of the Hungarian camp and on the first train out.

"He has your names. He'll see that you make it across today and find you on the Hungarian side."

"What if something goes wrong?" Jet asked. "Something unexpected?"

Bojan laughed, the sound ugly. "What do I look like, a magician? My job's to drop you off here and tell you about Josif. That's all. From here you're on your own."

Jet wasn't surprised by his tone. He'd been objectionable from the beginning, and the trace scent of alcohol that emanated from his pores, intermingled with the smoke, told her that they could expect no help from him beyond the ride.

The sedan bounced off the road and careened down a rutted trail to the field, where several thousand migrants were gathered in a long column. Jet eyed the line and gave Bojan a dubious stare. "We're supposed to wait in that?"

"Correct. They take everyone's names and verify their documents before turning the list over to the Hungarians. Some have been here for weeks. A few hours on your feet won't hurt you."

Bojan skidded to a stop on the dirt and turned to Matt. "This is it. Everybody out."

They piled from the car, and Bojan walked to the back and unlocked the trunk so they could retrieve their bags. Then he climbed back behind the wheel without a word and roared off in a cloud of exhaust, leaving them standing near the end of the queue, the Syrians staring at them with dead eyes.

They moved to the tail of the queue and shuffled forward periodically as more refugees were processed and took seats on the ground to await the calling of the names. The two-hour wait dragged to three, and finally they were at the head of the line, as fatigued by the sun and dust as by the demoralizing procession of misery.

They gave their names to a goat-faced man seated at a folding card table, holding a clipboard – Matt's passport identifying him as Givon, Jet's as Laila, and Hannah's as Hanna. When the man had checked their documents and scribbled down the numbers, Jet mentioned that they were friends of Milun. His face didn't change, but his eyes darted to the remainder of the line and then back to them. He nodded and leaned into her. "Stay close as you can, so you hear your names called."

And then they were being directed to the waiting area, where the press of refugees sat like expectant puppies awaiting a treat that would be insufficient for their number. Jet tried to imagine what it must be like to have this as an everyday reality and shuddered.

"It's unbelievable," she whispered almost inaudibly to Matt when they were seated cross-legged with Hanna near the edge of the field – the closest they could get to the folding table.

He nodded, glancing to either side, unwilling to talk in case one of the Syrians heard him and wondered why a refugee was speaking English. They'd already warned Hannah not to speak under any circumstances, and she sat mute as a log, her eyes closed, tired from the wait and from being woken in the wee hours of the morning.

Another hour passed, and the goat-faced man reappeared and began shouting out names through a bullhorn, his amplified voice distorted. Theirs were the last to be called, and they received glares from their neighbors when they stood and moved to join the new group of the lucky. Another man in uniform approached and called out in rusty Arabic to follow him, and led the ensemble past the Serbian border buildings toward the Hungarian station a thousand meters away.

When they arrived, they were herded into an area to the side of the road clogged with cars passing through customs, and directed into a fenced section, where two Hungarian officials checked refugee passports against the names on the list. They waited their turn, and when they arrived at the table, Jet handed their paperwork to the men without a word, wondering how Olaf would make contact.

If he was one of the officials, he gave no indication and swiped their machine codes beneath a scanner before handing the passports back to her after a cursory glance to confirm the photos matched the faces. The man pointed to where the rest of the processed refugees were clumped by a gate, and grunted something in Hungarian. Jet caught the drift and pulled Hannah along with her as Matt followed, his head hanging in his best imitation of a shell-shocked Syrian.

Another long wait ended when two heavy trucks rumbled up to the gate and shut off their engines. A stern-faced man they hadn't seen before neared the gatepost and read a short statement in Arabic from a worn yellow index card.

"Everyone onto the trucks. You will be taken to a camp, where you'll be held until arrangements can be made to transport you by train to your final destination. There will be no questions. That is all."

Jet didn't have to translate for Matt, who understood the sentiment of the declaration if not the exact content, and he filed through the gate with the rest of the throng and joined Jet at the rear of the closest flatbed, plywood attached to both sides to keep the cargo from falling or jumping off. Two jeeps sat a hundred meters away, their machine guns all the warning the refugees needed to stay on the trucks.

Matt clambered onto the bed and was helping Jet and Hannah up when a trio of men wearing army uniforms approached and barked at them in Hungarian. Matt froze, unclear on what the soldiers wanted, and then one of them marched to the rear of the truck and motioned at Matt and then the ground with his submachine gun, his message clear – Matt was to get off the bed.

He obeyed, concern writ large on his face, and Jet watched in horror as one of the officials walked toward them, clipboard in hand, pointing at them and speaking rapidly in Hungarian.

Whatever was happening, something had gone badly wrong with their documents, and the expressions of the soldiers conveyed that Jet and company were in trouble. The rest of the refugees stood watching the drama play out, and then an officer exited the customs building and hurried toward them.

An argument ensued in Hungarian between the officer and the official, culminating in much hand waving and disgusted gestures by both. In the end, the officer prevailed and pointed back at the truck as he addressed Jet in mangled Serbian.

"I'm Olaf. There was a misunderstanding. You are to get on this truck. Say nothing. I'll meet you on the other end."

Matt nodded and hoisted himself back onto the bed, pulling Jet and Hannah on board after him, and they pushed toward the cab to make room for more passengers. Their fellow migrants averted their eyes as they followed them on, nobody wanting to know anything more about their companions who'd been singled out by the Hungarians.

When both trucks were full, the drivers restarted the motors and the badly overloaded vehicles lurched off, followed by the jeeps and a dark gray staff car that presumably held Olaf. Jet watched their escorts as they rocked onto the highway, and then closed her eyes against the wind, Hannah hugged close, Matt's arm around her waist providing welcome, if slim, comfort.

CHAPTER 12

Szentmihály, Hungary

The trucks ground to a halt at the edge of an expansive muddy field, where tens of thousands of refugees were living in abject squalor in a sea of tents and filthy humanity as they waited for their chance to move on to a more hospitable destination. Armed guards patrolled the perimeter, and Jet caught sight of several oversized German shepherds straining at harnesses as groups of two and three soldiers walked the dirt path that ringed the area.

A tall Hungarian with a straw hat shading his face called out to them in Arabic. "Everyone disembark and line up for registration and to secure ration coupons and supplies."

Jet led Matt and Hannah off the truck amongst the other migrants and looked over to where Olaf was standing by his vehicle, watching them. That he was still showing an interest was the only positive in the experience as they were herded like livestock into another ragged line. Jet had been prepared for the hardship and the dehumanization, but what had taken her aback was how much of a refugee's time was spent standing in queues, doing not much of anything at the direction of some authority figure.

After a half hour shambling forward, they were given a single two-man tent for the three of them, several garbage bags to be used as rain parkas by tearing arm and head holes in the plastic, and a day's worth of coupons for sustenance. A gaunt man with an olive complexion handed Matt three one-liter bottles of water and instructed him to refill them as necessary at one of the taps by the latrines. Matt masked his lack of understanding, trusting that Jet had gotten it all, and then they trod to an open spot near the fence, which was apparently less desirable based on the number of people camped there.

Jet caught Olaf watching their progress through binoculars and was reassured that they hadn't been abandoned. That it was solely because of a profit motive didn't bother her a bit. She trusted greed as a catalyst and was looking forward to what would hopefully be their last negotiation –getting them on the next train headed for Italy and out of the cesspool that was the overcrowded camp.

They kicked the rubbish from the small patch of dirt they'd chosen, and Matt set about pitching the tent. A group of four young men watched with obvious amusement, and Jet heard several lewd suggestions from them, along with a proposal that the four of them show Jet and Hannah a good time. She ignored their taunts, but when they continued, obviously bored and with nothing else to do, Jet snapped at them in fluent Arabic, suggesting they perform the acts they'd described with each other's mothers rather than tormenting new arrivals.

That seemed to take the fun out of the exchange, at least for the time being, and Jet was congratulating herself on having nipped trouble in the bud when she saw the real reason the youths had suddenly fallen silent: Olaf was navigating through the tents to their position, trailed by a pair of armed soldiers with their submachine guns at the ready. The young Syrian men found other matters to pursue and made themselves scarce as the trio of Hungarians neared. Olaf's face was red from the effort of the walk, his well-fed frame clearly not accustomed to protracted exercise.

"All right," he said in Serbian, "Here's the deal." The soldiers stood out of earshot, looking around as though afraid of being mobbed. "I can get you on the next train out to either Spain, Portugal, France, Italy, or Germany. There's three of you, so the cost will be…fifteen thousand euros."

Jet gulped at the number. "I don't have that kind of money. That's crazy."

Olaf shrugged. "That's the price. The alternative is to wait your turn here. It's currently running a month or so, at least. Maybe more as the camps fill."

"Milun didn't tell me it would be so much," Jet protested.

"None of my business. That's what I charge. There are a lot of people who have to be paid off to accomplish this. The railroad personnel, the immigration people…it's complicated."

Jet did a quick calculation. They had eight thousand euros left. "I only have half that."

"Then you have a problem." Olaf turned, having lost interest.

She reached out and touched his arm. "How do I contact you if I can come up with it?"

He handed her a card with a cell number scrawled on it in pencil. "Don't lose that."

"Where's the nearest big town?"

"That would be Szeged. About six kilometers north of here." He eyed her dispassionately. "But don't get caught trying to sneak out, or I won't be able to do anything for you."

"Do you know anything about the guard schedules?"

"They patrol the perimeter every thirty minutes. If you watch them, you should be able to slip out after dark. Just be careful on the road. The natives are jumpy." He paused. "Call me when you have the money, and let me know where you want to go."

"I'll see what I can do."

Olaf walked back to the soldiers, and they retraced their route through the thronged migrants, distaste plain on their faces. Jet whispered a summary to Matt, whose face darkened when he heard the number.

"That's insane."

"I know. But we're not in any position to negotiate. I tried. He wouldn't budge."

"What's the alternative?"

She thought about Olaf's description of how long the average wait was running, and shook her head. "There isn't one. I'll slip away tonight and head to town and see if I can find a jeweler who'll buy one of the smallest diamonds. I don't see anything else we can do."

"You could have just offered him one."

"No. That would have had him wondering how many more we have. I don't want to get jumped by his henchmen. Better he think we pulled in favors from someone and had the money wired to us."

"I'll go."

"You need to stay here with Hannah. You'd be stopped in minutes. Again, most people discount women as a threat, so I'm less likely to run into trouble. Worst case, I speak way better Serbian than you do, and this close to the border, it seems like everyone's bilingual. I can bluff my way through anything, claim to be Serbian running away from an abusive boyfriend, whatever."

"What if you get caught by the guards?"

"Then they return me to the camp. How am I any worse off than where I started?"

Matt finished with the tent and glanced over at where the youths had been gathered. Two of them had returned and were making obscene gestures at Hannah. Matt offered them one of his own with a hard glare, and the pair laughed and continued baiting him.

Jet moved to his side and placed a restraining hand on his arm. "Don't, Matt. It's not worth it," she murmured.

"You know as well as I do that if we let them, they'll keep at it and escalate it. Better to stop it now."

"I'll go with you."

"No, I'll deal with this."

"You don't speak Arabic."

Matt had to concede the point, and Jet accompanied him as he made his way to the young men after telling Hannah to go into the tent and stay there until they returned.

"Appreciate it if you didn't do that anymore," she said, her tone friendly.

"You going to make us?" the taller of the two asked. A shadow crossed the ground and a third youth arrived, holding a length of wood like a club.

"We don't want any trouble," Jet tried.

"Then what are you doing here? And why are the soldiers making special visits?"

Jet's eyes narrowed to slits. "I beat a couple of men bloody. They warned me not to do it again. I promised I'd try."

That drew a sharp laugh. The man with the club grinned and ogled Jet. "You look like you need a real man, not this miserable old fool."

"I really don't want to have to hurt you," she warned. "Neither does he."

"You?" Another laugh. "Take those pants of yours off, and I'll show you how to hurt–"

Jet's spin kick caught the arm of the man with the club and he dropped it, the entire limb numb. She followed it with a lightning slam to the side of the head with her forearm and then stepped back as he collapsed in a heap, momentarily stunned. His two companions stood with mouths open, and Matt balled his fists, his legs spread slightly, weight on the balls of his feet, his hip turned slightly toward them in case either tried a kick.

Jet wiped away a lock of hair from her forehead and eyed the remaining men. "The only reason I didn't break his arm or his neck is because I didn't want to. A little more force behind the blows, and he'd be dead." She paused, letting that sink in. "You still want to get your kicks picking on us? Because I don't have a lot of patience right now, and if you're going to, we might as well get this over with now so you can leave the camp in a box."

The man on the ground groaned, and the pair exchanged a troubled glance. The smaller of them shook his head.

Jet took a step toward them, her eyes blazing. "Collect your buddy and move your camp. This is all the warning you'll get."

"We're not going to move," the second Syrian spat.

Jet's voice was so soft they could barely hear her. "You're either going to find somewhere else to pitch your tent, or you're going to learn to get around with a couple of broken legs. Either way's fine by me."

The man on the ground groaned again and rolled onto his side, holding his head with his good hand. Jet walked over to him, scooped up the length of wood, and hefted it as she turned back to the others. "What's it going to be, boys? Move, or learn you picked the wrong family to screw with?" She gave the downed man a kick in the ribs to drive home the point on the last word, and he yelped in pain.

The two youths walked to their tent and began dismantling it. Several older refugees had gathered around and joined in the spectacle. The youths were obviously unpopular with their neighbors, who muttered among themselves and occasionally jeered something derogatory as the punks broke camp. Five minutes later they were helping their friend walk away, their backpacks over their shoulders, the tent under one of their arms.

Matt leaned into Jet and whispered to her, "Well, that went well. Glad you let me handle it."

"You scared them off. My hero."

"Think they'll be back?"

"They're cowards. Probably not, although I wouldn't put anything past them."

When the men were out of sight, Jet and Matt walked back to the tent and called for Hannah. The little girl poked her head from the entry flap, her eyes radiating fear. Jet knelt down and hugged her as Matt stood by with his hands on his hips.

"It's okay, honey," Jet said. "They're gone. They won't bother us anymore."

"Really?" the little girl asked.

Jet nodded solemnly. "They decided to go somewhere else."

Hannah's soft features hardened for an instant. "Good."

Matt offered a smile and Hannah's face broke into a grin. Jet held her to her chest and looked up at Matt. "Think it's safe to go look for the mess area?"

"I'd give it an hour or two to calm down. I don't want to leave the tent and our stuff alone, just in case they decide to come back."

"Probably wise," Jet agreed. "Although I'm pretty sure I read them right."

Matt frowned. "They lost a lot of face in front of everyone."

Jet cocked her head and raised an eyebrow. "That can happen

when you're bullies and think you're picking on a defenseless woman."

"One of the many reasons I never try."

A hint of a smile tugged at her lips. "Bet you could take me."

Matt glanced at the Syrian spectators who, now that the excitement was over, had dispersed and were returning to their tents.

"Never know."

CHAPTER 13

Szentmihály, Hungary

Jet crept toward the fence encircling the refugee camp, her black cargo pants and long-sleeved top nearly invisible in the darkness. The stars and moon at two a.m. were obscured by a blanket of low clouds. She'd sat patiently, watching the patrols make their rounds, and after the last one had passed fifteen minutes before, had decided that there was no reason to wait any longer – she wanted to make it to Szeged while it was still dark, before there was likely to be any traffic on the roads, and if she delayed much longer, she'd be placing herself at risk.

Her fellow refugees had long since gone to sleep. She and Matt stuck close to the tent, preferring to avoid any encounters with the thugs. Matt had ventured to the mess area with their coupons and brought back three containers of vegetable stew they'd picked at with little enthusiasm before settling in as the light went out of the sky. The young men hadn't returned by the time the flood lamps shut off, so they'd gone down for the night with at least that danger suppressed for the time being.

Jet had snatched a few hours of sleep and then had slunk to a vantage point near the fence to watch for the patrols. If any of the nearby tents had been aware of her passage, they hadn't indicated it, and she'd drifted through them like a ghost on silent feet.

Now she would have to overcome the first real obstacle – the noise her climbing the fence might cause. She hoped that if the refugees heard her, they'd keep to themselves rather than sound the alarm, one of their number making a break for it hardly a personal concern.

She drew a deep breath and bolted for the chain-link fence, covering the final dozen yards of open ground in seconds. When she reached the barrier, she checked in both directions; seeing nothing, she climbed with slow deliberation. When she reached the top, she paused and then dropped to the ground below, thankful that the Hungarians had spared the expense of razor wire – finding something to cut it with would have been nearly impossible in the camp, and it would have slashed her to pieces if she'd tried to climb over it.

Jet landed with a thump and was up and running in a blink, making for the cover of trees a hundred meters off, where a road ran toward the town, fields of crops on either side. The ground was moist from condensation and she slowed as she neared the grove, cautious now that she was away from the immediate danger of discovery by one of the patrols and not wanting to risk twisting her ankle from a slippery misstep.

She neared the road and peered from the trees at the ribbon of black stretching into the gloom. She could just make out the lights of Szeged in the distance and cocked her head as she listened for any sound of approaching vehicles. The last truck she'd heard from the camp had passed two hours before; if she was lucky, the road would be empty until daybreak, when the agricultural vehicles began their day, carrying workers and supplies to the nearby farms.

When she was sure it was safe, she took off along the shoulder. The gravel beneath her boots crunched with each footfall, her gait fluid and easy, her breathing measured in the cool night air. It had been too long since she'd been able to do more than isometric exercises to maintain her strength, and after settling into a comfortable pace, she savored the responsiveness of her body to her demands, the exertion welcome after days of immobilization.

Fifteen minutes later she slowed at a rumbling behind her, and she swept the area in search of a hiding place. She darted toward the nearest field to her right and threw herself flat near a wooden fence, hoping she wouldn't be seen that far to the side of the road.

Headlights bounced along and the shoulder where she'd just been running glowed in the beams; and then the truck was past, continuing at a moderate speed, no sign of it having detected her. She waited until its taillights disappeared before she rose and brushed the soil from her pants, cursing beneath her breath. She'd hoped to avoid arriving in town looking like she'd slept in a culvert, but if circumstances conspired against her, she'd make the best of it.

She resumed her jog and over the next few hours was interrupted by three more vehicles – one personnel carrier from the border and two civilian work trucks loaded with produce, presumably for the town market. None spotted her, and she offered silent thanks as high neon peach and tangerine clouds streaked the eastern sky, the outskirts of the town now within easy reach.

The trek from the edge of the city to the commercial section by the Tisza River took another hour and a half walking at a moderate pace, during which time Jet stopped repeatedly to brush off her pants and top, the moist dirt drying as the sun rose. By the time she arrived at the downtown area, she was largely clean and didn't attract any undue attention from the locals as she ambled down the sidewalks in search of someplace to wait until the shops opened.

She found what she was looking for in a sidewalk café that was just putting out its tables, and ordered coffee and a breakfast roll in Serbian. Jet waited as the owner prepared her modest meal, eyeing the colorful spires of a nearby church jutting into the morning sky and taking in the townspeople making their way to work, each no doubt consumed with private concerns that were invisible to their fellows. A part of her envied the masses: their ignorance of how the world actually worked, their inconsequential part in it, the safety they all felt. Her problem was that she'd seen too much and knew how dangerous reality actually was. Most had no idea there were people like her among them, carrying out operations that benefited special interests at the expense of the many, doing the unspeakable as a routine part of their job.

The owner arrived with a steaming cup of coffee, and Jet banished the glum thoughts, choosing instead to focus on the simple pleasure of the strong brew and anticipation of her breakfast. It would do her no good to dwell on her situation, other than to find a way out of it.

When the owner returned, Jet asked whether there were any high-end jewelers she could recommend. The woman eyed her doubtfully and tossed out a couple of names, her Serbian heavily accented and difficult for Jet to understand. Jet repeated the directions the owner gave her to ensure she'd gotten them right and then dug into her roll, starving after the hours of exertion. Another cup of coffee and a glass of water rejuvenated her, and she lingered over her drink, killing time and watching the world go by.

At ten, she paid the bill and used the bathroom, retrieving one of the smallest stones from her pouch and folding it carefully in a paper napkin. She slipped it into her pocket and walked four blocks to the first shop, avoiding a pair of uniformed police at an intersection and taking a circuitous route on the off chance her escape from the camp had been discovered and there was a bulletin out.

When she reached the jeweler, she studied the offerings in the display window and her heart sank – the rings were obviously cheap, and the watches sported pedestrian brands. There was little chance that the store would be able to come up with the kind of money she needed, but she went through the motions anyway and pushed a button by the door and waited for the staff to buzz her in.

The shopkeeper was a woman Jet's age in perfect makeup, her outfit inexpensive but flattering. Jet approached her and offered a smile, which the woman returned before saying something in Hungarian. Jet asked her whether she spoke Serbian or English, and she nodded.

"A little English. From school."

"Do you buy diamonds?"

The woman's smile faded. "You mean from the public?"

Jet nodded.

The woman shook her head. "I don't think so. But I can call the owner if you want."

"Please."

The clerk fished a cell phone from her pocket and placed a call. After a rapid-fire discussion in Hungarian, she frowned and disconnected. "He says he doesn't."

It was Jet's turn to frown. "Do you know anyone that does?"

The woman's forehead creased as she thought. "You can try Luther's." She gave Jet directions to a shop near the river.

"Is that a jeweler?"

"Mmm, no, more like a, how you say, money lending?"

Jet nodded. A pawnshop. Probably not what she wanted, but it wouldn't hurt to see what the shop would give her for the stone – she had nothing but time until she could sneak back into the camp.

"Thanks," Jet said, and left, aware of the scrutiny she was drawing from the woman and wondering whether she still had mud on the backs of her legs. Once down the block she checked and was relieved to find her pants clean, and she set off for the pawnshop. The streets were busier now than earlier, providing welcome crowds into which she could blend.

When she arrived at the pawnbroker, she wasn't heartened by the array of sad baubles arranged in the window – scratched guitars, heirlooms of questionable value, old cameras, a scattering of cell phones, a tray holding cheap bangles. A terse discussion with the wizened man behind the counter made clear that he had no idea how to value a loose diamond and little ability to pay anything close to what the stone was worth. He offered to consign the stone without seeing it, but Jet politely declined and beat a path to the door after telling him that she didn't have the diamond with her – something about the man gave her the creeps, and she didn't want to contend with an attempted mugging after a call to a nearby accomplice.

The final jewelry store, in a tony section of town, appeared at first blush to be more promising – the inventory was reasonably expensive, at least. Jet entered the shop and was met by a young man in a suit with slicked-back hair.

"Yes. May I help you?" he asked, his gray eyes alert behind contemporary designer glasses.

"I'm interested in selling a diamond."

The man regarded her for a long beat, and then the hint of a smile played across his lips. "We're not normally buyers of stones from the public."

"This is an exceptional example." She paused. "Are you the owner?"

"No. But I'm familiar with his policy, and I can assure you–"

Jet cut him off. "Is he here?"

The man's expression hardened. "I'm not sure he'd appreciate being disturbed."

"There's only one way to find out. Please get him."

The salesman frowned. "I'm afraid I can't leave the showroom."

"If only there was an invention that enabled you to speak with people remotely," Jet replied, eyeing a telephone handset behind him.

The man rolled his eyes as he moved to the phone and pressed the intercom button. After a murmured discussion, he turned back to Jet with a triumphant smirk. "As I thought, he's otherwise occupied at the moment, but thanks you for your interest."

She checked her watch. "I'll wait."

"I'm afraid that won't do."

"I'm shopping for jewelry. Is my patronage not welcome? You're a jewelry store, aren't you? I'll just look around, and if he happens to free up, then the stars will have aligned."

The salesman's expression was a blank. "Was there anything in particular you were interested in?"

It was Jet's turn to smirk. "I'll know it when I see it."

She perused the display cases, humming to herself as the salesman stood by, his posture rigid. After an hour of scrutinizing every piece in the store, an aged man with a potbelly and dress slacks held in place by suspenders stuck his head from the rear of the shop. "Anton?" he called, and then spotted Jet.

"Yes, sir?"

"Oh, I didn't realize we had a customer."

Jet beamed a smile at him. "I'm actually here to see about your interest in a diamond. An amazing example," she said.

"Really? What makes it so amazing?" the older man asked, clearly interested.

"Near perfect color, clarity, and cut." She paused, eyeing Anton. "But I thought you were too busy to see me?"

The man appeared puzzled by her statement, and Jet's suspicion that Anton had faked the call was confirmed.

The man approached her. "No...Do you have the stone with you?"

She removed the napkin from her pocket and carefully unfolded it, revealing the diamond, which glittered under the high-intensity showroom lights. The jeweler bent to look at it and then asked Jet, "Do you mind if I inspect it? Won't take more than a few minutes."

"Certainly not. But I can't let it out of my sight."

The old man nodded. "Come back to my office."

Jet glared daggers at Anton as she collected her stone and trailed the jeweler into the bowels of the shop, passing through a narrow hall before arriving at an office with a workbench outfitted with a microscope and an array of tools.

"Have a seat," the old man said. "I'm Aram, by the way."

"Laila," Jet responded, handing him the stone.

Five minutes later, they'd agreed upon a surprisingly fair price in euros – easily enough to cover Olaf's fee with several thousand left over, although far below what Jet knew it was actually worth in the open market.

"I'll have to go to the bank to withdraw it," Aram said, when she insisted on cash.

"That's fine. I can go with you and we can do the exchange there, where there's security."

He nodded and refolded the napkin before handing it back to her. "I'd prefer if you carried it. I don't own it until I pay for it."

She pocketed the diamond. "Your man Anton pretended to call you about my interest instead of actually doing so," she said. "I had to wait almost an hour for you to come out."

Aram scowled but seemed unsurprised. "He's my nephew, so he can overstep. I apologize. He probably thought he was saving me from an unpleasant encounter."

"Just thought I'd mention it so you can have a word with him."

"I will."

They drove to the bank in Aram's car, an older BMW that shuddered over the cobblestone lanes. The manager offered to allow them to use her office to count the funds and do the exchange, and less than half an hour later Jet was hurrying along the street, putting distance between herself and the bank, eager to find a quiet restaurant where she could begin her wait for nightfall. Once darkness had descended over the town, she would return to the camp and sneak back in without any drama. Her study of their patrols had revealed that they weren't particularly alert to begin with, and the last thing they would be expecting was someone trying to enter the camp.

At least, that was her hope.

CHAPTER 14

The moon glowed overhead as Jet raced in a beeline toward the fence, the patrol she'd watched vanish into the ground fog five minutes earlier no longer a threat. She'd chosen the same section that she'd scaled on her way out, figuring she'd be able to find Matt and Hannah more easily from that spot.

The afternoon had passed slowly as she'd waited in another café, and after a hearty dinner she'd taken the road south, again dodging any vehicles so as to leave no trace of her passage. Now, just past midnight, she was looking forward to seeing her daughter and Matt again, the thought fueling her dash across the open perimeter and her climb up the tall chain-link fence.

A few startled faces greeted her inside the camp as she made her way to her tent, but she ignored them, secure that the difficult part of her adventure was over. Now that she had the money, Olaf would get them out of there, and they would soon be on their way to Italy, only a day's train ride from Budapest, which in turn was only a few hours from the camp by rail.

Matt started awake when she unzipped the tent flap, and then his teeth flashed in the moonlight at the sight of her. Hannah was slumbering beside him, wrapped in her jacket, eyes screwed shut.

Matt sat up and whispered to Jet, "You made it."

She made a face. "You doubted me?"

"Never."

She crawled into the tent and lay beside him as he zipped the flap closed and then reclined next to her. Jet nuzzled his ear and whispered to him, "I got the money. Any trouble here?"

"Nope. No sign of our friends, and we kept to ourselves. Luckily nobody's talkative in the mess line."

She exhaled softly and kissed him, his arms around her all the welcome she could have wanted. When their lips parted, he murmured to her, "You tired?"

"Beat."

"Then we should get some sleep."

"With Hannah here, that's the only option," she agreed, and closed her eyes, grateful to have made it back safely.

Morning arrived in a blink, and when Hannah awoke to find her mother nearby, she squealed in delight and hugged her close. Matt let himself out of the tent to allow them privacy and trudged along a well-worn path to the latrines. When he returned, Jet was up, cell phone in hand, waiting for the gadget to acquire a signal. After a few moments she dialed Olaf's number.

The Hungarian answered on the third ring. Jet told him she had his fee, and he grunted approval.

"I'll be there in about an hour. The lottery posts at one. I'll make sure your names are on it. Have you figured out where you want to go?"

"Italy."

"Good choice. Nice this time of year. I'll see to it." He hesitated. "You definitely have the money, right?"

"Correct. Where do I meet you?"

"By the lottery board, at noon."

"I'll give you half then and half when we're at the train station."

Olaf was silent for several moments and then loosed a hoarse laugh. "Fine. As long as you've got it all. I can just as easily arrange for you to be stopped and investigated if you stiff me."

"Don't worry. We didn't come this far to finish in this camp."

She disconnected, leaving the phone on in case Olaf needed to reach them. Matt raised an eyebrow and she whispered a summary of her negotiation. He nodded when she finished and grimaced at the tent.

"Then we'll be out of here today," he said. The trains departed from Szeged, where the refugees were trucked in the late afternoon, making way for new arrivals. The reading of the names chosen for travel took place over a megaphone after the list was posted, to avoid rioting by the board as desperate migrants fought for a glimpse of the roster.

"If all goes well," Jet agreed.

He studied her face. "You don't sound convinced."

"I don't trust anyone, especially not a mercenary prick like him."

"Sometimes those are the ones you can most rely on. They have a motive to do as they say."

"We'll know soon enough. Watch Hannah while I duck into the tent and count out the cash."

"Will do."

Breakfast was muted, the line endless, the food a tasteless and pasty glop unfit for pigs. Hannah made a face when she took a mouthful, and Jet winked at her and did her best to smile. "Just eat. Never know when we'll get the chance again," she said, and Hannah spooned another helping into her mouth, her distaste obvious.

Olaf was on time, eager to collect, and Jet surreptitiously passed him the wad of euros as his men shielded them from view.

"I'll see you at the station for the rest," he said, and then he and his men pushed through the crowd of refugees lingering around the board as though their physical proximity might improve their random odds of being selected for the trains. Jet turned to retrace her steps to where Matt and Hannah were waiting, and thought she saw the familiar face of one of the thugs before it vanished into the throng.

She scanned the crowd without spotting him, but her steps were heavy on the way back to the tent. They were so close to getting out of the camp she didn't want to risk another altercation, but if the men jumped her or her family, they'd be the losers for it.

Matt was more relaxed about it than Jet when she reported back. "Doesn't matter. We're history. All we have to do is keep our noses clean a few more hours, and this is all a bad memory."

"Doubtful they'll try anything in broad daylight, anyway. That's not how bullies work," she agreed.

"No. If they come, it'll be at night, and we'll be long gone."

The roll call took place at one and lasted an hour, and toward the end of the thousand names theirs boomed from the speaker. They were to be at the south gate with all their possessions at four, and once their IDs were checked against the list, they'd be on their way.

The queue at the gate snaked through the tents, and they shuffled forward as the guards verified each refugee's identity. Eventually it was their turn, and once through the gate, they were directed to one of fifty senile school buses, where they climbed aboard with their backpacks, the tent left at the camp for new owners. The original seats had been replaced by hard wooden benches, and they settled onto one near the rear, the acrid stench of unwashed bodies overpowering in the cramped quarters. Matt struggled with the window to get some ventilation, but the plastic safety latch came away in his hand. Jet shot him a warning look as he pulled at the window a final time, and he resigned himself to a miserable ride, breathing through his mouth.

The journey took the longest hour of their lives, and by the time they pulled to a stop at the station, Jet was choking down vomit. They gulped air when they descended from the bus and followed the others to where the soldiers directed them. Jet caught sight of Olaf and he nodded to her, but kept his distance as they herded into the station past barricades to one of four platforms already clogged with migrants waiting to board the trains.

The soldiers again checked their papers, and then Olaf materialized next to her, his bulk unmistakable among the rail-thin refugees. He pulled her aside and palmed the second half of the payment as he surveyed the chaotic scene.

"That's it, then. Good luck. You'll change trains in Budapest and be in Milan by morning," he murmured.

He gave her a final silent appraisal and then walked away, leaving her amid the crush to find her way back to Matt and Hannah, who were standing by the door of the passenger car they'd been assigned to.

The soldiers were growing more agitated as the platform continued to fill, and barked orders in Hungarian, pointing at the train, their meaning clear. Jet reached Matt and they pushed through the wall of bodies and ascended the steps, where another soldier indicated they should file into the car.

There were no seats left, so they stood, crammed together as they waited for the train to move. The only relief came from the open windows, which after the bus seemed like an almost impossible luxury. Hannah looked up at her mother with worried eyes, and then the train inched into motion with a roar from the locomotive far at the front of the column of cars.

"We'll be in Budapest before you know it," Jet whispered to her daughter, holding her close as the train rocked out of the station.

"Okay."

An older Syrian man eyed them suspiciously and then looked away, reminding Jet that they were still far from safe. She squeezed Hannah's hand reassuringly and then stared ahead, her eyes unfocused, resigned to several more uncomfortable hours before they boarded their final train to Italy.

Budapest turned out to be worse pandemonium than they'd yet experienced; theirs was only one of a dozen refugee trains that had converged on the hub for night trips out of the country. Conductors yelled indecipherable orders to them as they stepped from the car, and the ever-present armed soldiers directed them to a registration point for assignment to an appropriate platform. After another long wait, a red-faced official snapped a demand at them in Arabic, and Jet replied with their destination. The man waved a hand at one of the trains and then looked over Jet's shoulder at the next refugee with the long-suffering stare of someone who hated his job.

They moved to the platform, where a tall woman with the face of a buzzard confirmed their paperwork and told them to load into the nearest car and find seats wherever they could. Jet frowned but guided Matt and Hannah forward, glad that they'd used the bathroom on the prior train before it arrived – the next hours portended new levels of discomfort and unpleasantness, to judge from the appearance of the antique carriage and the number of people crowding aboard.

The trip to Italy stretched through the night, the train moving at barely more than a crawl much of the way, or so it seemed. A blood-red sun was climbing into the sky when they clattered into the Milan Central Railway Station. They were all exhausted after the long trip, the number of passengers making it impossible to sleep for more than a few minutes at a time.

The train lurched to a stop and the process of disembarking began. Jet held Hannah back as everyone rushed the exits at once, eager to be rid of the train's confined space. When the crowd had thinned to a safe level, they stepped from the train, where Italian police and soldiers prodded them toward a checkpoint, beyond which lay freedom. When it was their turn to be scrutinized by the immigration officials, they stood motionless while the men scrutinized their passports – and then they were stamped and through, part of the crowd moving against the early morning rush of workers headed for commuter trains.

The station was vast. They followed the rest of the migrants toward the main exit, where a group of soldiers eyeballed them with hostile glares. Outside they crossed to a plaza where hundreds of pigeons strutted in confused solidarity by a towering fountain. As they neared the water, Jet leaned into Matt and whispered a warning.

"I think we're being followed."

Matt's eyes widened, but he didn't look around. "Thieves?"

"Could be. Let's head for the boulevard. More people there."

They picked up their pace, and then they heard running footsteps approaching from behind. She grabbed Matt's arm in alarm. "Take Hannah and run. I'll buy some time."

"I'm staying," he protested.

"Get Hannah out of here," Jet snapped, and then spun to face the threat on their heels.

A trio of young Syrian men was bearing down on her, led by one of the migrants from the rail car that had carried them from Hungary. She felt at the pouch around her neck, slid the lanyard over her head, and tossed the diamonds to Matt. "Get going. I'll handle this," she said, her tone dangerously calm. Matt didn't budge, and then two of the men rushed her, coming in low, the flash of blades in their hands the only warning offered.

Jet whirled and parried the first man's clumsy thrust, blocking him with her forearm and rabbit-punching him in the throat with her free hand. The man dropped his knife with a gurgle and clutched at his voice box, and his companion slashed at Jet, nearly eviscerating her as she jumped back. The man recovered his balance from the foiled attempt, and his friend closed on her from the far side, his face twisted with a grimace.

A whistle shrieked and the pigeons took flight as one, flapping into the air in a gray and black cloud. "Matt, run," she yelled, and dodged another attempt to stab her by the nearest attacker before spin kicking him in the chest. She heard the snap of ribs, and the thug clutched at his sternum and wheezed. The whistles were joined by shouts in Italian as a pair of policemen came at a dead run. The migrant collapsed just as they arrived, Beretta 92s drawn, and stopped with their weapons trained on Jet and the downed pair.

Jet caught a glimpse of Matt hurrying across the street with Hannah out of the corner of her eye, and slowly raised her hands. "I'm unarmed," she said in Italian.

"What happened?" one of the cops demanded, his pistol unwavering.

"They attacked me." She paused. "I think they wanted to rape me. Or maybe rob me."

The man she'd kicked in the chest coughed a spray of bright red blood, and the policemen took a step back. One of them raised a radio to his lips while the other held his Beretta on the downed attackers, the third migrant standing frozen nearby, also with his hands in the air.

A minute later a motorcycle cop rolled up, followed by a cruiser with its siren blaring. An ambulance arrived shortly after one of the officers cuffed Jet and the man from the train. The other two Syrians were in bad shape, judging by the expressions on the paramedics tending to them.

"Why are you cuffing me?" Jet demanded. "They're the ones who attacked *me*!"

The cop who'd cuffed her looked at her hard and then shrugged. "That one doesn't look like he's going to make it. We're going to the station. We'll let my sergeant figure this out."

"Am I under arrest? What for?" she asked.

"Lady, I don't know what happened here, but I've got one man looking like he's about dead and the other with his windpipe crushed. Like I said, we'll let my sergeant decide how to proceed. For now, I'd keep quiet, because anything you say can be used against you."

CHAPTER 15

Matt was breathing hard when they reached the corner and turned to see the police arrive with their guns out. He debated going back for Jet, but knew that if she were taken into custody and they ran her prints, there was a good chance that she'd trigger Interpol, and then they'd all be cooked. Whether he liked it or not, his first duty was to keep Hannah safe – he and Jet had discussed every eventuality, and if one of them landed in hot water, the other's priority was the little girl. Jet was resourceful enough to be able to talk her way out of the situation – at least, he believed she stood a good chance, given that it was one woman who'd been attacked by three men.

Then again, her papers said she was a refugee, so she might be treated differently because of her immigration status. Matt didn't know how the law in Italy worked, but if the way the soldiers and officials had looked at them was any indication, it was unlikely to be kind to troublemakers fresh off the boat, regardless of who was at fault.

A police car screeched to a stop by the plaza, and he watched as a pair of officers leapt from the car, one with a submachine gun, the other with handcuffs. When the one with the bracelets approached Jet, that decided matters for Matt, and he pulled Hannah by the arm.

"No! Mama's in trouble!" Hannah cried, and Matt tightened his grip on her.

"Hannah, we need to go. Mama will be fine, but I promised her I'd make sure you're safe. Come on. Now. Before they see us."

"But Mama–"

"Hannah. Move."

His heart ached as he half dragged the little girl around the corner, and then he was jogging with her in his arms as she sobbed against his chest. He didn't stop for two blocks, and when he did, he set her down gently and knelt to bring his eyes level with hers. "Hannah, you have to help me, okay? We're going to find someplace to stay, and then I'll go help your mother, understand? Don't fight me on this. I need you to cooperate."

Hannah blinked away tears and snuffled as she nodded, her gaze accusing him of abandoning her mother, no matter what he claimed. He ignored the look and rose, offering his hand. She took it, and they walked east along the wide boulevard, Matt's thoughts a jumble of doubts, Hannah's sobs a reminder of his failings.

The first two hotels he tried claimed to be full, although the unfriendly and dismissive way the staff delivered the news made him doubt whether it was true. The third place, a run-down multistory affair in a questionable district, was happy to take his money after a cursory glance at his papers; the surly desk clerk showed no curiosity about why a refugee spoke American-accented English. The bellman escorted them up two flights of stairs to a long corridor and held the door of their room open for them with an expectant look. Matt slipped a five-euro note into his hand, and he muttered something in Italian before slouching off, leaving Matt and Hannah to themselves.

Matt locked the bolt and carried his backpack to one of the twin beds. He set it down and helped Hannah remove hers. "You want this bed, or that one?" he asked, trying to keep his voice light.

"I want Mama."

He sighed and nodded as he placed Hannah's pack on the bed closest to the window. "Me too, Hannah. But for now, let's get you showered and then we can grab something to eat, okay?"

"I'm not hungry."

Matt recognized the obstinate tone and elected not to fight that battle. "Let's see what the shower looks like," he said instead, and walked to the partially open door.

Like most European hotels, the bathroom was tiny, the stall barely large enough for him to stand in without his broad shoulders bumping against the glass door, but Matt forced a smile and opened the wall taps until a stream of warm water rained from the showerhead.

"This isn't so bad. Go ahead and get out of your clothes, and call if you need anything," he said, unwrapping a small bar of soap and placing it on the tray by the glass door, and then left her to her ablutions and sat by the window, pondering what to do next.

He turned on his phone, cursing himself for not remembering it earlier, and stared at the screen, hoping to see a missed call or message icon, but instead got only the roaming alert. He checked the charge and was relieved that it showed three-quarters full, but still ferreted in his backpack for the charger and plugged it in.

The bulge of the diamonds in his pocket reminded him to drape the lanyard around his neck for safekeeping, the weight of the stones trivial compared to their value. He counted his cash and was relieved to find over three thousand euros – plenty for the time being, even at the exorbitant rate the hotel was charging. The clerk had feigned contrition when he'd explained that there was a fashion show coming up, so all the hotels were full and charging premiums for any available space, but Matt had no fight left in him and gladly paid what was asked, his mind elsewhere.

Ten minutes later Hannah emerged from the bathroom with dripping hair, a towel around her torso. Matt rose wordlessly, removed clean clothes from her backpack, and handed them to her. She returned to the bathroom in silence, and Matt made a mental note to take her shopping for a top and some jeans, there being no further reason for her to dress like they were destitute.

He stared down at his pants and smiled sadly. He could use a change of clothes himself. If he didn't appear to be a refugee, perhaps he'd have an easier time of it and get more cooperation if he needed to hire an attorney to help Jet – assuming she'd been arrested. He was loath to jump to conclusions, but if she didn't call within another hour or so, he had to expect the worst and be prepared to go on the offense to free her before the system could identify her and their situation took an ugly turn for the worse.

CHAPTER 16

Baku, Azerbaijan

The outbuildings surrounding the vast grounds of the Muslumov steel factory were a drab gray that matched the sky. Taymaz Hovel walked with a retinue of aids and security men, guided by the factory director of operations, who was giving the president a tour of the grounds.

Part of Hovel's platform promise was to create jobs, and his trip to the plant was a gesture to show the seriousness of his intent – which ignored that during his two terms unemployment had skyrocketed and labor force participation plummeted. The official stats the government released painted a rosy picture of a healthy economy, in defiance of the data and simple observation. But like all good politicians, Hovel simply sidestepped inconvenient facts, simultaneously claiming the economy was robust while acknowledging that it needed more jobs.

The steel factory was one of the city's largest non-petroleum-based companies; the industry was considered a stronghold of Azerbaijani productivity and a lynchpin of the country's prosperity. That much of its work came from the government as a result of side deals negotiated in back rooms wasn't mentioned – the message was that the future looked bright under Hovel's strong leadership and that nothing could stop the country if it reelected him so he could continue his good work.

Hovel murmured to Hasanov as they neared the end of one of the long production structures.

"How many?" he asked.

The tour was to end with a rally in the mammoth parking lot, where Hovel's party had bused in supporters who'd been promised a hot meal and gift cards from the local supermarket chain in exchange for their appearance. Camera crews had taken up station near the stage to memorialize the event, and a small army of soldiers maintained order, ensuring that there would be no danger to Hovel or his entourage.

Hasanov did a quick calculation. "Couple of thousand."

Hovel's eyebrows rose. "That many?"

"Yes. Quite a few showed up unexpectedly. Which is good for the media coverage – speaks to your popularity."

Hovel was to give a twenty-minute speech to the masses, reading from handwritten notes, looking appropriately earnest and interested as he dispensed with the mandatory address. As the election drew near, his advisors had stressed that he be accessible and unafraid to appear in public, in contrast to the demonic figure the Nationalist Party had painted him as, in their relentless criticism of his regime and its policies.

Hovel checked his watch. "Are we on schedule?"

"Yes, sir."

"Good. I'm starving. I want to get this over with."

The factory director finished his tour, and the group made their way to the stage that had been erected near the central administrative office building. A sea of faces watched as Hovel arrived, and the cameras swept over the crowd as jubilant shills, in a staged spontaneous outpouring of support, held up signs emblazoned with Hovel's campaign slogans that had been distributed to them upon arrival.

Hovel walked to the microphone, where the director was introducing him with a laudable recitation of his accomplishments, and then it was showtime and the teleprompter blinked to life as applause rose from the gathering right on cue. Hovel waited until it died down and then began speaking, his voice evenly modulated with the practiced nuance of a professional liar.

"My fellow countrymen, thank you for coming. I've just received a tour of this factory and can honestly say that I'm astonished at how modern and competitive it is – truly a fitting symbol of the strides we've taken as a nation since I took office. If you recall, the country was in desperate straits then, but thanks to our collective efforts, we were able to build it into a powerhouse that is a beacon of progress in the region!"

A smattering of applause greeted his pause. Hovel had first taken power in a highly suspect vote a decade earlier, then was re-elected in an even more unusual contest five years later. There was no term limit, so he could theoretically continue to rule until he died of old age many years in the future.

"But we still have work to do. Our children deserve a bright future, a safe future, a prosperous future, where their voices are heard and count in their governance. It is that future that keeps me striving to improve our systems to meet the challenges of the new century. With your help, we will develop it together."

This time the applause was hardly audible, so Hovel picked up the pace.

"Every era has challenges; this one is no exception. I am committed to ensuring that the wealth of the nation is more evenly distributed moving forward, and that the corruption we have made progress against is eradicated by the time my next term is finished. That is my commitment to you, the voters, and it is shared by my cabinet and the prime minister."

Several boos echoed from the middle of the crowd, but Hovel soldiered through without acknowledging the outbursts.

"I'm painfully aware that some can't find suitable work, and I share their pain. Even in an economy that's prospering, there will be gaps, and part of our duty as a society is to find ways to fill those gaps so that every citizen can have a productive life and a decent standard of living. We're not there yet, but contrast today to where we were ten years ago and you'll see that much has changed. Is it enough? No. Of course not. It's never enough until every person can fulfill their promise, can raise their children with full bellies and in good health, and can enjoy the fruits of their labor with a minimum of government interference."

A red orb sailed from the throng. The tomato missed the podium by five feet but spattered colorfully against the stage. Hovel instinctively ducked at the inbound fruit, his body language fearful, and it was that image that was captured by the cameras trained on him and broadcast live. Shouts of protest erupted from somewhere in the middle of the press of bodies, and fists flew as supporters and protestors began fighting, while the front of the crowd surged toward the stage in an effort to get clear of the combatants.

Hovel's security team whisked him from the podium and down the steps at the back of the stage, and a cordon of armed soldiers closed ranks to prevent anyone from following. His bodyguards escorted him to a waiting column of SUVs and he climbed aboard the lead vehicle, the blood drained from his face at the unexpected outburst. The rallies had been peaceful up until now, but that the opposition forces were so emboldened as to disrupt a large one in the heart of his most supportive district boded ill for the election.

He glared through the bulletproof window as the driver dropped the transmission into gear and began rolling forward, Hasanov beside him with a strained expression.

"I want the troublemakers rounded up and dealt with. This is inexcusable. It will not be tolerated. We need to send a clear message," Hovel spat.

"Yes, of course."

The driver's handheld radio blared from the front seat, and a voice reported from the stage. "It's turning into a riot here. Get going."

"Roger that," the driver said, and tromped on the throttle.

"No shooting," Hovel ordered. "That wouldn't look good. Put down the protest, but don't kill anyone."

A mass slaying at his rally would destroy any remaining support he had, and Hovel's political instincts weren't so poor that he was willing to risk that. Better to let the masses beat themselves bloody and wear themselves out than to appear to be an authoritarian despot – precisely what the Nationalists accused him of on a daily basis.

Hasanov nodded and reached for the radio. "I'll relay your instructions."

Hovel's stomach rumbled, and he sat back fuming as the driver sped toward the complex gates, with the other vehicles keeping pace, the triumphant rally now an unmitigated disaster.

CHAPTER 17

Milan, Italy

Jet looked up from her position on the unyielding steel bench in the holding cell. The other prisoners gave her a wide berth, as though sensing danger even though she hadn't engaged with them.

She'd been taken in cuffs to the main police station, where she'd been questioned by a detective until they were interrupted by a uniformed officer, who'd whispered something to the interrogator before hurrying away. The detective had leveled a hard stare at Jet and shaken his head.

"One of the men you injured just died. A rib punctured his lung. Too far gone by the time they got him into surgery." He paused. "That changes things."

"How? I told you I was defending myself. Three men attack me, so what am I supposed to do? Give them a disapproving look? They had knives. Your men recovered their weapons."

"That's your story, and I don't doubt it. But they're saying you're the one who attacked them. You…and others."

"What others? That's preposterous. It's clear what happened. They tried to rob me, I responded to save my life, a couple of them got hurt. Being muggers is dangerous work. And now I'm in trouble?"

"Save it for the judge. We're going to process you and then you can contact an attorney, or one will be appointed for you. If you're innocent, you have nothing to fear. But with a dead man, this is far more serious, as I'm sure you can appreciate."

"So you're arresting me?"

"Yes."

Jet had clammed up at that point, silently cursing the man who'd died. She'd thought that she could talk her way out of the jam, but with a body in the morgue, she understood that the state had to do something – and it probably didn't help that she was a refugee and therefore suspect from the start.

She snapped back to the present as footsteps approached. Two guards neared the barred door and ordered the prisoners to step back. They opened it and motioned to Jet, who silently stood and walked out of the cell, surprised that they didn't cuff her. She considered breaking both their necks and making a run for it, but dismissed the idea; she'd never get out of the station alive.

The guards walked her to a steel door at the end of the hall, and the one on her right held it open for her. Inside, a man in his thirties sat on the opposite side of a steel table, the chairs bolted to the ground. Jet looked at him, her face unreadable, and he nodded to the guards, who closed the door behind them, leaving them alone in the room.

"What is this?" Jet asked in Italian. "Are you my attorney? I don't want a public defender. I want to make my phone call."

"Sit down," the man said in Hebrew.

Jet's eyes narrowed slightly, but she did as instructed. "How did you know I would understand?" she whispered.

"No games. I know everything. We've been tracking you for some time or at least trying to. You've led everyone on a merry chase. But your prints triggered a flag, which is why I'm here."

"And you are…?"

"My name is unimportant. You know who I represent."

Jet studied his unremarkable features; his dark, wavy hair; his neutral expression. She nodded slowly. "What do you want?"

"To help."

"Why am I not reassured?"

The man smiled. "The last words you ever want to hear coming from any government agency, I know. Still, I have a proposal, and you have yourself a very real problem. As you're no doubt aware, we're not the only ones interested in your whereabouts."

"One of the curses of celebrity."

"The same alarms that tripped when the prints were entered into Interpol's database are right now sounding in Washington." He paused, seeing a reaction in her eyes. "That's right. We know all about your friend's troubles with his ex-employer – troubles that are now yours as well. Not to mention that one of your victims here died."

"Victims? Attackers, you mean," she corrected.

"We both know they stood no chance. I've read your dossier."

"I have a dossier?"

"One we compiled after taking an interest in your latest exploits. Of course, there's no file on you from…before. That we pieced together."

Jet held his stare. "You say you want to help. How?"

"We'll walk out of here together, and you'll disappear off the radar again – this time for good."

"Is that part of the unofficial retirement package?"

"In a manner of speaking. We have a situation we could use some help on in reciprocation. One hand washes the other. Isn't that always the case?"

She shook her head. "I'm no longer in the game."

"Yes, well, your situation is a complex one. As you know, part of what you originally signed up for was a career you don't get to quit. We know why you faked your death, and your service to us in the terrorism matter since then hasn't gone unnoticed. So we're willing to strike a new bargain. It's simple, really. We'll keep you safe. You help us occasionally. Quid pro quo."

Jet frowned. "Why should I listen to any more of this?"

"Because if we can find you, so can your enemies, of whom you've collected quite an array. You and your new family will never be safe trying to hide the way you're doing it. The only way it could work is if you had state assistance – that's what we're proposing. You return with us to Israel; we create new identities for you and your family and put you into deep cover. Nobody will be able to find you, much less get to you. We can guarantee it." He paused. "The alternative is you decline, I go back and tell my superiors you're off the table, and you wait for the axe to drop."

They were interrupted by the door opening. One of the guards poked his head in, his voice tight.

"The AISI is at the front desk, demanding to see her," he said. The AISI was one of Italy's intelligence agencies, chartered with domestic security – the rough equivalent of the American FBI. "The desk sergeant is running interference, but he can't stonewall them for long."

Angry voices carried from down the hall, a heated argument coming from the administrative area. The Mossad operative nodded to the guard. "Okay. Is there a back way out of here?"

"Yes. I'll show you."

The operative eyed Jet. "We have to hurry."

The guard led them past the cells to a security door, where he swiped his card through a reader and pushed it open. They entered a stairwell that led into a basement and then another hall, longer than the first, that ran beneath the cell block.

"This leads to a maintenance access," the guard explained as they crept along the corridor. "There's another security door at the other end, and then you can exit through a pair of double doors into the central courtyard. From there, just walk out onto the street."

Jet remained silent until the guard had swiped the second door open for them. The Mossad operative nodded his gratitude to the man, who looked worried but calm. Jet followed her new friend upstairs and into the late afternoon sun. At least fifty uniformed officers were in the plaza, some talking in groups, others making their way to or from the headquarters building, and easily double that many civilians were going about their business. The Israeli led her at a moderate pace to the main street entry, where a pair of cops sat on stools, watching the stream of people come and go. The guards didn't give Jet a second glance, and a minute later they were a block from the building and walking faster.

"What about my papers, money, and phone?" Jet asked.

"I got your passport and phone. Money's part of the sergeant's take."

"I was going to ask how you penetrated the police so effectively."

He shrugged. "Everything's for sale. There will be a record found of you being accidentally discharged a half hour before the intel goons showed up. The security cameras have been down for most of the day, so no footage of your departure. Trail ends there. Of course there will be protests, but they won't go anywhere."

"What if somebody talks?"

"They won't. I pay well, and nobody wants to incriminate themselves. That's just how Italy works."

"Where are we going?"

He withdrew a cell phone with a digital scrambler attached from his pocket and dialed a number. After a short discussion, he gave her the handset.

"Hello?" Jet said.

"It's been too long," the director said, his sandpaper voice as distinct as a fingerprint. "But I suspected we might meet again. I felt we left things…unfinished, in Qatar."

"When Isaac tried to shoot me, you mean?"

"It was never personal. It was a tranquilizer gun."

"Same difference."

The director coughed, and Jet could hear him suck deeply on a cigarette before continuing. "Our man explained things to you?"

"You're offering sanctuary in Israel out of the goodness of your heart. But there might be strings attached."

"As good a summary as any. We have a situation. I can explain when you arrive."

"He mentioned my family as well."

"Yes, that's right. All of you. No extra charge for volume."

"How do you get us out of Italy without the authorities getting wise?"

"Let me worry about that. Put our man back on the line. I'll see you shortly."

She hesitated. "I'm not happy. We had a deal, which you reneged on."

"No, which prudence dictated I act upon, at the time, but which I subsequently kept. I haven't bothered you, have I? Although I've kept an eye on your misadventures, I haven't lifted a finger. As to Isaac, tell me that you would have handled that differently."

"Haven't lifted a finger until now," she corrected, ignoring his rationalization.

"There was no other way. Put him on the phone."

Jet hesitated, and when she spoke, there was steel in her voice. "I need to talk this over with…my partner. I can't give you an answer yet."

The director's breathing sounded labored as the silence on the line stretched for several tense seconds.

"We got you out of jail."

"I need to explain it to him. That's not negotiable. It's his life too."

The director's tone thawed a tenth of a degree. "There's a time element to the offer."

"I understand. I need…twenty-four hours."

The director laughed humorlessly. "Absolutely not. I can give you…twelve. After that, you're on your own, and believe me, with the Italians on alert and our American alphabet agency friends winging their way to Italy, you don't want to be."

"That sounds like a threat."

"It's not. We both know they want you dead, and they'll get you this time around. The EU's systems are too integrated for you to make it far. They'll take you down, and your daughter and your, uh…partner, as well. I understand they can be vindictive. You shouldn't risk it."

She ignored the menace in his words. "Twelve hours, then."

"We can't run interference for you if you're not in our custody."

"I appreciate your concern. But like I said, it's not negotiable."

The director sounded angry, but resigned. "You're making a mistake."

"It's mine to make."

"Put my man back on the phone."

Jet handed the operative the encrypted cell and slowed as he walked several steps away so she couldn't overhear his discussion, which lasted less than half a minute. When he finished, he pocketed the phone and extracted her slimmer burner cell from the breast pocket of his shirt. "Here," he said. "I'm to hold on to your passport." He powered on her phone, entered a number, and pressed send. Another phone chirped from his satchel. He terminated the call and handed Jet her cell. "That's my number. Call me. You have twelve hours. If you stiff us, there's nothing we can do for you, so forget you ever met me when they catch you." He paused and looked her in the eyes. "Which they will."

He veered off down a side street, and then he was just another pedestrian, indistinguishable from the rest. Jet continued straight, and when she'd put another two blocks between herself and the police station, she called Matt's burner. He answered on the second ring.

"Where are you?" he asked, clearly relieved.

She took her bearings from a street sign on the corner. "Safe. Where are you?"

He gave her the name of the hotel. She repeated it and then paused. "I'll find it."

"Is everything…are you okay?"

"I'll tell you in person. You'll need to pay the cab when I get there – I don't have any money. Wait for me in the lobby. I'm taking the battery out of my phone. It's probably compromised. Got to go," she said, and disconnected as she waved at a taxi, leery of spending any more time than she had to on the cell. The police might be crooked, but she couldn't bet they were incompetent – and she wouldn't have put it past the Mossad to have set up tracking on the cell, which made sense given it was the only thing of hers they'd returned. She stared at the little screen and memorized the number the operative had entered, and then pulled the battery and dropped it into the gutter as she climbed into the taxi and gave the driver the hotel name.

A block away, she hung the phone out the window and released it as the driver changed lanes, secure that it would be smashed to splinters within minutes beneath the wheels of the cars behind her, and then sat back, the director's words echoing in her ear. His offer was a bad one for her – but probably the only one that would keep Matt and Hannah alive.

CHAPTER 18

Tel Aviv, Israel

The director glowered at an abstract painting that hung on the far wall of his office. Smoke curled from his ever-present cigarette, his gray curly hair and basset hound face yellowed from many decades of chain-smoking. His gambit hadn't played quite the way he'd planned, but he was confident that the woman would come around to his way of thinking and take the deal. There was really no choice for her.

And besides, he knew her kind. She wasn't meant for civilian life. She was a highly trained killing machine, and you didn't just turn that off and walk away. She'd tried, but trouble had continued to find her, and now she was back at square one: either she cooperated with the Mossad and in return her family was sheltered, or she was hung out to dry and wouldn't live the week.

She might be stubborn, but she wasn't stupid. She would see things correctly once she spoke with the American.

He would be more of a problem. Keeping the CIA in the dark about the Mossad sheltering him was a delicate dance, but not an impossible one. After all, that would be about the last place on earth they would expect him to be: hiding in plain sight.

The director took a long drag on his cigarette and nodded to himself.

Jet was ideal for the task he had in mind. He needed someone deniable, skilled, highly efficient, who could pull off an extremely difficult mission without a hitch. He had others who might be able to do so, but no females of sufficient ability at present – and the opportunity they had required a woman.

Fortunately, the universe had provided, as it had so many times before. Jet would return to the fold, and he would have his super-operative to carry out the impossible.

Assuming she took the deal.

He inhaled another deep draught of toxic smoke and blew it at a discolored spot on the ceiling, his lungs protesting the ravaging, as they had much of his adult life. It was a filthy habit he detested – his clothes stank, his skin, his breath. His teeth were yellow and foul, his lungs scarred beyond recognition, and he'd stopped getting annual physicals because he didn't want to be told this was the year he was going to die.

He was honestly amazed every morning he came to and was still breathing. Given his stress levels, his abysmal diet, his nonexistent exercise regime, and his nicotine intake, every day was its own little miracle, and one he wouldn't take for granted.

Which brought him back to the problem at hand.

He'd considered the recommendations of his advisors on the Azerbaijan problem and had determined that the only suggestion that had any real chance of success, now that their assassination scheme had failed, was the one proposed by Amit Mendel.

But it would require a delicate hand, and someone who was expendable.

Jet fit that bill perfectly.

The director had long ago given up moral or ethical considerations of things like the taking of life to accomplish an objective. Those were for more innocent souls who didn't have to stare into the abyss over their morning coffee and determine the fates of regimes by noon. While he didn't order the assassination of someone lightly, he did so without hesitation if it was the best, or only, way to achieve an end. That was simply how the world worked, and there were plenty waiting to replace him if he ever lost the stomach for it. Powerful forces organized, manipulated, connived, and oppressed, all to get their way; and like it or not, his job was to achieve objectives set by his masters by whatever means necessary.

In this case, they had determined that the current president of Azerbaijan must win re-election, and had chartered the director's agency with ensuring that happened.

The only viable challenger to the president's bid was the head of the Nationalist Party. But the assassination plot against him had fallen apart, so there would be no chance to take him out in time.

Which was where Jet entered the picture. Mendel's plan was so audacious, so over the top, that nobody would see it coming, which ensured it would have the desired effect. Like a Russian doll, there were exquisitely complex layers to it, twists and surprises that would be pointed to as being too difficult for anyone to predict, and thus any conspiracy theory that approximated the truth would appear so outlandish it could be easily dismissed.

The director smiled as he lit a fresh cigarette using the lit butt of his last.

Machiavelli had nothing on them.

He reached forward and depressed the intercom button on an ancient handset that he'd been using almost as long as he'd held office.

"Get Mendel in here," he said. "Now."

CHAPTER 19

Milan, Italy

Jet spied Matt waiting on the street outside of the hotel, and the taxi pulled to the curb. Matt jogged over, money in hand, and paid the driver while Jet stepped out. They waited until the cab had disappeared into traffic before entering the hotel.

"Where's Hannah?" Jet asked.

"I had her stay in the room. Don't worry. She's trustworthy by herself."

"I'm not worried."

She covered her face while pretending to cough as they walked past the desk clerk, who seemed utterly disinterested in her as Matt led her to the stairs. When they reached the room door, she glanced down the hallway and pursed her lips. "Nice place."

"One step above cesspool," Matt agreed. "But at least it's expensive." He paused as he reached for the doorknob. "How are you?"

She tiptoed and kissed him. "I've had better days."

"You going to tell me what happened?"

"Let's get out of the hall."

Hannah came cannonballing across the room at the sight of her mother and hugged her tight. Jet returned the favor and then sat with her on the bed as Matt took a seat on the other.

"So?"

"They arrested me. One of the punks died. And my prints triggered the intelligence service…and my former employer."

Matt's face fell. "Then how…"

105

"Mossad got me out. Long story, but the short version is they're offering us a deal."

"Us?"

"They know about you and Hannah."

He nodded. "Right."

"And they seem confident that if I don't do as they ask, we're toast." She filled him in on her call with the director. When she finished, Matt's expression was drawn.

"You didn't agree?" he asked.

"No. I stalled for time. I don't trust them as far as I can throw them."

"Then what do we do?"

She looked at her watch. "We have seven more hours. They'll have my face all over the news soon. I need to dye my hair, at the very least. Go really dark, and maybe trim my bangs."

"So you want me to get you some dye and scissors?"

She gave him a tired smile. "Would you? That way Hannah and I can have some quiet time together. Oh, and maybe an eyeliner pencil and some darker base?"

"Okay. But if the system flagged your prints, you have to know that our immigration status, coming in together, will eventually surface."

"I'm betting on the chaos at the borders keeping them from being lightning fast in their data entry." She smiled again. "We are talking Italy, here."

"Good point. I'll go find a pharmacy."

Matt headed downstairs and was nearly to the entrance when the desk clerk called to him in heavily accented English.

"Sir?"

Matt slowly turned. "Yes?"

"I saw a woman with you, yes?"

"That's right."

"Rules say I need identification if she's staying here."

"Oh. Okay. When I get back, I'll see to that."

Matt exited the hotel and set off down the block, troubled by the clerk's request. Had he gotten a better look at Jet than they'd thought? Was he suspicious? Had her image already appeared on the television?

If so, their problems were compounding quickly, and they might not even have the seven hours Jet had indicated.

He found a pharmacy and went inside, hurried to the grooming and hair product section, and selected an ebony home dying kit that promised natural results in about an hour. At least that was what he intuited from the starburst and exclamation-pointed capitalized Italian. He grabbed a box and found hair shears on the same aisle, paid for his purchases, and retraced his steps to the hotel, his nerves shot to hell after the last few days.

The clerk looked up at him when he walked through the door. "Remember, the papers…"

"Yes. Of course. I'll see if she's going to stay past dinner, and if she does, I'll get you something. I trust you don't need anything if she's just here for an hour or two?"

The clerk offered a salacious grin and winked in complicit understanding, as only an Italian male could.

Jet had showered by the time Matt made it back and was wearing one of his shirts. He admired the way she filled it out and gave her a wan smile.

"Doesn't look the same on me," he said.

"I need to buy some clothes. The cops got my bag, too."

"That limits our moves."

"You have my other passports in your bag, right?"

"Yes. But if they distribute your photo, that could be a tough one to dodge."

"You get the dye?"

He handed her the bag and she padded to the bathroom with it and shut the door. Hannah followed her and knocked. Jet opened it a crack and she squeezed through, and then the door eased closed again, their voices muffled.

An hour passed as Matt channel surfed for news programs. Jet reappeared, her hair gleaming and wet, now raven toned and trimmed differently. She angled her head and raised an eyebrow.

"What do you think?"

"You've found your next career, if you need one."

"Will it fool anyone?"

"Better than nothing. I mean, it's different, but I wouldn't want to bet on it. I can't remember how close the passport photo was to how you actually look."

"I had heavier makeup on so it would mask some of my natural features. But there's a limit."

"What about the base?"

"That's next."

She returned to the bathroom and spread makeup in her palm, and then applied it from her neck to her hairline. After inspecting the results, she went to work with the eyeliner pencil, shading beneath her eyes and along her subtle frown lines. When she was finished, she looked easily ten years older than her twenty-nine years, the subtle shadows she'd created with the pencil hardening her face with a stern cast.

Matt inspected her work and nodded. "The clerk wants ID for you if we stay."

"I was afraid of that."

"We can give him one of your passports."

She shook her head. "We need somewhere we can go to ground while we figure out what we're going to do."

"Mama. It's you!" Hannah called from the television. They spun toward the screen, where Jet's booking mugshot was on the news, along with a sonorous voice-over advising the public that if they saw the fugitive, she was wanted in a murder investigation. When the program switched to parade footage, Matt eyed Jet.

"There's your answer about whether they were going to publicize things. Think the Mossad had anything to do with it?"

"Certainly turns up the heat."

"So what do we do?" Matt hesitated. "What do you want to do? You're the one who has to pay the price if you decide to take them up on it."

She sat down and pulled him beside her on the bed and stared deep into his eyes. "Do you see any way out?"

"We can bribe someone to ferry us over to Sicily."

"Maybe. But they found us again, Matt, and they know we're in the region. I'm getting the feeling the world's closing in on us. If it was just me, maybe I could vanish, but with you and Hannah…technology's not our friend."

"So you're leaning toward doing it?"

"I want you and Hannah to be safe. They're promising that."

"They've lied before."

"Yes, but this doesn't cost them anything besides a little house or apartment somewhere and some new documents. It's an easy one from their standpoint, and they get their operative back. They obviously need me for something serious or they wouldn't bother."

"And once you're done?"

"That's part of the problem. If I agree, I'll never be done."

Matt's frown deepened. "Then you'll be in constant danger. That's not a solution."

Jet sighed and considered Hannah's profile. The little girl was sitting on the floor, watching the screen, unaware of the drama playing out between them. "Seems like that won't be much of a change. It's not like we've been out of the crosshairs for long."

"Putting yourself in harm's way on a mission is different. We both know that."

"I'm all ears if you have any alternatives."

Matt proposed several, but even as he spoke, they sounded impractical to his ear. As they drilled through their options, the truth became apparent: the Mossad held all the cards. Jet rose and checked her appearance in the mirror again and, when she returned to the doorway, shook her head. "It's no good. They've got us in a box."

"And?"

She held out her hand. "Give me your phone. I need to make a call."

CHAPTER 20

Jet met the Mossad operative a block from the hotel with Matt and Hannah in tow. He pulled to the curb in a blue diesel Nissan van and waited as they loaded into the little vehicle, scanning his mirrors and the street with a vigilance Matt and Jet knew well. When they were seated and the doors closed, he signaled and accelerated into traffic with the daredevil machismo of the locals, the engine clattering like a can filled with pebbles.

"So what should we call you?" Jet asked him.

"Gino."

"Gino?" Matt repeated incredulously.

The operative switched to English. "When in Rome."

"Where are we headed?" Jet asked.

"It will be tricky getting out of Milan. There are reports of roadblocks."

"Isn't that unusual for something like this?"

Gino nodded. "It would appear that the CIA has exerted some pressure on the Italians since you disappeared. They apparently aren't happy."

"We knew they'd be in the mix soon enough."

"Yes, but we didn't expect them to be so aggressive."

"Then how do we slip past them?"

"You're to split up. They're watching for a woman, so you'll be smuggled to the coast in a truck with a false compartment. The girl and your friend will stay with me."

Jet crossed her arms. "No. We don't separate under any circumstances," she said.

Gino scowled and shook his head. "This isn't a negotiation. That's how it's going to go down. Either that, or you might as well turn

110

yourself in now, because if we're stopped leaving town, you're as good as arrested again."

"Why can't you get me a diplomatic passport or something?"

"We don't have time." He paused. "What's your concern?"

"My concern is I never see my daughter or Matt again, and I'm your prisoner. Obviously."

"Those aren't my instructions. You have the director's word you'll be treated fairly."

"All due respect, he's lied to me before, so his word means less than spit." She hesitated, thinking. "Matt and Hannah can ride with the driver."

Gino shook his head. "That would be a red flag."

"Then give them a car and they'll follow the truck. We can stay in contact via phones or radios. We're not going to be separated. Figure out a way," she said, her voice hard.

Gino placed a call on his encrypted phone and had a murmured discussion, and then hung up and caught her eye in the rearview mirror.

"Fine. We'll supply a vehicle. You do have a driver's license and passports if you're stopped, right?" he asked Matt.

"Don't worry about us," Matt said. "Just get us a ride and a phone."

They traversed the city and entered an industrial area with long warehouses stretching from the street, the road degrading with the neighborhood. Gino swung into an anonymous yard filled with bobtail trucks and a yawning gate, no signs of life anywhere. He ground to a stop on the gravel, shut off the engine, and unclipped his safety belt.

"Follow me."

They piled out of the van, Hannah and Matt with their backpacks, and made their way to a door near a loading dock. Paint was peeling from the walls, and discarded plastic bottles and wrappers clogged the drain grid that ran along the base of the building. Gino tried the handle and then knocked, and they waited as footsteps thumped inside, echoing off the high steel roof.

A man with no neck and pig eyes stared at them from the doorway and stepped aside without a word. Gino led them into the cavernous warehouse to where a truck was waiting near a stack of pallets. Another man in his thirties with a long ponytail and a goatee was leaning against it, listening to music on his phone. He looked up as they approached.

"You're late," he said.

Gino shrugged. "Traffic."

"Same problem leaving town."

"How long will we be on the road?" Jet asked.

The goateed driver shrugged. "Five hours. Maybe six."

"Where are we going? Genoa?"

Gino shook his head. "Porto Ercole, down the coast. There's a marina there. You'll board a vessel that will take you to Sardinia, where we'll have a plane waiting. The boat captain will give you the details." Gino glanced at the driver. "You have the car?"

He nodded and tossed Gino the keys. "Out back. Brown Fiat. Full tank. Registration's in the glove compartment."

Jet held out her hand to Gino. "Phone?"

The driver opened the driver's side door of the truck and returned moments later with a cheap disposable Nokia that was at least five years old. He gave it to Jet, and she turned it on and then entered Matt's number. She saved it and eyed the battery indicator with approval.

"You need to use the bathroom, now's your chance," the driver said.

Jet took Hannah by the hand, and they followed the driver to a door at the far side of the warehouse while Matt waited. When they got back, the driver shifted some of the cargo in the truck aside and opened a compartment in the floor. "There's cushions in there that should make it a little better than nothing, but it's not going to be a picnic. That's normally used for…special cargo, not people."

She looked to Gino, who shrugged. "Weapons. Contraband. Whatever."

"Hope you don't get claustrophobic," the driver said.

Jet met his eyes without flinching. "I don't." She turned from him, leaned over, and kissed Hannah. "Be good, okay? I'll be right here. You'll be following in a car with Matt."

"Can I go with you?"

"No, sweetie. Mama's got to do this alone."

Hannah's eyes welled with moisture and her lower lip trembled, but she nodded understanding, if not agreement. Jet swallowed a golf ball-size lump in her throat, gave Matt a peck, and climbed into the truck. She lowered herself in to the compartment and was reassured that it had sufficient space for her to adjust her posture somewhat and ventilation from a series of crude grills near her head. The driver looked down at her with a slight grin and slid the flooring back into place, and then she was enshrouded in total darkness.

Matt followed Gino to the rear of the building where the Fiat was parked. The Mossad operative climbed into the car, started the engine, and stepped out. He faced off with Matt, who was taller by a good six inches, and eyed Hannah.

"Stick on his tail. If he gets stopped, keep going and wait at the nearest place you can. There's only one main route down the coast, so you shouldn't have any problems once you're out of Milan."

Matt nodded and helped Hannah into the passenger seat, stowing their backpacks in the rear, and rounded the hood to the driver's side. He slid behind the wheel, adjusted the mirror and seat, and then pulled the door closed and eased the car into gear.

A rolling steel door rose at the back of the warehouse and the truck pulled out. Matt glued himself to the taillights and bounced down the drive, the afternoon light fading into the gloaming. His phone rang, and he reached for his shirt pocket.

"Hey," he answered.

"This sucks," Jet said, over the engine noise from the truck exhaust roaring in the background.

"You knew it would."

"You following?"

"I'm on your tail." He paused. "Good call on not splitting up."

"Over my dead body."

"You got enough air?"

"That's not the problem. It's the vibration and the bumps. Thing has no shocks."

"Well, good luck."

"Thanks. I'll call periodically to verify you haven't bailed on me."

"Now's our big chance."

There was a long pause. "I hope we did the right thing."

It was Matt's turn to hesitate. When he spoke, his voice was quiet. "We'll know soon enough."

CHAPTER 21

The truck braked to a stop at the end of a long line of cars. Ahead, police car roof lights strobed off the vehicles as officers scrutinized the occupants before waving them through. Matt's phone rang and he thumbed it to life.

"What's happening?" Jet asked.

"Roadblock. Appears the rumors were true."

"How thorough does it look?"

"They're definitely paying attention. Probably a couple hundred cars ahead of us, so they're taking their time."

Jet disconnected and Matt slid the phone back into his shirt pocket. Hannah was watching him with intense interest, and he forced a smile. "Mama called to say she's fine."

"Why is she hiding?"

"Bad men."

Hannah had heard the answer often enough before to accept it and nod knowledgeably. "Oh."

Matt felt for his fake Canadian driver's license and passport in his backpack with his right hand. The column of vehicles crawled forward as darkness fell, and he watched as the truck eventually reached the checkpoint. After several moments the driver appeared with two officers toting machine guns and rolled the door of the cargo bay up so they could see inside. One of the cops climbed awkwardly into the bed and rooted around the cartons, and Matt's breath caught in his throat – the police were taking this far more seriously than he'd have expected, no doubt due to the Italian intelligence service pulling out all the stops.

The officer hopped down and the driver pulled the door closed again, and then it was Matt's turn. A flashlight beam blinded him and a gruff voice growled a question in Italian through his open window. He shook his head and spoke English.

"I'm afraid I don't understand. No Italian."

The cop looked annoyed and shined the beam on Hannah for several seconds, and then on their backpacks. Matt forced his breathing slower as the cop appeared to lose interest, and then his phone trilled again, drawing the cop's attention.

Matt pointed to his shirt and smiled sheepishly. The cop gave him a disgusted look and waved him forward. Matt answered the call, his voice tight.

"We're through," he said.

"No problems?"

"Nothing fatal."

The drive south took longer than advertised, and it was midnight by the time the truck rolled into the tiny waterfront town of Porto Ercole and shimmied down the uneven road that led to the marina. The white hulls of private yachts reflected off the inky water in the pale moonlight that gilded the surface of the swells, the boats straining at their mooring lines with the Mediterranean surge as the trucker guided the bobtail the final yards to the parking lot and shut off the engine.

Matt wheeled in beside him and got out of the car. The area was still, the air redolent with the salty tang of the sea, and there were only a few lights still on in the surrounding homes. After glancing around, the driver moved to the rear of the truck and opened the bay. A minute later Jet joined Matt by the Fiat with Hannah, rolling her head to get a kink out of her neck, her muscles stiff from lying immobile in the confined space for over six hours.

A figure limped toward them from the marina gate, and a crusty man in his sixties with a hand-rolled cigarette stuck to his bottom lip approached, his blue turtleneck sweater and fisherman's hat black in the dim light. He inspected them with alert eyes and then turned to the driver.

"This everybody, right?"

"Correct. They're all yours now."

The old-timer grunted and looked hard at Jet. "You speak Italian?"

"Yes."

"My name's Giuseppe. I'm the captain of the boat that will take you to Sardinia. Is that all you have?" he asked, motioning to Matt's and Hannah's backpacks.

"Yes."

"Good. Then let's get under way. I want to be there by morning, but even with favorable sea conditions, it'll be a push."

The captain led them down a grade to the water, where a sleek Euro-style yacht was moored, its stern facing the jetty. A passerelle bridged the gap between land and boat. Jet went first, followed by Matt and her daughter, the captain bringing up the rear, his steps confident on the narrow teak gangplank.

Giuseppe depressed a button and the hydraulic passerelle retracted into a compartment in the stern with a whine, and then made for the pilothouse. The big diesel motors started with a rumble, and he returned to the stern and slipped the mooring line from a cleat before making his way forward and doing the same on the bow, his limp less pronounced as he moved with surprising speed, given his age and infirmity.

Back at the wheel, he slipped the transmissions into gear and idled to the breakwater at the mouth of the small harbor before pushing the throttles forward. The big boat surged ahead as the bow rose, and the captain's face glowed from the radar and instrument screens. The yacht picked up speed until the speedometer display read twenty-eight knots, and Giuseppe turned to where Jet was standing.

"There's food and drink below. Three staterooms. Use whatever you like. Self-explanatory, if you've ever been aboard a boat before."

"We have."

"Good. I'm single-handing this trip, so there's nobody to explain things to. Go ahead and get some shut-eye. We should be in Fertilia by nine."

"How far is that?"

"Four hundred kilometers. But the report says it'll get bumpy when we reach the middle, so we'll have to slow some."

"You've done the crossing before?"

"Often enough to never take the sea for granted." He paused. "Only thing worse than unexpected squalls would be an Italian patrol boat taking an interest in us."

Jet's eyes narrowed. "What are the chances of that?"

He shrugged. "Slimmer the further out we get. But it's always a risk."

"Then what do we do?"

"You have papers?"

She shook her head.

"How well can you hold your breath and swim?"

Her face was stony. "Is that a joke?"

Giuseppe grinned. "Don't worry. Most of them know me. I'm sort of a regular along this stretch of coast."

"Then why mention it?"

He winked. "Full disclosure, nothing more."

Jet threw him a dark look and edged to Matt. "We should try to get some rest."

A trace of a smile tugged at his lips. "I didn't want to interrupt your talk. You two seemed to be becoming best friends."

"He says to expect some ugly seas ahead, and I'm to swim for it if patrol boats board us – which is him being funny. Hopes to have us in Sardinia by nine. That about covers it."

Matt eyed Hannah and nodded. "Let's hit it. Lead the way."

The master stateroom was amidships, the full width of the hull, and was opulent by any standard, with polished exotic hardwoods and marble and granite everywhere. Jet plopped onto the bed, bounced twice, and winked at Hannah. "Last one asleep has to scrub the toilet."

"Ew," the little girl exclaimed, and threw herself beside her mother, giggling. Matt used the bathroom and then lowered himself onto the sheets beside Jet, suddenly as weary as he could remember.

"It'll be nice when we can actually sleep without being fully clothed," he said.

She sighed. "No argument."

The captain's warning of rough water proved prescient, and three hours into the trip the engine pitch lowered to reduce the hull from pounding. Fortunately, they were at the lowest point in the boat, so the rocking from beam seas was mitigated enough for them to snatch at least some uneasy rest.

When the sun rose over the azure horizon and Giuseppe inched the throttles forward again, Jet joined him in the pilothouse while Matt and Hannah slumbered. The captain had brewed a pot of rich Italian coffee, and they clutched steaming mugs as they eyed the sea, the water now nearly flat as they approached the strait between Sardinia and Corsica.

"How much longer?" she asked.

"An hour until we're between the islands, and then another hour until we moor. I was able to make better time than I thought, even with the slop."

"So…eight?" she asked, checking her watch.

"Or thereabouts."

"Are there customs agents or immigration at the marina?"

He laughed. "Not today."

She didn't ask how he could be so confident, satisfied that he was.

Matt poked his head from the salon half an hour later, Hannah by his side, looking a trifle green. Jet led her to a window and encouraged her to stare at the water.

"It's an old sailor's trick. Keep your eyes on the sea and you feel better. You'll see."

Hannah did as instructed, and they stood together as the big boat plowed along, engines rumbling beneath their feet, only a few cotton puffs of high clouds drifting across a turquoise sky. Eventually green and brown hills jutted from the water in the distance, and the captain turned to them with a twinkle in his eye.

"Corsica on the right. French. Sardinia on the left. Italy. Both of them crazy in their own way. Common on islands – the populations go nuts over the years."

"Bigger than I thought," Jet commented, taking in the massive island.

"Oh, sure. Corsica's almost a hundred and sixty kilometers long, and Sardinia's nearly twice its size."

"Wow."

"Most people don't realize what sits off the coast. I've always thought it amazing."

Another hour passed, and they rounded Sardinia's northernmost tip and made a course for Fertilia – where, Giuseppe informed them, they would be met by someone who would drive them to the airport. "We're going there because it's smaller than the larger marina at Porto Torres," he explained. "Porto Torres also has a big customs presence because of the ferry traffic."

Jet nodded. "Whatever works. We don't care."

The marina at Fertilia was filled with sailboats when they idled past the breakwater and pulled up to the fuel dock. They disembarked from the cruiser and were met on the dock by an unshaven young man with long hair, a grubby T-shirt, and a pronounced slouch, who nodded a greeting to them.

"Van's up there," he said, indicating the parking area above the fuel dock, and led them up the gangplank to an ancient VW van that was more rust than metal. "Toss your stuff in back and climb in."

Jet didn't ask the man's name and he didn't offer it, which apparently worked for all concerned. They loaded into the van and it started with a cloud of blue exhaust. He jammed the shifter into first with a grinding of gears before it settled into place, and tromped on the gas. The old van responded with a shudder and slowly picked up speed as it climbed the driveway to the street above. Matt made a face and looked at Jet, who shrugged and patted Hannah's hand.

Outside of the marina gates, a motorcycle policeman approached the van, hand on his gun, and Jet stiffened. Their driver remained relaxed and exchange pleasantries with the cop, who gave the passengers a cursory once-over before returning to his bike, belly sagging over his belt.

"Don't worry. I know him. He's harmless," the driver assured them, and ground the gears again before lurching forward unsteadily, the engine laboring like it was on its last legs.

It took them an hour to travel fifteen miles, the van rarely making more than jogging speed along the narrow roads. The airport turned out to be relatively modern and well outfitted, and the driver steered the van to the curb in front of a small building that served as the private terminal. There, a tall man with a military bearing wearing aviator sunglasses greeted them at the door with a smile that seemed unfamiliar on his thin lips.

"You made it! Congratulations. This way to the plane," he said abruptly.

A Citation X sat on the tarmac near the terminal. By the stairs a flight attendant in black slacks and a rainbow-colored blouse shielded her eyes from the sun. They ascended the steps, Jet strapped Hannah in beside her, and the woman raised the stairs as the man who'd greeted them joined the other pilot in the cockpit and started the engines.

Five minutes later they were pressed back into their seats as the small jet sped down the runway and streaked into the sky, Hannah peering out the window beside her in awe of the experience. The plane banked over the island and climbed to cruising elevation as Sardinia disappeared beneath its wings, and when it had stabilized, the attendant brought them breakfast, which they gratefully consumed.

Once at cruising altitude, the attendant returned to collect their plates and glasses and informed them in lightly accented English that the flight would take a little over three hours, and they should call on her for anything they wanted during the trip. Jet thanked her and reclined her wide leather seat. Matt and Hannah followed her example, and the drone of the turbines drowned out all else as they closed their eyes, the hardest part of their journey complete.

CHAPTER 22

The plane touched down on the landing strip of a military airstrip ten miles outside Tel Aviv with a puff of smoke from the tires and rapidly decelerated as it neared the end of the runway. It veered toward a collection of buildings where six fighter jets were parked, their windows glinting in the blistering afternoon sun. A black SUV was waiting near the jets, and two men emerged from the vehicle as the flight attendant lowered the stairs and guided Jet and her family onto the Tarmac.

Jet blinked in the sunlight, and one of the pair approached.

"Welcome to Israel. I'm Guy, and my partner is Doron. How was your flight?"

"Good. Smooth."

Guy regarded Matt and Hannah and nodded to them. "We're to take you to a safe house nearby."

"Perfect." Jet paused. "We'll also need to change some euros."

"The house comes fully stocked, so there's no rush. There are a number of money-changing places in town and along the waterfront that can do it for you." He motioned to the SUV and switched to English. "Need any help with your bags?"

Matt shook his head. "No, thanks. I've got it."

"Then this way, please."

The drive into Tel Aviv was mercifully short, and Jet was surprised when the truck stopped in front of a contemporary high-rise condo building near Ginat Zemach, a little park behind the theater in Habima Square. Guy sensed her puzzlement and twisted toward her from the passenger seat.

"Two-bedroom condo on the fifth floor. Security building. I think you'll like it. It's temporary, but it has everything."

She didn't comment on the temporary, instead opening her door and stepping out of the vehicle, Hannah right behind her. Guy joined her, Matt in the rear with the backpacks, and the Mossad operative led them into the lobby, where a security man sat behind a counter, a headset in place. Guy nodded to the man.

"Yosef, these folks will be our guest for the next week or two. Treat them well."

"Yes, sir."

They loaded into the elevator and stood packed too close together until it pinged and the doors slid aside, revealing a travertine hallway with doors on either side. Guy walked to the second one on the right and slid a key into the lock. He pushed it open and stepped inside. "I'll show you around and let you get settled, and then I need to take you to speak to the director," he said to Jet.

Matt leaned into her and whispered, "Does he even know we're here?"

She rewarded him with a smile and followed Guy inside.

The condo was nicely appointed and clean, with a view to the sea. The tour lasted only a few minutes, and Guy handed Jet two sets of keys and regarded her from the foyer. "We'll be waiting downstairs. Take your time."

The door closed behind him, and Jet pointed at the air-conditioning duct and then to her ear. Matt understood and moved close to her. "You want to take a shower before your meeting?" he asked.

"Of course. I'm covered with road dust."

"Me too. You first."

Jet led Hannah into the smaller bedroom, and Matt placed her backpack on the bed. "We're going to clean up, sweetheart. You should do the same, and then we can see what's in the refrigerator for a late lunch."

Hannah frowned. "I'm hungry."

"Me too. I'll be back in a few minutes."

Matt and Jet entered the master and he set his backpack down. "I've got two more clean shirts. You can borrow one."

"I wonder if this place has a washing machine? I'd expect so."

"Me too. I'll do laundry while you're gone."

She stripped off her clothes and walked to the bathroom, beckoning for him to follow. He did the same and she turned on the shower as she eyed the ceiling, where a fire alarm guarded the bathroom entry. Matt followed her stare and then they were under the warm spray, soaping each other under the luxuriant stream.

Jet kissed him hard. His hands lingered on her breasts, and then she pulled away, her jade eyes flashing. "Assume the place is bugged," she whispered.

"I got that."

"They might have cameras, too."

"Probably. Which means we'll be taking a lot of showers together."

"Grab a taxi to a money-changing booth while I'm gone. I want us to have options."

"I'm way ahead of you. I'll stop and get you some clothes, too, if you want."

"No, I can do that after the meeting. No offense, but we have different tastes."

"You afraid I'll get you short shorts and tube tops?"

"I wouldn't put it past you."

They finished bathing but left the shower running. "They still haven't given us any paperwork," she said.

"I noticed that. The message is pretty clear: we're under their control."

"Not entirely. You still have my spare set, and yours."

"Doesn't really matter, does it? They're either going to play straight, or we're screwed," he said. "As you pointed out when we decided to do this. So far it looks like they're being honorable."

She nodded and kissed him again, this time longer. When she broke away and gazed up into his dripping face, his strong jaw dusted with stubble, she licked her lips.

"We still have a few minutes to kill."

He pressed against her, his interest unmistakable.

"Anything for the cameras."

CHAPTER 23

Guy was waiting when Jet stepped out of the building. Matt's shirt was too big on her, but a relief after days in her own. Guy didn't comment on her ensemble and merely held the rear door open for her like a chauffeur. They drove for fifteen minutes and, after a brief stint in downtown traffic, arrived at the marina. Jet shot Guy a puzzled look, and he shrugged as he got out of the car.

"The director likes to look at the boats sometimes," he said by way of explanation.

Jet followed him past a massive public swimming pool to the yacht club, where the director was sitting in one of the private dining rooms at a small table near a floor-to-ceiling window. A cigarette lay smoldering in an ashtray in front of him, a cup of coffee beside it.

"Sir?" Guy called out, and the director twisted toward them.

"Yes, yes. Come in," he said. "Have a seat and some coffee, young lady. You could probably use it after your trek." He pointed to a coffee machine with a row of cups beside it. Guy closed the door, leaving them alone together. Jet walked to the coffee and poured herself a cup, and then carried it to the table and sat opposite the head of the Mossad – one of the most powerful men in Israel.

Jet waited as he puffed on his cigarette and squinted at a mega-yacht a few miles off the coast, sipping her black coffee, curious to learn why she'd been brought all the way to her home country but unwilling to show it. After several long moments, the old man grunted as though he'd just remembered she was there, and appraised her with a sidelong glance.

"I used to come out here as a boy. Everything was fresh and new, exciting. There was nothing but a wide-open future of possibility, and after the war, the atrocities, it seemed like we'd landed in paradise."

He paused, wetting his lips. "It's changed so much I hardly recognize it."

Jet saw no reason to comment. If this was the great man's way of leading up to whatever his point was, so be it.

He cleared his throat. "I mentioned on the phone that we have a situation."

Jet nodded.

"We have a delicate sanction that needs to be carried out. The assassination of a head of state in a former Soviet satellite."

Jet's expression betrayed no emotion. "You're all out of assassins? I find that hard to believe."

"My problem is that this assignment requires a woman fluent in Russian, capable of carrying out the hit under difficult conditions. Which means someone highly experienced. That narrows the pool considerably."

"Mossad is so threadbare they don't have anyone who speaks Russian?"

"Nobody that can pull this off." He blew smoke at the window and sighed. "You're here, which means you're in. The target is the president of Azerbaijan. He'll be appearing at a trade show as the keynote speaker in a few days' time. His security is competent and not to be underestimated. We'll fly you there tomorrow morning, where you'll meet our team in Baku. The rest is arranged. They'll fill you in on the details. You'll be posing as a member of an obscure Russian delegation from an outfit that signed up for the conference and trade show before they went out of business. The weapon will already be in the hall – a sniper rifle. I trust you still remember how to use one?"

Her eyebrows rose. "That's it? Blow him away and stroll out?"

"There's more, of course. We've taken care of all the details. You have nothing to worry about."

She shook her head. "I'm usually part of the planning process."

"Not this time. We don't have any choice. But we've put our best people on it. All you need to do is follow instructions. It should be easy for someone of your abilities – in and out. Clean." He paused again for another drag on his cigarette. "How's your daughter holding up?"

"She's fine. Thanks for asking."

"You know the outline of the deal we've offered you: your partner and daughter will be issued new identities, as will you, and you'll live in comfort here, protected by our forces. We'll provide you a safe house wherever you like, within reason. Your daughter will go to school here, learn Hebrew, grow up normally instead of being hunted like an animal. All is forgiven for our past differences, and we'll have more of a contractor relationship moving forward. An occasional assignment, and you're buying your family's safety."

"I need that in writing. As well as a contingency that they will continue to enjoy your protection even if something happens to me. That's non-negotiable."

His weathered face crinkled with a wry smile. "I anticipated you'd require that. I've drafted something for you," he said, and withdrew a white envelope from his jacket pocket.

She took it from him, removed the document from the envelope, and read it quickly before refolding it and nodding. "I see it's also signed by the chief justice of the Supreme Court."

The director grunted. "I figured you'd want at least one reputable party to the transaction."

Jet slipped the agreement back into the envelope. "Why do you want the president killed?"

"Does it matter? We do. That should be enough."

"I know nothing about Azerbaijan. That's why I'm asking."

"I'll see to it that you have all the background materials you require to become an expert." He eyed her. "How's your Russian?"

"Fluent. Which you know."

"Little rusty?"

She held his beagle-eyed stare. "Not at all."

"Good."

They sat in silence and Jet finished her coffee. She set the cup down on the table and studied the director. "Is that it?"

"I could bore you with operational details, but I see no point. You fly there, you carry out the sanction, you're back by the weekend, basking in the sun. A simple matter for one as skilled as yourself."

"I don't like that I'm relying on the planning of people I've never met."

"It's a necessary evil in this case. In the future, I'll see that you're part of the process."

She hesitated. "I recall our last operation didn't end well. I hope Isaac made it."

The director waved away the comment, as though it were beneath consideration. "That was a different situation. I feel far more confident with your family as leverage. Remember that we still had some lingering doubts about your motives at that point. Now there can be none. You'll do what's required to keep them safe. As to Isaac, he survived." He stubbed out his cigarette and felt for a pack in his jacket. "I'm a simple man as I get older. There are only a few things you can depend on. A mother's love is one. Greed is another. I understand that you're financially independent, so that leaves love. A powerful force, and one I trust will ensure you carry out your mission without any mishaps."

"I don't need to tell you what will happen if anything…if you don't honor your side of the bargain."

"No need at all. Remember, I'm more than aware of your capabilities. We're beyond vulgar threats."

She turned toward the marina. "I'm glad we understand each other."

The director exhaled heavily and stabbed a cigarette into his mouth, glancing at the lighter on the table before raising his eyes to meet Jet's. He lifted the lighter and nodded, his attention drifting back to the yacht in the distance, the flame dancing as he held the Zippo before him like an offering.

"Perfectly."

Jet let herself out of the room. Guy was waiting in an overstuffed chair and leapt to his feet when she emerged from the doorway.

"All set?" he asked.

"I need to buy clothes. I hope you have a credit card."

"Of course. Anything else?"

She thought for a moment and nodded. "What's the biggest toy store in Tel Aviv?"

He appeared perplexed and then held up his phone. "I'll check."

"Let's get clothes first and make that our last stop."

"Will do."

CHAPTER 24

Caucasus Mountains, near Tufandag

Sanjar Nabiyev's grip tightened on his rifle as he and Ygor Kazamov negotiated a mountain trail that rose at a near vertical grade. Greenery surrounded them, the high altitude air was crisp, and the weather idyllic. The only sound to be heard was their boots on the track and an occasional loose rock skittering down the side of the mountain when one of them misstepped.

Nabiyev, the prime minister, was the second most important member of the government; a wiry man in his forties with a birdlike face and cruel features, his eyes so dark as to be nearly black, his ebony hair cropped close to his skull, still thick as a teenager's but graying at the temples. He was the guest of Kazamov, a Russian oligarch who had a large mountain retreat in the Caucasus range, where the pair had spent the night drinking vodka before embarking on the morning hunt.

They had allocated four days to hunt Dagestan tur, a particularly prized ram with elaborate horns that sportsman from around the world sought for their trophy walls. But the elusive goats were difficult to spot, and the hunt required both stamina and guile – the former quality eluding the pair of hunters in the throes of their hangovers.

"What do you make of the political situation, my friend?" Kazamov asked at one of their frequent breaks.

"It is, as always, complicated. Nothing new there."

The Russian unscrewed the top of a leather-wrapped flask and took a long pull before handing it to Nabiyev. The vodka burned like fire going down, but began working its evil magic within moments, and the worst of the pain in their temples receded as the congener production that was partly responsible for the hangover stopped when new alcohol entered their systems.

"Hovel isn't playing ball any longer. That is troubling. The cost of continuing our operations is increasing, and the administration seems intent on creating obstacles at every turn," the Russian complained.

"I've tried to block the worst of his programs, but there are limits to what I can accomplish."

The Russian frowned and took another swallow of vodka before capping the flask and slipping it back into his hunting vest.

"I cannot sit by idly while this man dismantles what I've built. I understand the direction this is going. I can already see he's agitating to bring in foreign groups to compete for the new contracts that are coming due next year. That will mean even larger bribes, and there are no guarantees. That's unacceptable."

"I know. But what can be done? The man has his own agenda."

"Now that he's rich," Kazamov spat. "From money I, and others like me, paid him. He was all in favor of our patronage when he needed us. But of late, he's shown his true colors." The Russian paused. "As to what can be done, there are ways to eliminate those who oppose us. It wouldn't be the first time."

Nabiyev scowled. "I can't be involved in anything like that. You shouldn't even be speaking of it. It's treason and would be punished by death."

Kazamov looked around and spread his arms expansively to take in the surrounding mountains, the snowcapped peaks thrusting into the heavens like broken teeth. "There's nobody out here to hear us, my friend. Not even the damned goats are listening. We can speak freely. The man has to go."

Nabiyev sighed and chose his words carefully. "You sound like you've given this some thought."

Kazamov nodded. "I have. You have nothing to fear. We will hunt this week, you will enjoy my hospitality, and by the time your stay is over, everything will be resolved."

Nabiyev's eyes widened. "You're actually serious…"

The Russian nodded. "Have you ever known me not to be? This is my livelihood he's threatening, as well as the income stream for powerful interests in Moscow. They have exerted their power and set a plan in motion. It is a foolish man who confronts the immovable object, believing himself to be capable of besting it. He could have continued to have it all, but now will receive a death sentence as his reward." Kazamov ran his fingers over his face and winced at the lingering pain from the night's overindulgence. "Which brings us to you, my friend. You will assume an important position on the world stage. I trust you'll remember who put you there, and won't make the same mistakes as Hovel."

The warning was as clear as a cobra's hiss, and Nabiyev nodded, the color draining from his face as he considered the Russian's tone. He extended a trembling hand to Kazamov. "I think I need a little more of that damned potion you drink like water."

Kazamov laughed and felt for the flask. "You'll be a better man for it. Drink as much as you want, and then we'll track down one of these infernal goats for my wall. It's been two seasons since I bagged one." He smiled and handed Nabiyev the vodka. "You were with me on that trip, were you not?"

"I remember it well. You arranged for twins," Nabiyev confirmed.

"Ah, of course. How can I forget? The gymnasts. As I recall, they kept you enthralled for several days. I think you lost several pounds during your stay."

"You are a corrupting influence, Ygor. I'm ordinarily a virtuous man."

Both men laughed at the joke. Nabiyev was a profligate womanizer, a sadist whose tastes ran to the bizarre and the vicious. His career had been spent abusing his power to satiate his appetites, and Kazamov had been more than willing to supply him whatever he wanted. It was a relationship that worked well – a reciprocal transaction where each received what he wanted, and both understood where the power resided. Nabiyev continued to occupy the number two position in government, and Kazamov's oil empire prospered.

The Russian started at movement on one of the nearby peaks and pointed at it as he raised binoculars to his eyes. Nabiyev did the same, and they watched as a splendid example of their quarry climbed a nearly impossible ledge and disappeared over the ridge.

"Damn. We need to keep our voices down," Kazamov growled. "We spooked him."

"It wasn't his time."

"Very philosophical, but I want another ram for my lodge wall, and I'll get one this trip if it kills me."

Nabiyev took in his hunting partner's red face and the heavy bags beneath his eyes, and held his tongue. Kazamov's revelations about killing the president had shaken him – not because of the death of a man he despised, but rather at the thought of his sudden ascension to the throne. If the president died, the prime minister automatically became the nation's leader and, in the case of an assassination, might declare martial law and suspend elections until the guilty party was brought to justice.

Nabiyev could see that taking years.

During which time his own fortunes would grow due to his new position of power. While not poor by any stretch, his Swiss bank account could benefit from another ten or twenty million dollars, and as the decision maker on the awarding of lucrative contracts, he would be eagerly courted, paid off by Kazamov and others so they could continue pillaging the nation for their own enrichment.

"Well, then," Nabiyev said, "we'd best continue. The damned goats aren't going to come to us, that's for sure."

"No, they won't. Lead the way, my friend."

Nabiyev rose unsteadily, dizzy from the altitude and alcohol, and set out up the narrow trail, more than aware that the Russian was behind him with a high-power hunting rifle, and glad that he was useful to the man, lest he follow in his glorious leader's footsteps to the grave.

CHAPTER 25

Baku, Azerbaijan

The flight from Frankfurt banked on final approach and Jet checked her seatbelt. A flight attendant roamed the aisle, confirming that everyone was belted in, pushing seatbacks up and tapping on the tray tables of the inattentive before continuing along.

Jet's new passport identified her as a Russian, twenty-seven, named Katya Vilzak, born in St. Petersburg. The document was flawless, complete with several dated stamps from EU countries since it had supposedly been issued three years before. The level of detail was reassuring to Jet after her experience with the amateurs in Serbia, and she sat back and closed her eyes, recalling her last hours with Matt and Hannah as the plane dropped from the sky toward Heydar Aliyev International Airport.

They'd had a quiet dinner at a neighborhood restaurant, and Jet had filled Matt in on what she'd been ordered to do when Hannah nodded off after dessert. He had more than a few reservations, as did she, but neither of them could see any other way to ensure the safety of the family.

The parting, when Jet had tucked her daughter into bed, had been tearful for Hannah, who'd been on an emotional roller coaster for too long, and she'd still been sobbing when she'd fallen asleep. Jet had spent her remaining time with Matt, choosing to forego rest for most of the night in favor of lovemaking. When the car had shown up for her at dawn, she'd gotten only a few hours of sleep, but would try to slumber on the flights, first to Germany and then, after a three-hour layover, to Azerbaijan.

The flaps whined as they neared the airport and the plane shook.

The landing gear dropped into place with a clunk, and then the aircraft was bumping onto the runway and braking hard. The afternoon sky was beige from dust and pollution belching from lines of smokestacks near the Caspian Sea.

The futuristic terminal was a collage of glass and steel with a vaguely Eastern motif, with only a few planes at the gates. Jet filed off the plane and followed the rest of the passengers through immigration, where her passport was swiped and processed without a second glance by a pasty-faced clerk with a mustard stain on his uniform jacket. After clearing that hurdle, she waited in line to retrieve her bag from a carousel that groaned like a tired bear, and then submitted to a cursory search by customs.

She exited the arrivals area and found herself facing an expectant crowd pressed against barricades manned by three armed soldiers. Jet scanned the sea of humanity and spotted a sign with a travel company's name written in black felt pen, held by a tall woman in her thirties with auburn hair and a stern countenance.

Jet approached her and nodded a greeting. "ITV travel, right?" she asked.

"That's right. Are you in from the Rome flight?" the woman responded.

"I don't think that one's arrived yet," Jet answered, completing the verification sequence.

"That's it?" the woman asked, tilting her head toward Jet's checked bag. Jet nodded and then accompanied the woman out into the large lot to a decade-old black E-series Mercedes sedan. Jet placed her bag in the trunk and climbed into the passenger seat, and the woman twisted the ignition key and turned to her.

"I'm Leah. I'll be your handler while you're in Baku."

"Nice to meet you."

"We've got a safe house on the outskirts of town. Itai, our station chief, is waiting there. When we arrive, we'll explain the logistics of your mission."

"I'm surprised Baku has a station."

Leah gave her a grim smile. "It's a strategic area for us, but as you'll see from the resources he's been given, not all that important in the scheme of things."

"Are you permanent?" Jet asked.

"No. I'm like you, just here for the op."

They drove in silence, Jet taking in the dramatic difference between the Soviet-era architecture and the post-modern structures erected since Azerbaijan obtained its independence. Much of downtown was the latter, all shining panes and glittering steel, but as they ventured from the area, the buildings became heavy-handed drab gray monoliths with all the charm of a canker sore. Likewise, the people seemed to grow increasingly colorless and dull as they drove from the prosperity of the central district. The cars were now rusting and dented, and piles of refuse clogged the gutters.

Leah turned onto a residential street framed by a long row of identical square cinderblock and mortar homes. Corroding rebar jutted from their roofs, and an occasional dog roved the front yards in search of food among children who were amusing themselves by tormenting the hapless beasts. Halfway down the block, Leah pulled the Mercedes into a driveway and switched off the engine.

"Here we are. It's not the Ritz, but it's got everything," she said, and popped the trunk as she slid from behind the wheel.

A man in a green sweater and brown corduroy trousers greeted them at the front door, his tanned face deeply lined but his eyes alert and keen. Jet made him for well over fifty, which was ancient nowadays even for a field supervisor, and wondered what he'd done to drive his career into a ditch where he ran out the clock in an armpit like Azerbaijan.

"Greetings. Come in. I'll show you your room," he said in Russian, and Jet responded in kind.

"Thank you. Appreciate the hospitality."

He smiled and switched to Hebrew when the door closed behind Leah. "Your accent is flawless."

"Thanks."

The room was a ten-by-ten square with a bathroom down the hall, bars on the window, and a ceiling fan for ventilation. Jet stowed her bag and turned to face Itai. "I'm anxious to hear the details of the mission."

"I expect you are. Join me in the living room, and I'll fill you in."

Jet had been given a tablet with reams of material on Azerbaijan, so was up to speed on the geopolitical situation and the various factions struggling to dominate the upcoming election. She told Itai as much, and he nodded in approval as he sat with Leah on a sofa facing Jet, who'd taken a seat opposite on an upholstered chair.

"First, let's get some background out of the way," he started. "The trade show and conference start tomorrow, but the target isn't scheduled to deliver his address until the following evening at the close of the show. Leah will be in the field with you as your handler at the convention center. You'll each have latest generation comm gear that's virtually undetectable – micro earbuds with high frequency transmitters on private, matched channels. We've got sources inside security that have given us their protocols, and we know the number of guards, the placement of the camera systems, and the scanning gear they'll be using at the entrances." He continued for five minutes and, when he was done, eyed Jet. "Questions?"

"I want to look the place over," Jet said.

Leah shook her head. "That's not on the menu. We don't want you anywhere near it until it's game time."

"Why not?"

"In case they're using facial recognition software."

"I thought you said you had their protocols," Jet fired back. "They either are or they aren't."

Leah looked to Itai. "We consider it a possibility."

Jet frowned. "I don't walk into a live situation blind. Ever."

"You won't be blind. We've got photos and a blueprint of the layout," Itai said.

"It's not the same as walking the scene, and we both know that," Jet countered.

"The decision was made at a higher pay grade than ours. They probably know something we don't," Leah said. "At any rate, it's been decided."

"I wasn't informed, or I'd never have agreed to it."

"Take it up with your boss. I'm just following orders," Leah snapped.

Itai cleared his throat loudly. "Ladies, let's stick to the script, shall we? Leah, take Katya here through the steps so she understands how this will play out. Katya, save the objections until Leah's through."

Leah did as requested and, after thirty minutes of detailed minutiae, finished her briefing. Jet had a number of questions, which she answered without hesitation, and Jet grudgingly admitted to herself that it was a thorough and well-conceived plan.

"It pencils out, at least on paper," Jet said. "But I still want to snoop around and orient myself."

"We've already noted that, and I'll pass it up the chain for a response," Itai said.

Jet clearly wasn't satisfied with the answer, which sounded to her like a dodge, but she didn't fight it, preferring to let them think that she was fully on board. Itai fielded a few technical questions, and when it was obvious that he'd exhausted his knowledge of the convention center, he rose and walked with Jet to the door. He handed her a card with a shoe repair shop logo and a phone number on it. "If you have any questions Leah can't answer, you can call that number and the message will reach me. Ask for Krell, and say you have a delivery request."

She committed the number to memory and returned it to him. "I don't need the card."

He blinked in surprise and then nodded. "Interesting. You're full of surprises, aren't you?"

"I just want to do the job and leave. The rest, you can deal with."

"Hopefully it will go smoothly."

Jet didn't respond. Hope had no place in a wet op, and so far her handler's reluctance to allow her to visit the site had her doubting the setup, but she'd been told to stand down and saw nothing to be gained by arguing.

Itai opened the door and stepped out into the fading light. "If I don't see you again, break a leg."

Jet nodded without enthusiasm. "Will do."

Jet twisted the lock shut after Itai, and Leah called to her. "I'll be staying here with you. Let me know when you get hungry. There's food in the fridge, or I can go out for something."

Jet retraced her steps to the living room. "Is there Internet?"

"Sure. Although be careful what you search. The state monitors everything."

Jet smirked. "Not just the Americans, huh?"

"Everyone's spying on everyone else. The administration's learned well. It would have made the Soviets dizzy with eavesdropping possibility if there'd been a Web in the '80s."

"Whole different world now."

Leah studied Jet and nodded slowly. "Indeed. I'll find the code for the Wi-Fi and knock on your door if you want to rest in the meantime."

"That's fine. I'll unpack."

Leah pensively watched Jet make her way down the hall to her room, the assassin unreadable but radiating the self-possession of a seasoned pro. When Jet disappeared into her room, Leah fished a cell phone from her pocket and placed a call to a number in Israel and muttered in Hebrew.

"Ball's in the air."

There was a pause with nothing but the background hum of static on the long-distance line. Eventually a man replied before hanging up.

"Good. Keep me informed."

CHAPTER 26

The row house was dark at eleven p.m., as were most of the rest in the working-class neighborhood at that hour. A figure dressed head to toe in black darted from behind a shade tree in the tiny front yard and sprinted down the sidewalk toward an intersection where cars still drove by. When the figure reached the corner, it hooked right and slowed, and the blur of dark motion solidified into a woman wearing pants and a long-sleeved shirt.

Jet had decided before dinner that she was going to nose around the convention center no matter what her handler preferred – it wasn't Leah's life on the line, and Jet probably had more operational experience than the older woman, having packed three lifetimes' worth in her relatively few years of active duty. So she'd waited until Leah had retired, slipped from the house with a wad of the local currency the Mossad had been thoughtful enough to provide, and made a beeline for freedom.

Now, the challenge was to find her way to the convention center without getting mugged or picked up and questioned by the police. She didn't expect the latter; but given the neighborhood, had her doubts about the former.

The lights of a small market glowed on the far corner, and she set off toward it, waiting until there were no cars before running across the six lanes. At the store, she waited in front until she spotted a taxi approaching and waved it down. The driver appeared surprised to find a fare in that district, much less an attractive female with an impressive physique, and spent most of the drive ogling her in the rearview mirror.

Jet had him drop her off a block from the exhibition hall, which was adjacent to the world-famous futuristic white curves of the

Heydar Aliyev Center — a landmark in Baku and one of the most recognizable buildings in the region, as iconic as the Sydney Opera House or the Eiffel Tower. The area was surprisingly active, considering the time, with couples strolling together toward the waterfront and groups of youths meandering with no obvious destination.

The pedestrians made her job easier, and she circled the huge complex, eyeing the security that was already in place, relieved to see that the rear loading area was still bustling with truckers and contractors working to get last minute exhibit arrivals into the hall in time for the opening. The scene was pure chaos — loaders pushing dollies laden with crates, cleaning staff milling about, harried-looking exhibitors burning the midnight oil all swarming the open doors — and the guards stationed on either side weren't looking particularly attentive.

She watched the commotion for half an hour and, when a phalanx of cleaning people arrived, joined their ranks as they filed into the hall. She hunched over so her bearing wouldn't flag her as an outlier, kept her head down, and stayed toward the middle of the group of over fifty janitors, none of whom seemed thrilled about working the graveyard shift, many smelling of alcohol.

Inside the center, floodlights mounted on stands illuminated the hall, where a group of laborers was unfurling banners and rolling red carpeting into place in the lobby. After slipping on a yellow vest she'd lifted from a chair outside one of the bathrooms, she did a slow circuit of the trade show floor, where still more contractors were loitering and avoiding any actual work, laughing and joking, no supervision in evidence.

Jet spotted the stage where the president would speak, and turned to view the spot Leah had selected for her. It was off to the side of the hall, but too exposed for her liking, with no obvious egress that couldn't be blocked, and a knot tightened in her stomach as she considered the alternatives. The trick would be to make it out alive, not pull off the sanction; and she didn't like her odds, based on the layout. She called up a photo of the site blueprint on her cell phone and studied it. After several moments, she nodded to herself and thumbed the image away.

A glance up into the dark rafters confirmed her impression from the blueprint. Like in many convention halls, a series of girders and metal supports spanned the hall, the lighting suspended below them, the bones of the structure painted black so they wouldn't mar the impressive interior. She spotted a maintenance entrance hatch near the roof five stories above and made her way out of the hall and up a stairwell that led to the roof.

Another check of the plan identified the passage that terminated at the door, and she crept along the corridor, straining her ears for any noise of approaching workers. Satisfied that she was alone, she tried the handle on the hatch and it turned easily.

Jet found herself on a narrow steel walkway that ran along one of the primary structural beams, with a bird's-eye view of the hall and stage. Signage blocked her view of the podium, but as she edged along the platform, she found a spot midway that was hidden from view below by an exhibition banner that hung from a nearby girder yet had an unobstructed line of sight to the spot where the president would deliver his speech.

After confirming the location's viability, she returned to the door and identified two possible escape routes, the more promising one an access way beneath one of the elaborate ventilation system's air ducts. She pulled up the building schematic a final time and traced the ducting to a room in the basement, from which she could make it outside via one of the exits. In the pandemonium that would follow the assassination, she was sure nobody would be thinking of the air duct network as the concealment system for the shooter's escape, at least not at first – and that delay in sealing it off would be her window of opportunity to evade security and get clear of the complex.

She confirmed her impression by walking to the access door of the oversized air ducts and sliding it aside. Inside, as she expected, was a series of frames supporting the sheet metal that formed the duct walls. Jet didn't need to climb in and confirm that she could use the ribs in the vertical sections – she could see that the ribbing was uniform and that it would more than work.

Downstairs, she continued along the stairwell into the basement and was nearing the spot where the ducting entered the maintenance room when she heard voices approaching along the corridor. A glance at the passageway told her she'd never be able to evade detection, so she continued walking, studying her phone as though she belonged there.

Jet came face-to-face with four beefy maintenance men in orange coveralls and looked up from her phone in surprise.

"What are you doing down here?" one of them demanded.

"I…it's embarrassing. I'm supposed to meet my cleaning crew somewhere around here, and I think I'm lost," she said, batting her eyes.

"Where are you supposed to meet them?" another asked.

"They said the level below the loading area. They didn't tell me enough to find it, though." She hesitated. "I'm sort of running late, so…"

The men laughed. "Well, you're on the right track," the first one said. "Keep going down this way, and when you come to the T-intersection, make a left. That will take you to the rear loading area basement."

"Is it far?" she asked, checking her watch.

"Not that far. Maybe two minutes away." The speaker smiled at her. "You want me to show you the way?"

She returned the smile. "No, that would just make me look even more stupid. T-intersection, hang a left. I can find it."

Jet pushed past them and hurried away, feeling their eyes on her back as she picked up her pace. It had been a decent bluff, but she didn't want to push her luck, and if she stayed any longer, she risked one of the men asking to see her security pass or wondering why a woman with a perfect Moscow accent was working on a cleaning crew in Baku.

"Hey!" a voice called out behind her, and she debated continuing on. She opted for a more normal response and slowed while looking over her shoulder.

"What? I'm late."

"I'll be up by the loading area when the shift changes if you want to have a drink later."

She swallowed hard and shook her head. "Maybe. Let me see how the rest of the night goes."

"My name's Sergei."

"Okay, Sergei. If I see you, let's talk then."

Jet smiled to herself as she resumed her rush and, after a right turn, arrived at the T-junction. The basement widened into an equipment storage area packed with crates, pieces of machinery, and parts of exhibits that had been abandoned or were regularly featured. She moved among the pallets of boxes until she found a stairway and ascended to the ground level, where the beeping of backup warning alarms and the throaty rumble of forklifts drowned out the exhortations of workers muscling displays from the trucks.

She eyed the loading docks, counting two dozen trucks backed up against the platform, and shrugged out of her vest and tossed it into a trash barrel. Forty-five minutes later she was back at the safe house, tiptoeing to her room, satisfied that her foray had yielded fruit. She grimaced when her door handle squeaked as she turned it, and then she was in her room, stripping off her outfit, exhausted and ready for sleep.

Down the hall, Leah's door eased shut with a soft snick.

CHAPTER 27

Jet slept in, and when she emerged from her room with a yawn and ambled down the hall to the kitchen, Leah was seated at the dining room table, her laptop in front of her. Jet nodded to her handler and opened the refrigerator to see what she could find to eat, and Leah cleared her throat.

"Good morning," she said.

Jet looked over her shoulder at the older woman. "Morning."

"Sleep well?"

"So-so."

"You went out last night. Where did you go?"

Jet removed three eggs from the fridge and bumped the door closed with her hip. "What's it to you?"

Leah's tone hardened. "Everything you do is my business, Katya. Answer the question."

"I like to go for long runs when I can't sleep," Jet answered, the statement itself technically true even if not an accurate answer. "It helps my body adjust after all the flights."

"Where did you run?"

"I don't know the names of any of the places anywhere around here. I just ran."

"Can you be more specific?"

Jet exhaled in thinly veiled exasperation. "I don't know. Along the big boulevard. I tried to avoid anything smaller so I wouldn't get jumped."

"How long were you gone for?"

Jet shrugged, removed a bowl from the cupboard, and set it on the counter before cracking the eggs and dumping the whites into the dish, taking care that the yolks remained in the shells. "Beats me. I ran until I wore myself out. Maybe an hour or two."

Leah eyed her skeptically. "Big difference between one or two."

"Maybe to you. Not when I'm running." Jet paused. "Where are the pans?"

"In the big cupboard next to the oven." Leah's tone hardened further. "You were gone for two and a half hours."

"Then why bother asking me how long it was, if you already know?"

Leah stood, hands on her hips. "Look, Katya, I'm your handler, which means I'm your lifeline. Anything you do here is my business if it affects our mission. I can tell you resent that, but I'm surprised, because I was told you're experienced, and you should know how this works. My job is the successful outcome of the operation and your survival. If you don't cooperate, both might be endangered, and I can't allow that."

"I'm used to working on my own."

"That may be, but on this assignment, you report to me, so if I ask about your whereabouts, it's not some passive-aggressive power play, it's because I need to know what you've been up to."

Jet placed an iron skillet on one of the gas burners and lit the flame. She waited a few moments for the butter she'd dropped into the pan to melt, and then poured the egg whites in with a sizzle.

"Fair enough. I went for a run. Which you now know. Anything else?"

Leah snapped her notebook shut, her lips a tight line. "I don't want you leaving the house until tomorrow. That's an order."

Jet raised an eyebrow. "Why not?"

"Because I said so."

"I was planning on going for another run today." Jet decided to extend an olive branch. "Maybe you can go with me? I don't do well cooped up before a mission."

Leah regarded her, trying to figure out whether Jet was playing her or not. Eventually her expression softened. "When?"

147

"This afternoon, before dusk, when it's cooler. I can find ways to occupy my time inside until then." Jet paused. "I like to work out any nerves before I go into action. There's no reason for me to be forbidden from running. It's not like I'm in deep cover or anything."

Leah gathered her computer and the power cord and nodded. "Fine. But don't leave the house for any reason before then. Clear?"

Jet stirred the eggs with a fork, busying herself with cooking, and waited just long enough to annoy Leah without seeming to do so on purpose before answering, "Sure. Whatever you say."

Leah stood beside the table and appeared to be debating reprimanding her further, but opted to leave instead of giving voice to any objection. She and Jet weren't there to become best friends, and she didn't have to force the issue of who was in charge. Most importantly, Leah needed Jet to trust her enough to rely on her; otherwise the op might be jeopardized, and proving a point over something that had already occurred wasn't worth it.

When Leah had disappeared into her room, Jet's face didn't change other than an amused glint in her eyes. She'd never been good at being ordered around, which was why she'd been at home in the Team, where everyone operated autonomously except for instructions issued by their control, David, whom they all respected.

Leah's problem was that she was dealing with a different kind of operative than the usual Mossad agent who would blindly obey and not think for themselves. She probably wasn't a bad handler, but she didn't know enough about Jet's background to understand why her attempt to assert dominance was the wrong approach to take.

Jet hummed as she shut off the burner and scraped the eggs onto a plate. She'd have to cut Leah a little slack and play nice. There was nothing to be gained by antagonizing the woman, and it was in Jet's best interests that they get along.

She carried the plate to the table and returned to the kitchen for a cup of coffee before taking a seat and waiting for the eggs to cool. Jet needed to focus her attention on the task at hand, not get sucked into diversions. The assassination was tomorrow, and she needed to be a hundred and ten percent on. Leah's suspicions or dislike of her tone

148

couldn't interfere with that, and Jet resolved to push the interaction aside and rally her resources for the job she was there to perform: to kill a president.

CHAPTER 28

The following afternoon, Jet was striding toward the exhibition hall, wearing a smart black pantsuit, her micro transmitter sewn into the lapel and a tiny flesh-toned earbud concealed by her fall of hair. She'd spent the morning getting outfitted by Leah and Itai, who'd put in an appearance at lunch to participate in her final briefing before the main event.

"You're to show up several hours before the speech, walk the floor, and collect samples and literature from the exhibitors," Itai had said. "When Leah gives the word, move to the booth where our people have the rifle. It was smuggled in as part of the piping that supports the backdrop and the signage, and they'll have removed it today and concealed it in a pair of cardboard tubes that look like samples of their lighting products."

Leah had taken over from there. "The rifle has a sound suppressor and subsonic ammunition, so your firing location will be undetectable. It's got a three-round magazine, but my advice would be to use only one, because it's unlikely you'll get off a second or third shot with any success."

The gun was a modified 5.56mm rifle with ammunition that had been engineered to explode on impact, causing lethal damage even though a small round – more than the typical tumbling that round would experience once it struck. Accurate to three hundred meters even with the subsonic load, her firing position would be from a hundred and fifty meters, so the execution should be a cakewalk from a functional standpoint.

Her escape would be more difficult, but Leah had a convincing plan: Jet would join the exhibitor crew of the lighting company, where the staff would swear that she had been standing during the shooting if anyone questioned her whereabouts. Jet hadn't been as enthusiastic about relying on the authorities simply accepting that the assassin had dematerialized as if by magic, but Leah had insisted that the combination of Jet's gender, coupled with the witness testimony, would be sufficient for her to slip into the parking lot, where the Mercedes and Leah would be waiting. From there she would be smuggled to a private airstrip in the Dagestan Republic, and a turbo prop would fly her back to Israel.

That had all sounded fine in the dining room of the house, but now that she was nearly at the exhibition hall, the little voice in her head was poking holes in the plan, which largely relied on everyone being so entranced by the president's speech they wouldn't notice her getting into position or assembling the rifle. The idea was that his ten-minute oration would give her the chance to make her move, and that she would execute him once he was seated with the rest of the dignitaries on the podium following his keynote address, while others waxed eloquent about free trade and the relentless march of progress. That was the only good part, in her opinion, because he would be immobile, making the shot one even a rookie could easily accomplish.

She snapped back to the present at the sight of the cordon of soldiers in black combat gear, replete with flak jackets and automatic weapons, positioned on the path to the hall and at strategic points along the exterior of the building. None of this was unexpected, and it had been part of her briefing, but the reality of it still sent a momentary chill down her spine.

At the entrance, she presented her passport and credentials, which a tall man studied carefully before scanning her ID and sending her on to a metal detector. Her purse had nothing that would raise any suspicion – a few cosmetic items, a wallet, extra business cards, pens, a cell phone, a trove of other expected odds and ends – and she handed it over so it could pass through a scanner while she walked through the detector without setting off the alarm.

The hall was a different place than the chaotic scene she'd visited two nights before – carpeting now blanketed the exhibition area, and the booths were elaborately lit and manned by interchangeable wonks in shiny suits and beaming professional salesman's smiles. She took an oversized plastic bag with the logo of a pipeline company on it from a woman passing them out, and proceeded to make a circuit of the floor, collecting information from exhibitors as instructed.

Her earbud crackled, and Leah's voice buzzed in her ear.

"I can hear the attendees. You must be inside by now."

"*Da*," Jet said, covering her hand with her mouth while pretending to cough.

"Okay. You have an hour and a half before he's onstage. I'll go dark until then, but I'll be monitoring the feed. Pretend to make a phone call if you need me. I'll hear everything you say."

The earbud went silent, and Jet returned to her apparently random wandering, pausing at each booth and listening to the canned pitches before thanking the staff, bagging some more handouts, and continuing to the next, exactly as a genuine attendee would do.

She was nearing her final destination booth, which was a Romanian front company that distributed electrical products, when an overbearing, well-padded man in a cheap suit cornered her in a pipe-fitting booth, his intent obviously not limited to professional interaction. He reluctantly tore his eyes from the badge lying against the bulge of her breasts from a lanyard around her neck, and offered an oily smile.

"I see you are Russian," he said, his tone friendly.

Jet nodded, ignoring the liberal dosing of cheap cologne that barely masked the smell of partially metabolized alcohol from a liquid lunch.

"That's right. There are quite a few here."

"Which part?" He paused. "Moscow, from the accent, am I right?"

She fingered her watch pointedly. "Yes. Now I live there."

"That's where I'm based as well," he said, his eyes darting to her hands to check for a ring. Seeing none, his smile broadened. "What part of the city do you live in?"

Motion from near the street drew her gaze, and she spied a group of obvious security personnel getting into position earlier than she'd expected. She looked back at the salesman and gave him her best blank stare. "I'm sorry, what did you say?"

"Oh, I was just asking where you live."

She mentioned one of the most expensive neighborhoods, her tone suddenly frosty, hoping that he would get the message – he was trying to fight far above his weight. Unfortunately, he wasn't the brightest and persisted in his clumsy overture.

"How long are you in town for?"

"I'm leaving early tomorrow." Jet began edging away, but he matched her steps.

"So you have time for dinner?"

Jet offered him a wide smile. "Of course. With my boyfriend. I'm looking forward to it."

Cold water poured on his pass, he stood flatfooted as she walked away to the next booth, where the fascinating topic of water filtration was receiving a thorough exploration by a speaker with a headset to a less than rapt audience of six. She debated taking a break from her rounds, but afraid of encouraging the Russian in the next booth to slip over and try again, she instead made for the bathroom to freshen up. As she was opening the door, Leah's voice sounded in her ear.

"Apparently you're making an impression. You have half an hour before the president arrives for his speech. That is all."

She frowned and entered the restroom, where she joined a line waiting for the stalls, the women mostly younger and attractive, with the hard expressions of predators that corporate salespeople often developed over years of high-pressure pitches and incessant lying. The woman in front of her tried to strike up a conversation when she saw Jet's badge, but Jet refused to engage, limiting her responses to monosyllables. The woman quickly took the hint and returned to inspecting herself in the mirror while Jet stared off into space.

Jet shuffled forward, her mind elsewhere, counting the minutes until she would retrieve the rifle and get down to business, wondering whether this would be the one time something went wrong, and if she'd ever see her daughter or Matt again.

CHAPTER 29

Jet made it to the electrical fixture booth with ten minutes to spare and caught the eye of the manager, who was watching for her, she knew. He walked over and glanced at her name tag, his expression tense, and nodded.

"Welcome. Can I show you some of our products? We've got everything you can think of for your electrical needs, at the most competitive prices in the region."

"That sounds great," Jet said. "Do you have any samples? I'm specifically looking for lighting fixtures and fluorescent bulbs."

"This way," he said, and after looking around, led her to a curtained area near the rear of the booth, full of briefcases and boxes of literature. He reached inside and extracted a box the size a cell phone might come in and an unmarked cardboard tube, sealed on each end. Jet held out her bag and he placed the box inside and then handed her the tube like he was releasing a live snake.

"Thanks. This looks like exactly what I was hoping for," she said, annoyed by the man's visible nervousness. If this was the quality of the field operatives the Mossad had devoted to the effort, they were in trouble. "Might want to take a few deep breaths," she whispered, and he stiffened before forcing his stance into a more relaxed posture.

"Right. Got it."

"I'll be back shortly. You going to be all right?"

"Sure. Absolutely."

Jet walked away, unwilling to remain in the booth any longer than necessary. The knot in her gut twisted as she carried the tube and bag toward the front of the hall – not to the position she'd been instructed to fire from. Everything about the setup struck her as wrong. She knew from experience how easy it was to make critical mistakes working from drawings and pictures, which was why she always walked the location of a hit before, if possible.

She exited the hall and looked around and was greeted by a wall of suited business people heading toward the cavernous space for the keynote speech. Jet walked with measured steps against the tide and paused at a steel door that fed onto the corridor leading to the stairwell. She pushed it wide enough to slip through and eased it closed behind her, waiting to confirm that there was nobody nearby in the hallway.

When she was confident she hadn't been observed, she sped to the stairwell and took the steps two at a time, breathing evenly as she climbed five stories. Outside the hatch to the rafter passageway, she paused and flipped the top off the cardboard tube. Inside was a length of barrel with a suppressor screwed onto the end, which she quickly removed and set by her feet. She shook the tube and felt the weight of a small scope and some sort of stock. Jet pulled them from the container and inspected the heavy wire that would serve as the stock – obviously homemade, as was the barrel and suppressor.

Jet inspected the threaded end of the barrel and then ferreted in her bag for the box her contact had given her. She found it, slid her thumbnail along the seal, and opened the top. Inside was a trigger mechanism and breech, the magazine already in place. She inspected it and confirmed there was a round chambered, and then screwed the barrel into position. Jet finished by clipping the wire stock into two holes drilled in the back of the breech.

She eyed the weapon and fit the scope onto the rail and tightened it down. Only ten power, she noted, but that would be more than sufficient at the range, assuming it had been zeroed accurately. One of her concerns was that she hadn't been allowed to sight it in herself. Under any other circumstances, she would have never allowed that, but because it had already been smuggled into the trade show, she hadn't had a choice.

Jet set the bag down, removed the lanyard from around her neck, and unsnapped the badge and slipped the plastic rectangle into her pocket before opening her purse and removing a pair of nail clippers. She snipped the clip off the end and tied one end of the lanyard to the barrel, and secured the other end near the breech. Satisfied it would hold the rifle, she held it overhead and smashed the lightbulb that illuminated the landing. The area instantly went dark, and she shouldered the rifle, listening for a few moments before cracking the hatch and peering into the hall.

Applause rose from the floor as the president took the stage and shook hands with several men. After some backslapping and good-natured grins, he moved to the podium. Jet waited until she was sure that all eyes were on him before pushing the hatch open, secure that she wouldn't arouse attention from any light emanating from the hatch behind her. The president began speaking and Jet inched forward, each step placed with the caution of a tightrope walker, careful to avoid banging the gun against the railing that kept her from plummeting to her death.

Her progress was interrupted by another outburst of applause, and she realized that the president's speech had been little more than a short welcome to the attendees and a self-serving recitation of all the progress the country had made since he took office. He waved to everyone, obviously finished, and strode from the podium to shake more hands and slap backs.

No matter, she figured. He would soon be seated with the rest of the dignitaries, where she would have a clear shot without complications. She continued edging forward, wary of moving too fast lest she draw the eyes of the security men who were standing by the stage, arms crossed, the bulges in their suit jackets as obvious as neon signs.

Jet's breath caught in her throat when Hovel reached the line of seats, shook hands with yet another suit, and then ducked out of sight. She froze in place, waiting, and then resumed breathing when he returned twenty seconds later, holding a plastic water bottle, and took the end chair in the long row. The game back in play, she crept toward the spot she'd determined was ideal for the shot as another man began speaking at the podium, his voice booming through the hall, causing a screech of feedback before the sound technician dialed the volume back to compensate for his bellow.

Her eyes narrowed as she peered toward the stage, and then she unslung the rifle and brought it to bear. She peeked through the scope and swept the faces of the dignitaries until the president's head filled the Zeiss optics, the crosshairs centered on the bridge of his nose. She eased back the bolt of the firing mechanism and it snapped into place, ready to be released by a pull of the trigger, the spring driving the firing pin into the cartridge at high speed – a simple device at heart that she could have built out of parts from a hardware store and a few hours of time with some basic tools.

She would jettison the rifle when she was done, leaving it to be found, its homemade nature eliminating any chance the assassination would be linked to a state actor. She had no idea who the Mossad intended to frame for the killing, nor did she care. It wasn't her job, and she didn't involve herself in geopolitics. All she cared about was getting away clean and not leaving any prints with which she could be traced, the latter taken care of by a thin coating of a polymer she'd sprayed on her hands before leaving for the convention center, its microscopic coating sufficient to eliminate DNA or fingerprints.

She returned to eyeing the soon-to-be-ex-president through the scope, and her finger was moving to the trigger when Leah's voice rang in her ear. "Abort. Repeat. Abort. There's been a switch. The man on the stage is a double."

Jet held her finger over the trigger guard and whispered, "What? Are you sure?"

"Yes. The president is at the back of the building near the loading dock. They're bringing his motorcade around."

"How do you know?"

"We have a mole."

Jet was already in motion, moving back along the walkway as quickly as she dared. "What do you want me to do?"

"Get to the loading dock area as fast as you can. You should be close from your position. We'll create a diversion."

"Diversion?"

"Just move."

"How am I supposed to do that with a rifle?"

"We situated you where you could easily move along a maintenance hall to the loading area without being seen. It's right behind you. Now get going."

Jet did a quick calculation in her head and realized there was little chance she could traverse the hall using the basement as she had the other night and make it in time. Leah was assuming she was in the original firing position, from which she might have been able to make it to the dock within a minute – but it wasn't possible from her current location. With the basement hallway out of the question, that left only one option – one that exponentially increased her odds of getting caught.

She took a deep breath, uncocked the rifle, slipped the lanyard over her shoulder, and set off along the walkway, reconciled to having to cross the entire hall above the heads of the heavily armed security force, only an errant upward glance away from being stopped in a hail of bullets.

CHAPTER 30

Jet was halfway across the hall when the first explosion boomed from outside the rear of the building, followed closely by two more detonations – grenades by the size, she guessed. The crowd on the floor milled in panicked confusion as the dignitaries onstage were instantly surrounded by bodyguards, guns drawn but nothing to shoot at. Screams pierced the air as she continued along the beam, undeterred by the commotion, and when she passed the halfway point, she tapped her lapel and spoke in a quiet voice.

"Was that you?"

"Yes. Grenade launcher. We took out the lead vehicles in the motorcade. That will slow them down. Where are you?"

"Almost to the dock. Where's the target?"

"Still inside, per our source. What's taking you so long?"

Jet ignored the question. "What's the new plan?"

"Neutralize him however you can," Leah snapped.

"Not if it's suicide."

"Just do it."

Jet increased her pace, grateful for the exhibitors below adding to the chaos of the attack outside. The armed guards were trying to restore order, but their efforts had the opposite effect, their weapons serving only to further frighten an already spooked crowd. Her hope that nobody would see her seemed to be paying off, and she realized that the glare from the lights below her, pointing downward into the hall, created an effective shield for anyone not specifically looking for her.

She reached the area over the back loading area and swore – there was a drop ceiling preventing her from seeing the dock. Jet studied the cabling that held the ceiling in place and then swung herself over the balcony and threw herself into space.

Her hands locked onto a girder, and she pulled herself along until she was close enough to one of the cables to reach out and grab it. Once she had it tightly gripped, she levered her legs forward and wrapped them around it. She released the girder and began sliding down the steel cable, but slowed her descent enough so that when she landed on the ceiling frame below, she was stable enough to remain on the steel frame and not put a foot through the soft acoustic tile between the metal supports.

Jet inched along until she reached one of the big ventilation ducts. She squinted along its length in the dim light and spotted an access hatch. She moved to it and slid it aside, and then unshouldered the rifle, placed it inside the vent, and followed it in. Once inside she crawled along the vent, thankful that the metal was thick enough to support her weight, until she reached an exhaust grid, cold air rushing past her with enough force to blow her hair into her eyes. She brushed her bangs aside and looked down into the loading area, but couldn't see much. The grid wasn't sufficiently large to give her a decent view of the surroundings, so she'd have to find something else.

She crawled back to the hatch and Leah's voice rang in her ear again.

"Well? Where are you?"

"I'm above the loading dock, but I don't see him."

"Soldiers are running toward it, so he's there. No vehicles have left."

Jet decided not to dilute her attention by giving Leah a blow-by-blow and instead pulled herself from the duct, rifle in hand. She stood and tested the frame beneath her feet; then, hands out to either side for balance, she hurried along the thin rail to the far wall to where she'd seen another duct. She knelt where it terminated into the ceiling, set the rifle aside, and pulled the duct with as much force as she could muster. The ducting shifted, and she redoubled her effort until she'd created a gap six inches high through which she could see a swarm of men below. She scanned the loading dock and spied the president surrounded by his entourage of guards, their handguns pointed at anyone and anything as they warned the laborers to keep their distance.

Jet felt for the rifle and brought it to bear. At that angle it would be a tough shot if the target moved, but easy if he remained still just a little longer. She cocked the bolt and peered through the scope at the president, no more than fifty yards away, confident that if she was successful, all hell would break loose, the sound of shouting more than sufficient to mask most of the sound of the shot.

Hovel turned as though sensing imminent danger, but Jet adjusted her aim and her finger felt for the trigger. She exhaled evenly and squeezed it with steady pressure, and then the wire stock bucked so slightly it was almost unnoticeable, and the upper half of the president's skull blew against the wall in an explosion of blood and brains.

Jet didn't linger to watch the security detail lose its collective mind, but instead returned along the rail, her pulse steady, the rifle discarded where she'd lain as she raced the guards' confusion, praying silently that the origin of the shot wouldn't be identified until she'd had time to get away.

She pulled herself up the cable, the climb slower than the descent, and then she was at the girder and swinging her legs to gain momentum for a vault that would take her close enough to the walkway to make a grab.

Jet almost missed the railing and her fingers slipped before locking tight; and then her legs were below it, the toes of her boots feeling for support on the beam below. She pushed up and heaved her torso over the railing, and paused for a second to take a deep breath before leaping to her feet and moving unhurriedly back to the far side of the hall, the hubbub back at the loading dock no longer her concern.

"Well?" Leah demanded in a strangled voice.

"Mission accomplished," Jet said as she reached the halfway point. She was just beginning to believe she would make it when a cry sounded from beneath her, followed closely by gunshots. Sparks flew from ricochets off the steel beams beside her, and she abandoned her measured progress in favor of a wide-open sprint for the safety of the maintenance door. Rounds whined and pinged off the metal, and one of the lights to her left exploded in a shower of glass. She kept running, the elevation and the fact that the shooters were using handguns her only advantage, and had just made it to the maintenance hatch when a submachine gun opened fire and the concrete around her exploded in a shower of chips.

Jet hauled herself through the hatch and swung it shut, breathing heavily in the darkness as the gunfire continued, and then scooped up the purse she'd left by her exhibition bag and ran to the ducting assembly she'd discovered the other night. She paused to catch her breath and then pulled the hatch wide and climbed in.

She slid it closed behind her and was plunged into darkness. Hearing no indication of guards, she felt for her purse, located her phone, and switched on the flash to use as a light. Jet pulled herself along, gaining speed when she spotted the first vertical junction, and thumbed the screen to life so she could eye the schematic. After confirming that the duct was the one that terminated in the basement, she activated the flash again and moved to the lip of the junction to look down.

A series of ribbed intervals she could use for support stretched downward into darkness, each no more than a couple of inches deep, but adequate if she was careful. If she lost her grip, she would drop five stories to where the heat pumps connected to the ducts in the basement, but the thought didn't faze her. Jet slid the phone into her breast pocket so some of the light still shone over the top of the fabric and lowered herself into the duct, pushing her feet against one wall, her back against the other.

Five minutes later, she was at the bottom of the duct and listening at another maintenance hatch. After a cautious pause, she opened it and lowered herself to the floor of the equipment room filled with heating pumps the size of cars.

She made her way across the room and put her ear to the steel door, eyeing her phone screen as she strained to hear. The blueprint showed an exit to the street at the end of the basement corridor to her right, and if she could make it the twenty-five meters and get out of the building, she'd be in the clear.

"What's the situation?" Jet whispered.

Nothing.

"Leah. Status?" she demanded.

No response.

"Damn," Jet muttered. The thick reinforced concrete in the basement had to have blocked reception. So she might be walking into just about anything when she emerged into the hall. Without the benefit of intel on what was happening outside, she was flying completely blind, and for all she knew, there could be squads of soldiers covering the exits.

Her options were limited to either making a break for it from the maintenance area or working her way back to the hall and subjecting herself to the hours of interrogation that were sure to come. Neither was particularly appealing, but her instinct was telling her to get as far from the exhibition center as possible while she had the chance.

Jet twisted the lever and opened the door to find a dimly lit empty hallway. Her luck having held so far, she trotted to the security door and pressed her ear against it. A groan from the far end, where a stairwell led to the ground floor, startled her, making her decision easy. Jaw clenched, she slid the heavy bolt securing the door open and pushed the slab with all her might. A man yelled from the stairs behind her and then she was through, just in time to hear more screaming before the door slammed shut, leaving her standing beneath the dark sky, night having fallen while she was making her escape.

She looked around and, seeing nobody, took off at a flat-out run. The lights of the building receded behind her, any snipers no doubt on the other side of the complex where the explosions had detonated.

"Leah, I'm out. Where are you?" she gasped as she poured on the speed.

Silence answered her, and she frowned as she reached the edge of a large parking lot, where a symphony of horns from the wide boulevard beyond signaled that something was happening beyond the events in the hall. Footsteps ran by from the other end of the lot, and she saw a group of young men wearing hoodies, scarves covering their faces, racing along the street. A crash of glass triggered a car alarm, and then another crash from farther away preceded an orange fireball that exploded into the sky.

Jet shook her head. The civil unrest that Itai and Leah had warned would be the immediate response to news of the president's assassination was already starting, and she couldn't help but wonder at how quickly word had leaked. She was too seasoned to believe that any of what was to come was organic – there was only one reason to assassinate a head of state, and even if she hadn't been told, she understood that regime change was the goal. The Mossad had probably had a team to communicate the assassination instantly, and if Baku followed the pattern of any of the other regime changes she'd been involved in, there would be rioting and civil disobedience that would give the military an excuse to clamp down, eliminating dissident voices and silencing any opposition.

None of which was her problem. She needed to get to the Mercedes, where the clothes that were more in keeping with what the Azerbaijani women wore had been stashed by Leah, and then make it to the safe house. The first wave of rioters passed the lot, leaving a trail of broken windows and burning vehicles, and Jet waited until she couldn't see any more approaching before moving toward where the car sat in the center of the lot.

"Leah, come in. What's happening?" she tried a final time, but received no answer.

Something had gone wrong, obviously. Possibly connected to the explosions. Maybe her handler had somehow been hurt or captured while creating the diversion?

Jet didn't dwell on it and instead peeled the earbud from her ear and shrugged out of her suit jacket, wary of the transmitter now acting as a potential tracking device if Leah had been taken into custody. She emptied her pockets of her passport, cash, and phone, and removed the battery just in case, jettisoning the jacket beneath a truck and sliding her belongings into her pants pockets.

Whatever was happening, her imperative was now to survive and reach the safe house. She paused by a SEAT sedan, and after peeking over the hood to confirm that there were no more miscreants headed her way, she took off at a run toward the Mercedes, which thankfully had been spared the first wave of destruction by the angry mob.

CHAPTER 31

Jet reached the car and tried the rear passenger-side door handle, only to find it locked. She frowned – it was supposed to be open. She quickly rounded the vehicle, trying the other handles, and found them all the same. Jet shook her head. Nothing was going according to plan. Maybe the car had an automatic locking function after a certain period of time? She couldn't believe that Leah would have forgotten that critical piece of the escape plan, but didn't allow it to throw her and instead slammed her elbow into the driver's side window again and again until it shattered in a shower of safety glass.

She reached in and popped the trunk, and there were her black cargo pants and a dark blue windbreaker with the logo of a local sports team emblazoned on the breast. Jet slipped out of her suit pants and pulled on the others, and then loaded the pockets with her belongings before donning the windbreaker. She balled up the suit bottoms and tossed them into the trunk, and then the whump of a Molotov cocktail at the end of the lot shook the ground, signaling that things in the vicinity were spinning out of control.

Sirens keened in the distance, and a few shots rang out from the convention center. Jet knew better than to remain a second longer and wended through the parked cars to the main thoroughfare. Military vehicles were approaching the complex down the wide boulevard, their lights bright in the deepening night. Jet darted across the lanes and made for the university grounds a few blocks away where there was a taxi stand and, if nobody was willing to take a fare, buses running in the direction she needed to go.

Crowds of students gathered on the sidewalks as she neared, their expressions excited and fearful. Jet overheard loud discussions about what had transpired – it was a coup by the military, the president had been shot, the prime minister was nowhere to be found. One of the clumps of youths was listening to a broadcast blaring from his phone: a newscaster advised that the authorities were clamping down on any opportunistic looting or rioting and to stay indoors until the civil unrest had been quelled.

Jet approached a quartet of young women who seemed scared but harmless. "Have you seen any taxis or buses?" she asked.

One of the women shook her head. "We just got here from the housing building. I haven't seen anything, but I doubt the buses will be running if there's rioting."

"Thanks," Jet said. The scenario was worsening by the minute. If the student was right, Jet would have to try to make it across town on foot – the six kilometers to the safe house wasn't the problem so much as the unknown of police patrols and rioters between the university and her destination. It could have been worse, she supposed – she was just one woman among millions in Baku, and as far as she knew, there was no surveillance footage of her. Her plight had more to do with being a lone female in an unstable environment than being hunted – presuming she was correct that she hadn't been filmed in her headlong dash from the building or by a camera she'd missed in the lot.

She skirted the university grounds, which were filled with more students arguing about the upheaval and the president's assassination. They were surprisingly orderly, given what she'd seen just a few blocks away, leading her to suspect that the seemingly spontaneous rioters had in fact been part of an orchestrated campaign. Jet hoped that would be confined to the convention center area and not spread – at least not until she'd made it back to the house.

Jet got the first inkling that it might not be that easy when she spotted several trucks rolling down the street that bordered the university, their beds filled with armed men with scarves wrapped around their faces and balaclavas concealing their identities. Her impression was reinforced when one of the men held a bottle aloft and let out a whoop. Streets filled with roving gangs of drunk, armed hoodlums would make matters much more difficult for her, even if they would also provide confused cover.

She waited until the street was empty and then sprinted across, eyes scanning the far sidewalk. Being female and on the street in an environment that was in flux, even temporarily, meant being a target for any predators looking for a chance to misbehave.

At the far side of the street, she paused in the doorway of a tall building, seated the battery in her phone, and powered it on. After it booted up, she activated the map function, located her position, and traced the most direct route to the safe house, which she saw would take her past a sports arena and a couple of large hotels. She set off in the direction of the coliseum, which was dark, and fifteen minutes later arrived at the larger of the hotels.

A pair of security guards with shotguns by the hotel main entrance didn't bode well, nor did the empty taxi stand in front. She approached the lobby, and the guards looked her over. One of them, with a puckered white scar running down one side of his face, stepped into her path, weapon at present arms. "Are you a guest?" he demanded.

"No. I need a taxi, and I'm hoping the concierge can call one."

The man chuckled dryly. "Fat chance. Haven't you heard what happened? The president's been shot. City's under martial law. They're saying they're going to shoot looters."

"Which is why I need a cab. I can't walk, obviously."

"Lady, there are no cabs. City's locked down."

"Then how am I supposed to get where I'm staying?"

The man shrugged. "Not my problem. Move along."

Jet frowned. "What if I want to check in?"

"Reception's closed. Everyone's gone home to their families except for security and a skeleton housekeeping crew."

Her tone softened. "Come on. Don't turn me away. There's got to be some way to get where I need to go. I have money. Maybe one of you knows someone who could give me a ride?"

"How much money are you thinking, and where are you going?" the other guard asked.

"A hundred manat?" She named the neighborhood.

The guards exchanged a small smile. "Two might get it done."

"That's all my money."

"Then have a nice night."

Jet sighed. "Let's say it was two hundred. You know anyone who could drive me now? I'm in a hurry."

"I can make a couple of calls."

"Please."

"Go on into the lobby and wait there. You don't want to be outside."

Jet thought the guards were overstating the risk, but agreed and pushed through the revolving door. Four more armed men stood inside, stationed in each corner of the lobby, and regarded her curiously, weapons in hand.

She contented herself with watching a big-screen TV broadcasting a live news feed from outside the convention center, cutting occasionally to helicopter footage of the city, where bonfires had been started in several districts by rioters who had begun looting some of the shopping areas. A serious newscaster echoed the earlier radio warning that the authorities were under orders to shoot first and ask questions later, and that everyone should stay off the streets due to gangs wreaking havoc. The footage changed again to what was clearly a firefight between government troops and armed looters taken from above, the muzzle flashes of the civilian weapons orange blossoms in the gloom, quickly answered by overwhelming automatic rifle fire from the government forces.

Her attention was pulled from the screen by the scar-faced guard outside waving to her. She stood and returned to the entrance, where the man had a somber expression.

"Sorry. Nobody will do it. Too weird out there right now. Maybe in a few hours…"

"That's it? Just…no?" she asked.

"Like I said. All I promised to do was try." He eyed her. "No tip for the effort?"

Something about the guard gave Jet pause. "Sorry."

"Then beat it," the man growled, turning mean.

"Yeah. Thanks for nothing."

Jet resumed her slog along the main street, troubled by the interaction at the hotel. When headlights bounced along the street from behind her, she quickened her pace and turned onto a side street just as a dark sedan rolled to the curb behind her. She considered whether to run, but elected to capitalize on the situation by standing her ground and playing the weak victim.

Two men emptied from the car and ran after her. They pulled up short at the sight of the young woman in black, standing with her hands at her side, purse strap slung over her shoulder. A stiletto snapped open in one of the men's hands. The other wielded a small semiautomatic pistol with an ugly snout and snarled at her.

"Give us your money. Now."

Jet smiled. "You don't want to do this."

"Give us the cash or we'll cut that pretty face of yours."

"I don't have any money."

"We know you do. Last chance."

Jet's suspicions were confirmed. The guard had made calls, all right, but to alert some hoodlums that there was prey on the street.

"If I give you my money, you'll leave me alone?" she asked, noting that they were inching toward her.

"That's right. Unless you want some company," the other man said with a leer.

"I actually need a ride."

The men looked at each other and laughed, the sound ugly. "Hear that?" the first said. "She wants a ride. I think we could help her, don't you?"

"Oh, definitely. Been a while since—"

Jet covered the ground between them in three steps and leveled a kick at the man with the gun, catching him in the side of his ribs. His breath blew from his mouth in an O and she followed through with a forearm strike that caught him in the nose, breaking it and sending a spray of blood down his chin as he struggled for breath. He burbled and slumped to the ground, the pistol dropping harmlessly beside him. The other slashed at her, but she was too quick, and she followed a hard knee to his groin with both palms smacking his ears, rupturing his eardrums. He reeled away, and the knife skittered into the gutter.

Jet didn't wait for the men to recover, and instead scooped up the pistol and made straight for the waiting car around the corner. The driver looked up in surprise when she threw the passenger door open and slid beside him.

"Your friends said you'd give me a ride," she announced. The man, his wide face and pig eyes those of a bully, fought for comprehension at the words, and then she punched him in the throat, the blow so fast he never saw it coming. He gurgled and pawed at his neck, and she delivered another brutal strike and leaned over, jerked his door handle, and pushed him onto the street.

She crawled behind the wheel, pulled the door closed, and roared off, her transportation problem temporarily solved – at least until the muggers reported it stolen. She eyed the gas gauge and shook her head; it was nearly empty. Jet frowned in the darkness. She'd be lucky if it made it to the house. It figured that a pack of lowlifes so desperate that they'd mug a woman for a few hundred manat would be too broke to put gas in their car, and she cursed as the car sped through an intersection and past a filling station that was dark as a tomb.

Sirens howled from a larger boulevard ahead, and she shut her lights off and braked, waiting to see what was coming. A procession of police vehicles turned onto the street. She stood on the throttle and turned hard right between a pair of buildings and yanked up on the emergency brake so her brake lights wouldn't illuminate. Moments later the column of squad cars and armored personnel carriers sped by, going on forever, roof lights pulsing red and blue.

When the last of the vehicles had passed, she stepped out of the car and chanced a look around the corner of the building. The street was once again empty; but if there were mass troop movements coinciding with the rioting, she was risking arrest, or worse, by driving. She paced behind the car as she thought through her options and, after checking her phone and calculating the remaining distance, resolved to continue on foot. Tempting as it was to drive as much as possible, it would be easier to dodge patrols or criminals if she stuck to back streets and the shadows under her own steam, whereas any car on the road given the circumstance would be automatically suspect.

Jet removed the battery from her phone again, pocketed it and the cell, and set off down the strip of pavement, grateful that the streetlights were largely nonfunctional, the only sound the steady pounding of her boots and the ululating of sirens in the night sky.

Chapter 32

Yashar Bahador looked up from the television screen as Sergei entered his office. Bahador's dour features were grim, mirroring Sergei's, both men experienced enough to know that the murder of the president was a game changer.

"I'm glad you made it. Looks bad out there," Bahador said.

"And getting worse. The streets are crawling with army and police, and there are some pockets of armed resistance."

"Who would be stupid enough to take up weapons now?"

"There's always a fringe that waits in the wings. We both know that. Probably the Anarchists or the Revolutionary Party." Both groups had been suspected of attempting to assassinate Bahador and were known to appeal to extremists of all stripes.

"Well, if it's them, they deserve what they get." Bahador eyed Sergei and tipped his head toward a bookshelf behind him. "Drink?"

"I could use one."

Bahador rose and fetched a bottle of premium vodka and two tumblers. He poured both half full and sat back down. Sergei reached for one of the glasses and toasted his master, and then they swallowed a third of the liquor, eyes brightening at the bite.

Bahador shook his head and set the drink down. "Who do you think is behind this?"

"The assassination? Could be any of a half dozen culprits. Hovel was widely hated, so narrowing it down is the challenge."

"What does anyone gain by his demise, though?"

"I'm hearing rumors that it is a coup attempt by a faction in the military."

"We would have been alerted, no?"

"Not necessarily. That bunch tends to be secretive, and God

knows there are enough cliques in the top brass for one of them to get it into their heads to take over."

"But with the elections so close, it makes no sense."

"I understand. However, a better question is, what's our response going to be?"

Bahador's brow furrowed and he took another swallow of vodka. "Obviously we must condemn the assassination. I've been working on a draft to issue within the hour."

"Obviously," Sergei agreed.

"Further, I'm calling for all members of our party to refuse to participate in any unrest. I don't want to be lumped in with any agitators in the coming clampdown – we cannot afford to have anything to do with rioting or looting or the administration will come at us hard and manufacture a reason to dismantle our party. That must be avoided at all costs. We both know they would like nothing better than to eliminate us."

"Are you going to do a broadcast?"

Bahador nodded. "I'm waiting to hear back from the national radio station. The television outlets will pick it up live, so we'll get maximum coverage."

Sergei nodded slowly. "Good idea." He eyed the Nationalist leader over the rim of his glass. "Who do you think did it?"

"I honestly have no idea. Nobody wins with Hovel dead, except perhaps Nabiyev, but only if he suspends elections long enough to campaign."

"You think he would do that?"

"The man's a weasel. I wouldn't put anything past him. But I don't see him orchestrating an assassination." Bahador hesitated. "One thing I find troubling is how fast the unrest has begun. Someone knew in advance and wants lawlessness."

"Why? Who benefits?" Sergei asked.

"I'm trying to figure that one out. If it's a faction in the military, perhaps they want cover while they consolidate their power."

"The country would never go along with it. And the international community would reject any attempt to seize the reins. I don't see that as viable."

"Neither do I. I'm just throwing it out there."

"What about foreign interests? With the contracts scheduled to reset next year, a change in leadership might be part of a larger strategic reorganization."

"I can't see the Americans being behind this, and they're the usual suspects. Do you see anyone else being foolhardy enough to assassinate a democratically elected head of state simply so their corporations benefit?"

"Not immediately. But the sums involved are huge."

The subject was a sore point for both men, who felt that the nation's wealth was being stolen from its people by foreign interests. It didn't matter what flag flew over the oil fields, if the profits largely flowed to foreigners, the people were the ultimate losers, exactly as had played out all over the rest of the world where international conglomerates pocketed most of the benefits from impoverished populations' resources. Whether mining in the Congo, with the wealth transferred to Belgium, or oil in Argentina to a consortium of international interests, the same predictable pattern repeated again and again.

"It's possible it was a private effort, but I don't think we should speculate. They haven't found the shooter, and until they do, it's all guesswork."

Sergei frowned. "Oh, I know, officially. I was just asking what you thought."

Bahador finished his drink. "I think I need to polish my speech so it hits all the right notes. Which is why you're here. You have a talent for these things. Here's what I have so far," the older man said, and slid a notepad to Sergei.

The younger man read, nodding in places, frowning in others, and held out his hand when he was finished. "Do you have a pencil? I can see a few spots that might be improved."

Bahador handed him one and sat back, his mind racing. Even after fifteen years in politics, this night would go down as the most stunning in his career – where everything had changed in a blink, and the nation's future had gone from predictable to precarious in a heartbeat.

He watched Sergei scribble and erase, and mulled over the possibilities Sergei had raised. The next hours would have to be handled with the delicacy of a neurosurgeon, and if Bahador managed things correctly, he would emerge as a clear leadership figure at a time of unfathomable crisis. The truth was that Hovel's death had benefited one group far more than any others, if they didn't blow it, and that was the Nationalist Party, at least at first blush. Whether they could leverage that into a win on election day was really the question, but one Bahador felt optimistic about the more he thought the idea through. No matter how mild the police and military response to any unrest, it would create tremendous resentment with a segment of the voting public, and the more draconian their actions, the worse it would be for them.

All Bahador had to do was wait for them to shoot themselves in the foot, and then step in as a voice of reason, advising his supporters to work within the system rather than attempting to take matters into their own hands.

Bahador couldn't have scripted the opportunity better if he'd tried, and he didn't plan to blow the godsend that had fallen in their laps. Whoever was behind the assassination had just done Bahador the biggest favor of his career, whether intentionally or not, and now he was ready to step onto the world stage and speak with conviction.

Until then, he would caution restraint and let the administration dirty itself with the fallout.

The phone on his desk rang. He answered, his voice velvety, his calm unflappable after four fingers of vodka.

"Yes, my friend. It's shocking, no doubt. Thank you for the chance to address the nation in this tumultuous time."

CHAPTER 33

Jet tore across another street after verifying that nobody was observing her and there were no emergency vehicles on the road. As she had made progress, she'd become less concerned with being attacked, most Azerbaijanis apparently preferring to stay behind closed doors in their apartment blocks rather than running amok after dark. That made sense – it was usually a tiny minority that viewed upheaval as an opportunity to loot. Judging by the cars, most people in this area of Baku were hardworking middle-class families, and while Jet had no doubt that things might get bad in the slums, the middle class tended to be well behaved.

That assessment changed when she saw a man gun down another in the middle of the street, the crack of his pistol shattering the quiet of the residential area. She shrank into the darkness of a doorway as the man kicked the body several times and then spit on it and walked off, his gait unsteady, obviously inebriated or injured.

There would be those who used the opportunity to settle scores – drug turf disputes, criminal rivalries, jealous crimes of passion – but she wasn't worried about her safety because miscreants were scrabbling over territory or someone was getting even for wooing his girlfriend. Her big fear was the men she'd seen in the trucks near the convention center. They'd seemed organized and well-armed, if undisciplined and drunk, and that implied foreknowledge and a plan. If she ran afoul of a group like that, it wouldn't be as easy as it had been with the muggers, who were obvious amateurs with no skills. Even an idiot could be deadly with an AK, she knew from harsh experience. Once the gunman had vanished around a corner, she continued toward the safe house, the temperature dropping as the hour grew later.

She activated the phone again to check her progress and frowned when it displayed no service – not completely unexpected, as police and government agencies in many countries shut down the cell system during times of chaos to prevent gangs from communicating with each other.

Jet closed her eyes and recalled the image of the map in her head, and guessed that at the rate she was going, she'd be at the house within minutes. Hopefully Leah would be there, ready to transport her to safety. Jet had no idea what had gone wrong on her handler's end, but she would know soon enough. If she'd been apprehended or injured, Jet would call Itai. The station chief would have a backup plan; they always did.

Jet pushed herself harder in the final stretch, anxious to make it to the safety of the house as the neighborhood deteriorated. She spotted a couple of young men down the block as she turned onto the safe house road, but if they saw her, they ignored her.

She slowed as she neared the darkened house, no sign of Leah's Mercedes in the drive. A scattering of vehicles was parked on the street, and Jet automatically scanned them for occupants, grateful for the dark and the dearth of streetlamps. Seeing nothing to alarm her, she strode purposefully toward the house, senses tingling, her nerves raw.

When she reached the front door, it was locked, and she glared at the wood slab. Nothing had gone right the entire night. She wrenched the handle again and then moved to the front window, stopping in frustration at the bars that protected it.

She tried the tall iron gate on the side yard, but it was padlocked shut. Jet looked around again and then stepped away from the barrier and took a running start at it. When she reached it, she vaulted upward while scrambling against the side of the house. Her fingers clamped onto the top of the gate and she hoisted herself over it, landing on the dead grass in a crouch.

Jet rounded the back of the house and surveyed the small yard, and then turned to the walls separating the property from other homes abutting them. After taking several deep breaths, she moved to the rear door. The handle didn't budge, and she slid her purse off her shoulder and rooted in it until she found a credit card in Katya's company's name. From what she remembered, the locking mechanism was ancient, and she'd made a mental note that a schoolgirl could have opened it with a little time and almost no skill.

She slid the credit card along the jamb until it found the curved part of the bolt and, with a swift motion, pulled it and the handle toward her. The door swung wide and she smiled in the dark. At least that had gone well.

Jet stepped into the house, her eyes roaming over the hall, and called out with little hope of a response. "Leah?"

Nothing.

Jet reached for the light switch, but stopped when she saw a tiny red LED blinking by the front door. She moved toward it, passing her and Leah's rooms, and stared at a small box mounted near the ceiling.

A box that hadn't been there earlier.

She couldn't make out what it was, so removed the phone from her pocket and used the flash to illuminate the device. Her eyes widened when she identified it.

An alarm.

Which she'd triggered opening the rear door.

Jet could think of several reasons Leah might have wired the house after Jet had left: if she'd feared a robbery attempt, or a hostile actor breaking in and lying in wait, or an intruder bugging the place. But why wouldn't she have alerted Jet that she was doing so? Jet recalled Leah's arrogant tone when addressing her and shook her head in disgust. Because Jet had no need to know. She was just the hired help – a pair of hands to operate the gun, nothing more.

Of course, Jet was assuming it was she who'd triggered the alarm and that nobody had been there before her.

The thought sent a chill up her spine, and she backed away from the front door and stopped at Leah's room. The door was closed. Jet tried the knob and it opened easily.

Inside, there was no trace Leah had ever existed. The bed had

179

been stripped, and the closet cabinet doors stood open, the interior empty.

She was interrupted by the faint squeak of metal in the front of the house.

Brakes.

Jet darted to a window by the entry and spied the dark form of a personnel carrier, its police markings visible in the dim moonlight. She didn't hesitate, but ran as fast as her legs would carry her to the back door and pulled it softly closed as the sound of boots on the sidewalk in front reached her. She glanced around and then tore toward the rear wall and ran halfway up before locking her arms over the top and hauling her body over it.

She heard the front door battered in with a ram and raced along the side of the home that backed onto the shared wall. When she reached its gate, it was also locked, and she repeated her maneuver from earlier and pulled herself over it. She hit the ground and rolled before pushing herself to her feet, and checked to ensure her purse was still in place before scrambling away.

The sound of engines from the end of the street urged her to greater speed, and she put every ounce of energy into reaching the homes across the way. If she made it, she could disappear into their yards, leaving the police empty-handed, raiding a house with nobody in it. Why they would do so had only one ugly answer: Leah had been captured and had given up its location, or some item she'd been carrying had given it away. Nothing else made sense.

She reached the front wall of the house across the street and raced toward it, again pulling herself to the top, but this time remaining there and forcing herself upright. Jet moved carefully along the wall, feet placed one in front of the other like a gymnast on a balancing beam. She stepped over a gap at the rear and continued to another street before dropping to the ground and taking stock.

There were no further signs of anyone searching for her, which was a positive, but when the police discovered the house was empty, they would broaden the net, she was sure. That left her precious little time to get clear of the neighborhood, which she could do without being caught, assuming the streets stayed deserted. Seeing no option but to continue, she darted house to house, pausing at each to listen before moving to the next.

A dog barking at the fourth house made her cringe, and she was back to flat-out running, distancing herself from the animal's baying as she drove herself hard. If the police heard the animal, they might come to investigate. She had no way of knowing how determined they were, but had to assume the worst, and forced herself to breathe easily as she ran, arms and legs pumping like pistons as she traversed the suburban street, making for the apartment blocks in the near distance where she could vanish into the jumble of buildings.

She made it to the larger street at the end of the row of homes, and froze, chest heaving, at the sound of blades beating the air to the south. Of course, she thought belatedly, they'd bring a helicopter into the fray. Any slim lead she'd had was rapidly disappearing, and once the helo was overhead, possibly with infrared sensors and night vision equipment, her odds of remaining undetected were zero.

The thought galvanized her into action, and she tore down the street, abandoning any caution in favor of putting distance between herself and the aircraft, her mind churning along with her stomach as she ran, praying silently for just another few minutes of luck before all hell broke loose.

CHAPTER 34

Tank treads ground against asphalt as a column of armored vehicles rumbled down a wide avenue toward the city center. Jet watched the procession from the shadows of an apartment complex entryway with a knot in her stomach, still gasping from the exertion of the adrenaline-juiced run. The faint pop of gunfire from miles away echoed in the night like fireworks over the tall buildings that ringed the convention area, nearly inaudible but as distinct as Morse code to Jet's trained ear.

If there was a battle raging a few miles away, then the situation had shifted from unstable to actively dangerous, and she needed to find someplace to hunker down and wait out the power struggle she presumed was under way. The death of the president had created a vacuum, and rivals were shooting it out to determine who got to next loot the country under the guise of governing it. In an oil-producing nation like Azerbaijan the stakes were high, each year's production a fortune, and he who controlled the tap controlled the purse strings.

Jet didn't care about politics except to the extent that they affected her, but she more than understood that most wars and coups weren't so much about power or ideology as they were about money. That didn't bother her, and she didn't think about the ramifications too deeply, because at the bottom of that rabbit hole was the conclusion that the clandestine maneuvering of all governments had little to do with good or bad, and everything to do with profit and loss.

If she followed that reasoning through, then her role as the instrument of one of those governments became deeply suspect, and she couldn't afford the luxury of doubts. She was doing what she had to in order for her family to survive, and if she'd refused, someone else would have done it.

More vehicles pulled into view, and Jet counted another twenty tanks rolling toward the gunfight, escorted by a fleet of personnel carriers, no doubt with hundreds of soldiers. She briefly wondered whether the chatter she'd overheard at the university about a coup might be true – had the Mossad terminated Hovel in order to facilitate a takeover by the military?

She didn't know that much about the intricacies of Azerbaijani's government, but it seemed unlikely. That wasn't how the Mossad operated, at least that she was aware of. But anything was possible, and she was sure an explanation for the army's presence on city streets would surface soon, if only to reassure the public that their country hadn't been taken over by its military.

Her mind turned to where she could go that might be safe, and she kept coming up with the same answer: the large hotels, where her status as a Russian attending the trade show would serve her well. The problem was that if Leah had been compromised, Jet's Katya identity might be flagged, and all that would do was lead any pursuers to her. The police at the safe house had unnerved her, and Jet had to assume the worst, which meant that appealing as they might be, hotels were out of the question.

That left breaking into a car and putting the city behind her, or finding someplace that didn't ask questions where she could stay until morning. Ordinarily, she was trained to find a nightclub or bar and flirt with one of the men looking for love, using their place to lie low. But nothing would be open on a night like this, and she doubted she looked particularly appealing with scuff marks, grime, and dirt residue covering her clothing.

The car option was also off the table until the curfew was over, likely at daybreak. She checked the time and shook her head. At least eight more hours until dawn. If she was careful and avoided conflict, she might make it, depending on where she holed up.

An idea occurred to her and she seriously considered it, even though it was the most unappealing possibility she could think of. The local junkie population might have shooting galleries – abandoned buildings they used to buy and sell drugs, and inject or smoke them. Every developed economy in the world had an area in its larger cities where the police didn't venture into, and she was sure Baku was no exception, based on what she'd seen of the poorer sections.

Her phone vibrated in her pocket and she remembered that she hadn't taken the battery out the last time she'd used it, seeing no point since there was no signal. She retrieved it and eyed the indicator, and saw that there was service. Jet pulled up the map and located her position, searching for any landmarks that might be promising before settling on the marina. There would be private yachts there, and most would be painfully easy to break into. The idea was more appealing than spending the night among heroin or meth addicts, and she quickly did the math on the distance and figured she could make it to the waterfront in an hour or less.

Jet remembered Itai's instruction when handing her the shoe repair business card, and she dialed the number from memory and waited as it rang. It was answered by voicemail, and she left her number and a message that Katya needed to speak to Krell about a delivery as soon as possible. When she hung up, she was startled when her phone chirped and vibrated almost immediately, announcing a call from a Baku number she didn't recognize. She thumbed the phone to vibrate only and answered with a whisper.

"Yes?"

"Katya. It's Leah. Where are you?"

Jet frowned. "I'm safe. Why didn't you answer my transmissions?"

"Technical problem on my side. Where are you?"

"I tried the house."

"I was going to warn you. Don't go there. We've been compromised."

"Too late."

"Are you there now?"

"No."

Leah paused. "I'm going to give you an address. It's a residential building that's being renovated in the Sovetskaya section of town, near the Sultanbey Mosque. Are you mobile?"

"I can get wherever I need to be."

"Not hurt?"

"Thanks for asking. I'm fine."

"Write this down." Leah gave her a street name and number. "You'll have to be careful. The police and army are everywhere, but mainly near the city center."

"I know. I hear shooting."

"You familiar with where Sovetskaya is? How long will it take you to get there?"

"Yes, I know where it is. Maybe…an hour and a half."

"Okay. Call me when you're on approach."

"The car was locked," Jet said. "The Mercedes."

"That's not important. I have another one."

Jet bit back the anger that surged through her at the woman's dismissive tone. "It was important to me."

"Just get to the building and I'll explain what happened."

"Are we still leaving tonight?"

"Absolutely."

"Why can't you pick me up?"

"Only military and police vehicles are allowed on the streets."

Jet frowned. "Then how are we going to leave town?"

"I've got that handled."

"How?"

"I said I'll explain everything once you're here. Now get moving."

The line went dead, leaving Jet staring at the phone in wonder. The woman's arrogance knew no bounds. She was treating Jet like a junior cadet, not an experienced operative. Jet choked back the resentment that rose in her throat and quieted her mind. Leah's personality defects weren't her concern. She was the handler, and if she was a complete bitch, that was just the way it was. Jet would never see her again after the night was over, so she would have to stomach the insulting tone and short responses in the interests of getting clear of Baku.

Jet knew from her reading where the Sovetskaya section of town was located, a borderline slum north of the original old town, which dated to the twelfth century. She pulled up the map on her phone and entered the address Leah had given her, and a pulsing dot glowed on the edge of the district, most of the area closed to automobiles per the map legend. That made sense given the age of the neighborhood – the alleys had been created long before cars, and most of them were just wide enough for a horse-drawn cart or a couple of pedestrians standing abreast.

If Jet pushed, she could make it in under an hour. That would give her the time to nose around the area to ensure she wasn't walking into a trap. Leah's non-explanations hadn't done much to reassure Jet, especially after the raid on the safe house, and it was always possible that she'd made the call to Jet under duress, to lure her into an ambush. Leah hadn't used any of the standard trigger words that would have indicated that was the case, but given that Jet had assassinated the president only hours before, she could afford to take no chances.

She slipped the phone back into her pocket and cocked her head, listening for any more engines. When she heard nothing approaching, she moved along a hedge that ran the length of the apartment complex to the next street. At the road, she paused to confirm it was empty and then jogged across to another series of monolithic dwellings. Only a few lights shone in the windows, as though the residents feared making themselves targets. The memory of the Soviet years was probably still strong with the locals, the generations of oppressive rule as fresh as yesterday's rain.

The streets were deserted as she trotted south, serenaded by sirens and gunfire, two sounds she knew as intimately as a lover's touch. She reached the end of a block and glanced in both directions before she vanished into the darkness, the sound of her boots echoing off the buildings, her mind working furiously as she plunged headlong into the dead of night.

CHAPTER 35

The Sovetskaya district was a jumble of squalid homes, many of them decades old, and in some cases, centuries. Jet crossed a construction site to the west of the neighborhood, where heavy equipment was parked in clumps near maintenance sheds. The area was devoid of other structures and appeared deserted; whatever security had been in place must have fled after the first explosions from the convention center.

Jet reached a chain-link fence at the edge of the site and scaled it, eyes on the homes before her, most of which were dark, with only the glow of televisions flickering behind curtains. When she landed hard on the gravel, a flash of pain shot up her ankle and she grunted. The misstep was a complication she couldn't afford. She tested her weight and the pain receded, but she was limping slightly as she worked her way along the winding alleys past charmless buildings with laundry lines and bootleg electricity wiring streaming from utility poles.

The streets narrowed as she neared the center of the neighborhood, and became the expected medieval walkways, the cobblestones beneath her feet worn smooth from the passage of time. She followed a promising passageway toward the dome of the mosque in the near distance. Moonlight glowed off the glazed tile washed clean by the prior day's rain. Dogs barked from behind walled yards at each rattle of distant gunfire, but she ignored them and pushed on, her ankle reminding her that she needed to keep her mind focused and be more careful if she was to survive the night.

Jet paused at a junction and checked the phone map. The address was no more than a hundred yards away now, on a winding street that ended at the mosque grounds. The surroundings improved slightly as Jet crept along the route. Her eyes roved over the windows above her, the buildings older but multistoried and larger than the single-family dwellings she'd passed through. Many were abandoned, the area clearly in transition, and construction fencing barricaded several of the crumbling façades. An occasional whiff of stale urine from one of the doorways told her that there might be some vagrants within the more presentable buildings, but they were the least of her worries at this point, and she was glad to be the only one on the street.

She veered down an even narrower alley that ran behind the building, keeping to the shadows. Jet stopped twenty yards away and checked her watch – it had taken her longer than she'd thought, but she was still a few minutes early and had time to reconnoiter before going in for the rendezvous.

There was no evidence of an armed force anywhere nearby; the few vehicles she'd spotted were decades-old economy models with fading paint and dented exteriors and all empty that she could see. Her nose wrinkled at the stench of garbage from an overflowing can and she skirted it, staying close to the walls as she surveyed the alley. She rounded the corner and made her way back up the street that the building fronted upon. As she approached the entrance, she slipped her phone from her pocket and placed a call. Leah answered on the first ring.

"Where are you?" Leah asked.

"Almost there. Everything okay?"

"Of course. Why wouldn't it be?"

"It's just a question."

"Well, hurry up. We don't have all night."

Jet hung up and jumped back as a flash of black and gray fur shot from an empty doorway and tore away, the cat emaciated and feral, disturbed by Jet's unexpected intrusion. Jet breathed deeply, slowing her heart rate back to normal. When she was composed, she walked the rest of the way to the building entrance, where she could now make out a dim glow deep in its recesses.

She pulled a plywood door aside and stepped into the foyer of the two-story structure. Every surface was covered with dust, and she had to pick her way through rubble and construction trash underfoot. Jet crept toward the glow, the hall lined with scaffolding, the walls bare, and passed into a large room with a workbench in the center. Several crates of tile stood nearby, and a primitive crane system rested by the doorway.

"You made it," Leah said, from where she sat on one of the crates. A freestanding work lamp provided light from a fading bulb.

"Yes."

"Good. Let's get the debriefing out of the way, and then we can hit the road."

"Where are you parked?"

"A block away." Leah studied her. "Take me through the scene at the hall. I know you made the hit, obviously. But what took you so long?"

"I decided to change position after scoping out the original location. So I was further away." Jet gave a dry report of her reasoning, the assassination, and the subsequent escape. When she was finished, Leah was frowning.

"You were given a specific set of instructions and you disregarded them," she said flatly. "Disobeyed, to be exact."

"I carried out the sanction successfully and lived to tell about it. I wouldn't have been able to get clear if I'd done it your way." Jet paused. "Now I have a few questions. What were the explosions I heard – the diversion you arranged?"

Leah turned from Jet and removed something from her pocket as she answered. "We had mercenaries waiting if you were unsuccessful, and I put them to use. He was going to get away, and that would have ruined everything."

When Leah turned to face Jet, there was a pistol in her hand with a long suppressor attached to it. Jet's face remained impassive at the sight of the gun.

"What's going on here, Leah?" she asked softly.

"You were supposed to be killed in the hall, you stupid bitch. It was all arranged. But you had to do things your own way."

"Killed?"

"Whether or not you were able to take out the president, they would have had their lone gunman. Now it doesn't matter. What's done is done."

"What if I'd failed?"

"Then one of his security detail would have been two million euros richer instead of two hundred thousand for alerting us of the double switching places with the president."

Jet nodded. "So I was the patsy? That was my true role?"

"You're stupider than you look." Leah withdrew another pistol, this one a revolver, and tossed it toward Jet. It landed on the dusty cement floor five feet from her. "Pick it up."

"Why?"

"I'm not going to argue with you. Pick it up or I'll shoot you where you stand."

Jet stepped forward, closing the distance to the revolver, and crouched down to reach for it. Three shots rang out, deafening in the room, and Jet threw herself to the side as she withdrew the little .32-caliber Russian pistol she'd taken from the mugger and continued firing until the magazine was empty. Leah crumpled to the floor, at least six of the shots having struck her; her own shots at Jet had gone wide. Leah twitched as she tried to raise the gun to fire at Jet again, but her arm failed her, and all she managed was to shift it against the cement. Leah opened her mouth, and blood ran from both corners in crimson rivulets, her breath a wet croak.

When Jet was sure that Leah was dying, she stood and crossed to her, eyes on the silenced Beretta still in her hand, and then toed the weapon aside. Leah's fingers were now limp, and Jet stared down at her handler and then at the mugger's pistol.

"Piece of cheap junk, but hard to go wrong at this range," she said, and tossed it aside before scooping up the Beretta and studying it.

Leah answered with a gurgle, her shirt now stained red from the multiple chest and stomach wounds.

"The director set me up to be killed?" Jet demanded in a soft voice.

Leah closed her eyes and winced in agony, her face whitening as shock set in. Jet knelt near her and prodded her with the gun. "Answer me and I'll end this now. If not, I'll leave you to drown in your own blood. We both know how that goes."

Leah fought for words, but all she managed was another gush of blood and a groan. Jet frowned and stood, shaking her head at the dying woman. She would get no further information from her, and what she'd heard had more confused than clarified anything.

A rustle from the entry echoed through the building and Jet spun, pistol clutched in both hands in a military grip.

Itai stepped into view and took in the scene at once, a shocked expression on his face.

"Hands where I can see them or you're dead," Jet hissed.

He nodded and slowly raised them to shoulder level. "What happened?" he asked.

"As if you didn't know. She tried to kill me. She failed."

"She what?" he blurted, eyes wide. He eyed the pistol in Jet's hand and his voice quieted. "I'm unarmed."

"Put your hands behind your head and turn around so I can frisk you. So much as breathe and you're next."

Itai did as instructed, and Jet closed the distance between them and did a fast search. He was clean. She stepped back far enough that he couldn't reach her with a strike or kick, keeping her weapon trained on the station chief.

"Turn around," she ordered.

Itai complied. "You going to shoot me, too?"

"Give me a reason not to."

"Tell me what happened here. Exactly what happened, step by step."

Jet regarded him curiously. "You know what happened. Your handler tried to execute me so the trail would end here. I got the jump on her – she didn't know I had a gun. And then you showed up right on cue."

"I showed up because she called me and told me you were coming in. That you'd deviated from the plan, and she believed you were working against the Mossad."

"Against it? You sent me in to be killed. She admitted it."

"So you say. Doesn't look like she can contradict you now that she's dead, does it? Convenient for you."

Jet withdrew her phone from her pocket and stopped recording. She thumbed it into playback mode and set it to speaker. The discussion with Leah ended with the shooting, and Jet switched it off. "Let's stop playing games. Mossad wanted me dead. She was clear about that. Got any glib lies for me now?"

Itai slowly lowered his hands, visibly shaken. "You don't understand. That…nothing about this makes any sense."

"If you have something to say, spit it out, Itai. Because even with all the gunfire outside, the shooting in here might draw someone, and I'm not sticking around for that."

He held her stare with bloodshot eyes and shook his head. "This is a disaster. I need to talk to HQ immediately. If you're going to shoot me, get it over with; otherwise let's move someplace safe while I figure out what the hell is going on."

Something about Itai's tone resonated with Jet. She didn't think he was faking. He sounded genuinely confused by the turn of events…and more than a little afraid.

Jet held the gun on him for a few moments as she tried to decide how to proceed, and then lowered it and raised an eyebrow.

"Where would you suggest?" she asked.

He looked around. "Anyplace but here."

CHAPTER 36

A Brahms violin concerto drifted from hidden speakers in Ygor Kazamov's hunting lodge as Sanjar Nabiyev watched live coverage of the assassination aftermath on his computer, his mouth agape at the helicopter footage of moving gun battles and tanks rolling down Baku's streets. Much as he'd been prepared for what was to come, seeing it in real time stunned him speechless, and he was glued to the screen as the situation worsened.

"Well, my friend, the game is afoot, eh?" Kazamov bellowed from the doorway of Nabiyev's room, a sturdy structure of rustic log walls. The entire six-bedroom home was a study in testosterone-driven design: bearskin rugs replete with snarling heads lined the floor of each bedroom, and a dizzying array of game trophies stared down from the walls with beady glass eyes. Outside, the soft purr of a generator provided power for the house and the satellite communication system that delivered high-speed Internet, television, and phone service to the wilds of the Azerbaijani mountains.

"You actually did it," Nabiyev said softly. "At first I thought it might be some sort of ruse, but he's actually dead."

"That's right. And you are now the new leader of the Azerbaijani people. Congratulations." Kazamov held a glass of vodka up in a mock salute. "Never come between a Russian and his work, right?"

"A valuable lesson," Nabiyev agreed. "I need to get back to Baku as soon as possible."

"Nonsense. Let it all play out. There's no rush. Perhaps in a day or two – but what's the point of putting you into harm's way before the military has had a chance to restore order?"

"The people need to see me, to hear my words, to be reassured…" Nabiyev said, his tone doubtful.

"And so they shall. I have a broadcast-quality camera system available for your use, and I've taken the liberty of having some of my best people draft a statement for you." Kazamov paused. "With your approval, of course."

Nabiyev smirked. "Of course."

"I'll email it to you shortly. We can film it as many times as we like and then send it to the networks. You'll want to strike just the right tone – confidence, determination, sadness, hope. This will be the first time the nation really pays any attention to you in the biggest crisis it's experienced during our lifetime, so it should put your poll numbers on top."

"Do I cancel the elections?"

Kazamov laughed. "Of course. But you don't say so tonight. There will be plenty of time once you've met with your cabinet. For now, your role is to pound the table and commit to bringing the parties responsible for this atrocity to justice, and to punish the opportunists who have seized the tragedy as a chance to challenge the very democracy of this fine land. That will lay the groundwork for postponing the elections until the smoke has cleared, and should play well to those who were on the fence between your party and the Nationalists. I've had my people sprinkle in hints that you suspect the assassination may be politically linked, and if so, that you will go to your grave before you allow the disruption to be successful. Fire and brimstone. They'll eat it up."

"Who are we going to blame it on? Officially?"

"Foreign powers attempting to overthrow the democratically elected leadership. Trying to subvert the will of the people. We'll position you as anti-corruption, anti-manipulation. It's just you and your determination against the barbarians at the gates, and it will take a strong and committed leader – like yourself – to ensure that Azerbaijan remains sovereign and free."

Nabiyev clapped slowly, his usual cynical smile in place. "I'm tearing up."

"By the time this is over, you'll be a hero."

"I could use a drink."

Kazamov eyed him. "Maybe a half, just to steady your nerves. We can't afford any missteps."

"That's all I was thinking."

"Then come, my friend, and sample some of my private store." Giggling echoed down the hall, and it was Kazamov's turn to smirk. "I trust you have enough energy left to lead the country after two nights with the girls?"

"They are remarkable. More inspiring than draining. The fountain of youth, to be sure."

"I've always thought so. Come, let's get you some medicine and you can review the speech. It will be a ten-minute address, no more, organized to hit all the right high notes without saying much of anything."

Nabiyev nodded. He'd been mouthing platitudes his entire career, so was adept at the dog and pony show he was about to put on. That the Russian was orchestrating the entire thing didn't trouble him in the least. Politicians were always servants of powerful special interests that pulled their strings from behind the throne – one didn't last long in the political world if one fought that reality. The trick was to negotiate a suitable reward for services rendered, which Nabiyev certainly would. That was the least of his problems with Kazamov, who had always been generous.

"Lead the way."

The great room was a two-story-high cavernous space filled with overstuffed sofas and still more trophy heads. Three flat-screen televisions were droning from a massive dining room table that could seat twenty. The two men approached the slab, carved from a single tree, and sat. Kazamov snapped his fingers and a servant appeared from the swinging kitchen door, where he'd been waiting in anticipation of his master's wishes. The Russian pointed at his glass and held up two fingers. The servant nodded in understanding and disappeared, leaving Nabiyev to watch the news feeds.

Kazamov looked around and sniffed at the air. "What's that smell?"

Nabiyev sniffed as well. "Oh. That's my cologne."

The Russian made a face. "Smells like a French whorehouse."

"Two thousand dollars a bottle."

"You're joking."

Nabiyev colored slightly. "I'm glad you like it – I'll send a bottle over once I take office."

Kazamov shook his head in bemusement and pointed at one of the televisions streaming CNN. "The Americans have already issued a canned statement about standing in solidarity with the people of Azerbaijan, and condemned the assassination and coup attempt. The Russians have done the same. Everyone's waiting to see what happens before they pick a side." Kazamov grinned wolfishly. "I was thinking we can always salt the next few days with hints of Wahhabi extremists being behind the unrest. That's a delicate balancing act, though, given your mostly Muslim population."

"Probably best not to go there," Nabiyev warned. "We'll need as much support as possible, and there's no need riling up anyone over religion."

"I was just thinking it would be a nice way to get a dig in at the Americans." It was commonly accepted in much of the Muslim world that the Saudi brand of extremism that was responsible for radical Islamist terrorism had been manufactured to further the interests of the U.S. and Saudi Arabia.

"Yes, but it could cause significant blowback. Better to do that via social media. We can lace the alternative sites with hints of it. They'll publish just about anything."

They laughed as the servant reappeared with a glass of vodka on a sterling silver tray, set it in front of Nabiyev with a flourish, and left without a word. Nabiyev took a grateful swallow and smiled at his host. More giggling emanated from the hall, and Kazamov waggled his eyebrows, unruffled by having just engineered a coup of a major oil-producing nation. "Better pull the speech up on the screen and have a look before the girls get bored and come out to put on another show."

Nabiyev nodded at the recollection of the last performance they'd been treated to. "Wise counsel."

Kazamov clinked the edge of Nabiyev's glass with his own and winked. "That's what I'm here for – to keep you out of trouble."

"Not too much, I hope."

"Of course not."

CHAPTER 37

Jet allowed Itai to lead her along the alley, unsure whether to trust the man, given that his subordinate had just tried to kill her. They avoided a noxious puddle of black water, and he tacked right down another small road, moving with a conviction she didn't feel.

"Where are we going?" she demanded.

"I have an office by the mosque. We can talk once we get there. Keep your voice down until we do. No telling who's lurking out here."

Jet followed the station chief until they arrived at a four-story structure in a block of commercial buildings. He produced a key ring from his jacket, opened the steel grid over the entrance, and ushered Jet through before locking it again and proceeding to a glass front door, which he unlocked with a flourish. Once inside, he led her up the stairs to a second-floor office with the name of a travel agency painted on the door.

The office was just an outer secretary station, a medium-sized room with a steel desk and a few generic prints on the wall. Jet shook her head and raised a finger in warning as Itai made to round the desk and sit down.

"How about I sit where I can access the drawers instead of you, for now?" she said.

"No problem. I don't keep any weapons here, unless you count a letter opener and stapler."

They sat and Jet fixed him with a hard stare. "You said nothing about this makes sense. What did you mean?"

"The operation was designed to eliminate the body double, not Hovel. It was to be an attempted coup, which would then allow him to emerge as a hero, having prevailed in spite of nefarious parties unknown trying to take him out. You were never supposed to kill him," Itai said, his voice gravelly and tired.

Jet absorbed the station chief's words and sat forward. "Leah didn't get the memo. She directed me to Hovel. Warned me that the man in the chair was a double. Claimed she had an informant in Hovel's security detail, as you heard."

He nodded. "I did. That means she was working against the director's express orders and the Mossad's imperatives." His frown deepened. "You were never supposed to be killed. You were supposed to take out the double, escape without issue, and then Hovel would emerge, still alive, after a token coup attempt played out. He'd already arranged with some of his trusted military to pretend to be leading a coup in order to sway public opinion in his favor."

Jet's eyes never left Itai's face. "Would have been nice if someone had told me."

"You understand how this works. Need to know. If something had happened and you'd been captured, the less information you had, the better."

Jet shook her head. "Leah knew about the double and had a backup to kill Hovel if I failed. Sounds like you have a real problem on your hands. There's no way she was working alone."

"Of course she wasn't. But since you killed her, we'll never know who was behind this."

"Not necessarily. There's always a thread to follow. You know she was bent now. That will lead to a trail. Something will surface." Jet paused. "It wasn't a bad plan from her standpoint. She could shoot me, supposedly in self-defense, and then it was me who went off the reservation, not her. That would have worked, I suppose. Why I did so would be a matter of conjecture, but I wouldn't be around to contradict her, and she'd be home free."

"I got that part of it. The real question is why she wanted Hovel dead in the first place. That obviously isn't in our best interests. Hovel was sympathetic to our agenda. That's why we were trying to help him get reelected."

Jet snorted. "I suppose that made sense in whatever conference room it was cooked up, but it didn't work so well in reality. How well did you know her?"

"Leah? Not at all. She was assigned here a few days before you arrived – no, make that a week before."

"Who assigned her?"

"HQ."

"No name?"

"That's above my need to know." He rubbed his face and sighed. "I have to call the director. I don't trust anyone below him. This operation came from his level."

"Then do it. We're not going anywhere right now with the army on the streets." She hesitated. "We're safe here?"

"As safe as anywhere."

"You said that she called you and wanted you to rendezvous at the construction site?" Jet asked.

"That's right. My guess is she needed a witness to the aftermath of the shooting."

"She tossed an old revolver to me and demanded I pick it up. You heard her."

"I'm not questioning your story, Katya. Thick as I may appear at times, even I can put this together." He indicated his jacket. "You mind if I retrieve my phone?"

"Be my guest."

A sound from the front of the building interrupted them, and Itai's hand froze halfway into his jacket.

"What's that?" Jet whispered.

"Someone at the front gate," he said, his voice soft.

At the distinctive sound of the barrier sliding to the side, Jet rose, weapon drawn. "We need to get out of here. Shut off the light."

Itai did as instructed, and they waited several long moments as their eyes adjusted to the darkness. When they could make out the furniture by the moonlight streaming through the window, Jet moved around the desk just as the sound of glass breaking downstairs reached them.

"Is there a back way out?" she asked.

"No."

Jet thought for a moment. "The building next door. Does it abut this one?"

"I...no, I don't think so. There's an alley that runs between them."

"How wide?"

"Maybe...six feet?"

She studied him in the gloom. "You much of a jumper?"

"Not for about thirty years."

"Show me the roof."

Itai moved surprisingly quickly for a man of his years, puffing only slightly as he climbed the rear stairs. They could make out the sound of footsteps from the front of the building and Jet closed on him as he ascended. "Hurry," she hissed. "They're inside."

"I'm doing the best I can," he whispered with a glare tossed over his shoulder, but picked up the pace.

They reached the fourth-floor landing and he rushed to the back of the hallway, where there was a maintenance closet and a door that led to the roof. He pushed through the roof door, but Jet paused by the maintenance room and peered inside. She nodded to herself, grabbed a plank of wood, and shouldered an aluminum ladder leaning against the wall, and then followed Itai onto the roof, pausing to close the door, and wedged the plank against it at an angle, where it would make opening the door difficult, if not impossible.

Jet accompanied Itai to the edge of the building and stared over at the adjacent roof, a few feet lower and more like eight feet across. She extended the ladder to its full length and lowered it across the gap, leaving a foot on either side for support.

"Can you do this?" she asked, noting the queasy expression on Itai's face.

"Don't see any choice, do you?"

"I'll go first. You hold this side so it doesn't slide on me. I'll do the same for you once I'm across."

"Got it."

Itai knelt and gripped the end of the ladder, his head turned away from the edge of the building, as though just looking over the rim would sicken him. Jet slid by him, holding his shoulders, and then lowered herself feet first, backing toward the far roof, her eyes locked on the ladder. She was on the other side within moments and then stabilized her side and motioned for him to follow her across.

He attempted the same maneuver, but his greater bulk and age worked against him, and the ladder sagged alarmingly as he crept along its length, eyes clamped shut. His right foot misjudged one of the rungs and he gasped as he locked onto the ladder for dear life. She looked over him at the roof door and whispered encouragement to him.

"Come on, Itai. Almost there. You can do it. Only another meter. Come on, they'll be on the roof any second."

Her final words spurred him into movement, and he continued his snail's-pace crossing, the ladder trembling from his effort. Then his feet touched the roof and he was moving faster, eager to be back on stable ground.

Jet didn't wait for him to get his bearings, instead lifting the ladder and running with it to the door at the other end of the building. She tried the handle and it swung open. Itai joined her, roof tar and gravel crackling under his shoes, and then they were over the threshold and in the building. Jet leaned the ladder against the wall and twisted the bolt before rushing down the steps after Itai, who'd gotten a second wind.

At the ground floor, Jet pointed at the rear of the building, where there was a steel fire door with an exit sign. They sprinted to the door and pushed the bar that ran across it. An alarm sounded in the hall, deafening in the confined space. Jet exited into the alley, trailed by Itai, and they bolted down the alleyway as voices called out from above.

The first volley of assault rifle fire rattled from the rooftop as they neared the corner, and ricochets whistled by them, the shooters' aim off or the rifles out of range. Jet rounded the building with Itai and they zigzagged toward the mosque, now out of sight of their pursuers, the darkness shielding them as they ran for their lives.

CHAPTER 38

"Who was that?" Jet demanded as they made their way toward Itai's apartment building, a half mile from the Sultanbey Mosque.

"Your guess is as good as mine."

She gave him an ugly look. "That narrows it down."

"It wasn't the police. They wouldn't have fired on us."

"Then…?"

"Likely part of the group Leah was working with."

"How did they find us?"

Itai scowled. "Leah met me at that office when she first arrived in town. It would be a natural spot to look for us if they found her body at the construction site."

"We should have seen that coming."

"My fault. But nobody's been to my apartment. It's completely off the radar. I pay for it myself in cash every month, so it isn't even in the Mossad system."

"Are you going to call the director?"

"Yes. But only once I'm home. I have an encrypted scrambler on my landline I can hook up. I don't like how intermittent cell coverage has been tonight, nor do I trust the system not to be logging calls. Depending on how sophisticated Leah's group is, they might have the ability to triangulate a call to Israel if they know what to look for."

"That seems like a long shot," Jet countered.

"Not if they're in the government. They buy a ton of technology from us, as well as from Russia. Trust me on this – they're as advanced as anything on the planet in that regard."

Jet didn't argue, preferring to remain silent as they trudged toward his apartment. When they arrived, he unlocked the front door and let them into the lobby, and then pointed to the stairwell. "You willing to risk being stranded in the elevator if there's a blackout, or take the stairs? I'm on the fourth floor."

"Stairs."

"I was afraid you'd say that."

The apartment turned out to be comfortable but Spartan, Itai a confirmed bachelor without many needs that she could see. He offered her a bottle of water, which she accepted after checking the seal to confirm it was unopened, and Itai noted her caution with a smile.

"You're going to have to decide whether you trust me or not," he said.

"Not right now, I'm not."

He nodded, acknowledging the reasonableness of her doubts. "Not sure I would, either. Want to accompany me to my study so you can ensure I don't come out with an Uzi?"

"You read my mind."

Jet was coming around to the idea that Itai was what he looked like and that the treason stopped at Leah, but she wasn't about to bet her life on it, not only minutes after nearly being gunned down in the street. A thought occurred to her, and she eyed Itai skeptically. "Your cell. Did you ever call Leah with it?"

His smile was sad and utterly without humor. "I'm not a complete rank amateur. No, nobody has my cell. That's not how they found us."

"What about in Israel? Anyone there?"

His eyes narrowed. "A few people…" he admitted.

"Pull the battery." Jet paused. "We don't know who's involved in this, Itai. They probably have access to Mossad resources back home. If so, you can't assume anything is safe."

He nodded and removed the battery. "Following your logic through, we shouldn't linger here, then."

"I'm afraid not."

"Okay. Let's go make that call."

He looked at a wall clock as he entered his office. "They're an hour behind us. He's not going to be happy to be woken up."

Jet took a seat beside his desk, her hand on the pistol in her pocket. "No chance he's asleep with the mission going upside down on us."

"Good point."

The station chief plugged a gizmo into the telephone on his desk and dialed a number. When the line answered, he recited an authorization code and told the operator he wanted to speak to the director, urgency level one. Sixty seconds went by, and the director answered.

"What went wrong, Cohen?" he barked.

"Everything," Itai said, and then gave a succinct summary of what had transpired and what they had discovered. When he was done, the director was silent for a half minute.

"Is she there?" he eventually asked.

"Yes. She's sitting beside me with a pistol in her pocket trained on me."

"Put her on," the director ordered.

Itai held the handset out to Jet, who took it like it was radioactive and held it to her ear. "Yes?"

"First, my apologies. This is an unmitigated disaster, but it's not of your making."

"I'm glad you realize it. I was double-crossed by your operative."

"Yes. I know. I'll get to the bottom of that shortly."

"You have a leak."

"At the very least. It might be worse than that. Again, not your issue."

"Fine. So what now?"

The director exhaled, and she could hear him sucking on a cigarette before he answered, "I don't know. I'll have to get back to you."

"That's it? You haven't been able to come up with a plan B since hearing he was assassinated?"

The director's voice had an edge to it when he replied, "I appreciate your impatience, but there are quite a few moving parts we need to consider. I'll let you know what we come up with shortly."

"I'm afraid Itai's apartment may be compromised."

"Then get out of there."

"There's a curfew. Martial law."

"He'll figure something out. Let me talk to him."

"You confident he's clean?" she asked softly, her eyes holding Itai's stare.

"Absolutely. This is localized to your handler. Itai's above suspicion. Don't waste your energy in that regard. Now put him on."

Jet handed the station chief the phone and sat back, thinking. Itai listened for a good minute, asked a couple of questions, and then signed off. He placed the handset in its cradle, disconnected the device, and pocketed it as he addressed Jet. "All right. If we're going to get moving, we'll need a few things. You have your documents with you?"

She nodded. "Yes."

"I need to open the safe in my bedroom. Inside there's a wad of cash, some paperwork we'll want, a sat phone, and a few weapons. You satisfied with your pistol?"

"I haven't fired it. But it's a Beretta, so it should be bulletproof. I could use some more 9mm, though. She got off four shots."

"I have a pair of H&K 9mm's in the safe with extra magazines and a box of cartridges. I'll bring those, too. Use what you need."

"The question is where we can go."

Itai walked to his bedroom, accompanied by Jet, who for all the director's reassurances was still on guard. The station chief seemed to intuit that and didn't protest when she sat on the bed and watched him open his closet and spin the dial on a medium-size gray metal safe.

He opened it and removed two pistols, setting them on the floor with a spare magazine for each, and then placed a half-empty box of 9mm bullets beside them. Next came a passport from a small stack and a bound document on official stationery. Finally, he removed a satellite phone and a fat wad of local currency before closing the safe and spinning the dial.

"What's the document?" she asked.

"A release from arrest or prosecution. Signed by Hovel and the prime minister. It's my get-out-of-jail-free card. Might get us past any roadblocks, assuming there still are any by the time we get on the road."

"Any idea where we can hole up?"

He smiled, and this time it had some genuine warmth. "You know, if you don't mind damaging your reputation, I do have an idea."

"Reputation?"

He nodded. "I have a friend…" he started, and by the time he'd packed a small bag with the pistols and his belongings, Jet was smiling too.

"Call him. I can play a fallen woman with the best."

Itai regarded her and grunted. "Or the worst."

Chapter 39

Rabbi Dor Herzog opened his front door and nodded a greeting to Itai and Jet. "Please," he said, "Come in."

The rabbi's home was next to the only synagogue in Baku, which fronted on a long park and plaza, rock-throwing distance from the winding alleys of the old town. He stood aside, and Itai motioned for Jet to enter first, the rabbi silently taking her measure as she passed.

Itai had called Herzog when they'd left his apartment, and the rabbi had been gracious in extending his hospitality, inviting them over immediately in response to Itai's explanation that he and a special friend were in a spot of trouble and needed a place to stay the night. The station chief hadn't elaborated on what the nature of their special friendship might be, and the holy man hadn't asked, instead insisting that they come by and enjoy his hospitality, apparently untroubled by a call in the middle of the night.

Itai had explained to Jet that he played chess with Herzog on a biweekly basis, and while Itai wasn't the most observant of the small Jewish population in Baku, he and the rabbi had a good relationship and had become friends.

"Does he have any idea of your...entanglement?" Jet had asked.

"None. He thinks I run the world's worst travel agency. I don't disabuse him of that, although I take my share of grief from him over it."

"Anyone else know of your friendship?"

"No. Nobody in the life."

"What story are you going to tell him?"

Itai had laughed. "With Dor, all I have to do is show up with you. He'll assume the rest."

Jet waited for Itai and the rabbi to join her at the threshold of the living room, her clothes now mostly clean after a hurried rubbing with a wet towel at the section chief's apartment. The rabbi closed the front door and walked heavily to where they stood admiring the décor and the breathtaking art framed on the walls.

"These are troubled times," Herzog said. "You hear the shooting? Terrible."

"Any news on that?" Itai parried.

"They're saying it's criminal gangs. A few websites are saying it's a coup attempt by disgruntled military officers. All I know is that nobody's sure what's going on, but the shooting continues – although it's slowed in the last hour or so." The rabbi shook his head. "I've never seen anything like this in my entire time in Baku. Twenty-six years, and this is a first. And what they did to the president? Shocking. Animals. I mean, don't get me wrong, I was no fan, but still…"

"Thank you for letting us stay," Jet said.

"Oh, any friend of Itai's is a friend of mine," Herzog said, appraising her in the brighter light of the living room. "He's a good man, even if a little worn around the edges."

"I know," Jet said, leaving it at that.

Herzog and Itai exchanged a knowing look, and the rabbi busied himself giving them a fast tour of the house. His family was away in New York on vacation, so he was alone, with the large home all to himself.

"I have a bedroom for each of you," he said, underscoring that they wouldn't be staying together. "Simple, but it should do," he said with a shrug.

"I'm sure it will be more than fine," Itai said.

"Let me show you your rooms."

When Herzog indicated a smallish guest room for Jet, she thanked him and yawned. "I hope you don't mind, but I'm beat."

"Of course not," the rabbi said. "Good night."

Herzog guided Itai to another room at the opposite end of the hall and put a hand on his shoulder. "She's awfully young, isn't she?"

"It's not like that, Dor."

"It never is. Look, it's none of my business, right?" Herzog paused. "What kind of...trouble...is she in?"

"It's private."

The rabbi eyed him. "You're a little old to be skulking around in the middle of the night with a girl half your age, my friend. Not that I'm judging you."

"Clearly not." Itai cleared his throat. "And we're not skulking."

"Just the first word that came to mind. I retract it."

Itai exhaled and eyed his room. "Thanks for doing this."

"My pleasure. Just name the little one Dor if it's a boy and we'll be even. Are you planning on getting married?"

"Very funny."

"If I didn't laugh every day, it would be all tears."

"I know the feeling."

Herzog nodded at Itai with pursed lips. "Seems like you've found ways to keep yourself amused. I will say I'm constantly surprised by life. You amaze me, my friend."

"If you knew the half of it, I'd have to kill you."

"I've seen what you charge for a flight. That's close enough."

Itai stepped into the room and looked over his shoulder. "Good night, Dor."

"Likewise."

CHAPTER 40

The director glowered at his staff; the tension in the conference room was palpable. Amit Mendel and Maor Lachman were bearing the brunt of his anger, but that was only fitting, given it was their operation.

"So now what? The entire mission has gone upside down on us, Hovel's dead at our hands, and the exact outcome we were trying to prevent – a scenario where he's not at the helm – is suddenly our reality."

"There was no way of foreseeing this," Lachman protested. "We couldn't have incorporated being betrayed into our plan."

"That's a related issue we're going to get to the bottom of, but it doesn't solve our current problem," the director snapped. "With Hovel out, our interests are in jeopardy, and the choices we're now faced with range from bad to terrible."

"Do we actually know what went wrong?" Mendel asked.

"Yes," the director said without elaboration.

"How do we know that this woman, this assassin we sent in, wasn't working against us all along?" Mendel pressed.

"I'm confident she wasn't. But that isn't what we're here to discuss. The question is what we do now, not how any of this happened."

"I think it's relevant," Mendel said.

The director lit a cigarette and eyed him. "Again, it's late, I'm old and tired, and I need a solution. That's why I called you, my experts, in. Not to waste time covering ground that will be analyzed later. So final time. What. Do. We. Do? Let's hear some suggestions. Our people on the ground are waiting to hear from us."

"Where are they?" Lachman asked.

"Safe. In Baku."

"You're not giving us anything to go on," Lachman complained.

"Perhaps I wasn't clear. I've gathered you here to propose how we dig ourselves out of this hole using the resources at our disposal. Do we simply do nothing? It's fine if that's the safest course. Or is there some action that would result in a less unbalanced outcome? Everything's on the table here, gentlemen. Everything. I want some creative solutions, and fast."

"Well…we could always knock the prime minister off."

Mendel shook his head. "No. That would be a mistake."

"Why?" the director asked.

"Because it would leave an even larger vacuum and would place the outcome of the election in jeopardy."

"I think it's safe to say it already is," Lachman argued.

"The real question is which would be worse for us – Nabiyev holding the reins or one of the other parties?" The director puffed at his smoke, serpentine coils drifting to the ceiling as he eyed the men thoughtfully. "Lesser of two evils time."

"We can't attempt another assassination without drawing international attention we can ill afford," Mendel said. "So we need to eliminate that possibility out of the gate. Perhaps…perhaps we can reach out to Nabiyev and feel out how interested he might be in playing ball?"

"Too risky," Lachman said. "No way to do that without him suspecting us."

"We could use a third party."

"He's clever like a fox. He'll see through it, and then it's game over for us."

The director listened to his subordinates argue back and forth for fifteen minutes and then thanked them for coming and abruptly left. A tall, thin man with black curly hair and a mustache was waiting for him in the outer area of his office when he returned, the inner sanctum locking automatically upon the director's departure and requiring a retinal scan to open. The director nodded to him and escorted him into his office, where they sat at a small round table in the corner.

"Avi," the director began, "I explained the situation. I want a proctology exam on this Leah. Everything you can learn. She wasn't working alone. Someone, possibly a group here in Israel, had a hand in it. Your job is to discover who her accomplices are."

"I've already run a background on her and there's nothing obvious, sir. Who picked her for the posting?"

"As I recall, she was selected by committee for the slot in Baku," the director said.

"It's possible that the entire committee was in on it, then," Avi said drily.

The director shook his head. "Maybe, although I doubt it. Too many disparate personalities. My money's on her having been co-opted once she received the assignment, but I've been wrong before. Come at it from all angles. But I need to find any other traitors, and find them quick."

Avi nodded. "And when we do?"

"We'll deal with them appropriately."

"Yes, sir. Is there anything else?"

"A practical matter." The director explained what he wanted to know.

Avi thought for a few moments and then sat forward with a smile. "Here's how I would do it," he said, and spoke for two minutes.

The director asked a number of pointed questions and then nodded once he had the answers he was after. "Very well. Keep me informed of any progress. There will be a trace, I'm sure. Find it and you'll make the connections."

Avi rose. "Will do. I'll be in touch."

The director watched his most trusted internal affairs investigator leave and reached for his packet of cigarettes. He had the outline of a plan in mind, but needed a backup in case for some reason it failed. He smoked, thinking his scheme through, and then made a phone call on a secure line to Itai's cell phone.

When Itai answered, the director spoke quietly, explaining what he needed the station chief and the woman to do. When he finished, Itai had questions of his own, which the director fielded, taking notes.

"We're working on a location and should have it shortly. As to getting the material to you, I'll call you back," the director concluded, and then hung up and typed instructions on his terminal. He checked his watch – his staff would be at their desks, working crisis hours, so he'd have responses within minutes.

When he was done, he chewed away a piece of skin from his thumb and eyed the monitor expectantly. The plan wasn't perfect, but it was achievable, and sometimes that was better than the most elegant, but improbable, approach. If it failed, they were in no worse shape than they were now.

His computer pinged and he leaned forward, his eyes sharp in spite of the hour. He read a missive and grunted approval. He reached for the keyboard and typed a response, only to be pinged again. After a furious back and forth, he lifted his phone handset to his ear and called Itai again. This time the station chief sounded alert.

"All right," the director said. "This is what we're going to do."

CHAPTER 41

Jet blinked away sleep, checked the time, and rolled toward where Itai stood in the doorway. "What's happening?"

"It'll be light in half an hour. No more curfew once dawn breaks. It was on TV."

"Great. So where are we going?"

Itai glanced down the hall and stepped inside. When he spoke, his voice was a hoarse whisper. "I spoke with the director."

"And?"

"I'll tell you in the car. For now, let's clean up and eat so we can hit the ground running."

"You're not going to tell me where we're running to?"

"It's complicated. Let's enjoy the morning while we can."

She frowned. "That bad?"

"It won't be boring."

Jet yawned and stretched. "Anything on the tube about the situation on the streets?"

"They're saying it was a failed coup attempt. I'll fill you in downstairs."

"Is your friend up?"

"Not yet. But he's an early riser."

Jet showered and pulled on her clothes, annoyed at Itai's reluctance to tell her anything but resigned to it. She'd been on her own for too long and had gotten used to self-determination rather than following orders, and it stuck in her craw no matter how much she reminded herself that the treatment she was receiving wasn't personal.

When she came down the stairs, Itai was seated in the dining room, looking like he'd aged five years overnight, and Dor was standing by a window, watching the sun come up. He turned toward her and nodded a greeting.

"Good morning, young lady."

Jet managed a smile. "Morning, Rabbi."

"Itai here has made coffee and tea and managed to toast some bread by himself. It isn't half bad for a first effort."

Itai tilted his head at his friend. "Old dog, new tricks. It's a time of miracles."

Dor looked Jet up and down, and a hint of a smirk played across his face. "Indeed it is."

They ate quickly and said their goodbyes, and then were on their way back toward the mosque, Itai leading the way. Neither of them spoke. A few cars passed on the street, and it was obvious that the night's excitement had already died down as the mundane business of earning a living claimed the population's attention. Jet waited on the sidewalk for Itai to enter his apartment building's subterranean garage, eyeing the vehicles on the street as a reflex, her nerves frayed after little sleep and the prior day's tumultuous events.

An ancient gold-toned sedan rolled from the garage, belching poorly combusted exhaust, its motor sounding like it was ready for the scrapyard, and Itai rolled down his window. "Hop in."

Jet pulled the door open and the hinges protested with a groan. She seated herself on a cracked leather seat and slammed the door, and then inspected the aged interior as she fastened her seatbelt. "A classic, I see."

"No point in squandering my fortune when this runs like a top."

"Beauty is in the eye," Jet agreed. "What do I do with my gun?"

"There's a compartment under the backseat. We'll stop somewhere away from prying eyes and you can stash it."

She patted the dashboard and was rewarded with a cloud of fine dust. "Don't drive it much?"

"I prefer walking. Good for the soul."

"Uh-huh. Are you going to tell me where we're going and what we're up to?"

The station chief's face grew serious as they rattled along the narrow street. "As I said, I spoke with the director. We're to head north, into the country, and…terminate the prime minister."

"What?!"

"You heard me. They can't allow him to take power, and apparently he's still in the Caucasus Mountains, at a friend's house. That will be our only opportunity to do so. Once he's back in Baku, he'll be surrounded by security."

"How do you know where he is?"

"He made a broadcast last night. Our tech team was able to get into the network's system and trace the IP address to where it originated."

"How do we know he's still there?"

"We don't. But we've dispatched a watcher who will report if anyone leaves."

She shook her head. "This doesn't strike you as madness?"

Itai nodded. "I should say not at all, but you know better. This is a business of contradictions. I'm just following orders."

"So they orchestrate a phony coup, get double-crossed and the president winds up dead, and the answer is to kill his second-in-command?"

"The prime minister is ten times worse than Hovel. But his greatest sin is he doesn't play ball with our team. He's actively pro-Russian, and this week we aren't. So he has to go."

"That's the whole logic?"

Itai nodded grimly. "Best I can make out."

"And nobody thinks it's going to look odd when the two leaders of Azerbaijan are eliminated within a day or so of each other?"

"That's the other thing. We're to make it look like he died of natural causes."

Jet closed her eyes and exhaled in resignation. "Of course. Because that's so easy to do. Did they articulate how we're supposed to accomplish that? Scare him to death?"

Itai eyed her. "The director said you might not respond like a typical agent."

"He knows me better than I thought."

"We're to drive out of the city and take the road up the coast. A drone with supplies is being dispatched and will drop its cargo near the mountains. We're to retrieve the goods and rendezvous with the watcher at dark, and you're to penetrate the house tonight and take him out."

"Did he mention how, exactly, I'm supposed to slip past whatever security is in place and accomplish all that?"

"They're going to have satellite imagery sent to my phone this afternoon. We'll know more about the layout from that and from the watcher's reports on the number of guards, shifts, and so on."

"And if I say no?"

"I'm to remind you that the director will be extremely grateful if you agree. He said to use those exact words."

"I want to talk to him myself."

"Which you can. Later. For now, I'm under instructions to get to a field in the middle of nowhere by a specific time, and it's going to be touch and go making it anywhere close to when I'm supposed to."

Jet frowned. "How are they going to fly a drone into the wilds on this short a notice? From where?"

"All the director said was that he'd lean on our allies to assist. Mine is not to question why…"

"What are they sending?"

"A cutaneous nerve agent that was developed by the Soviets. Apparently just a few drops is all it takes. You swab the target or drip a couple of droplets on him, and it's nearly instantaneous. He'll seize, and then respiratory paralysis sets in, and then his heart stops, all within twenty seconds. It will look like a massive heart attack when he's autopsied – it leaves no trace unless you know exactly what you're looking for."

She nodded. "I've used something like that before. But that doesn't answer the question of how I'm supposed to get close enough to him to deliver the dose."

"The director said he has tremendous confidence in your resourcefulness."

"He should also know the best way to get yourself killed is to do inadequate research on a target, the layout, and the logistics. This is beyond half-baked."

Itai's expression was glum. "I'm not disagreeing with you."

"I've already been stuck with one near suicide mission. I won't do another."

Itai sighed. "What would it take for you to say yes?"

"I'd need to have confidence I could make it in and out and get away clean. Otherwise it's a nonstarter."

"Fine. Let's do what we need to do, check out the layout in person, see what my man has to say at the site, and take it from there, okay? No need to do anything but look it over."

She eyed him distrustfully. "Sounds like you're trying to ease me into a yes."

"I'm with you. If you can't pull it off, we go to plan B."

"Which is?"

Itai gave the car more gas, and it responded with a tired wheeze and more smoke before reluctantly accelerating. "I'll let you know as soon as I figure that out."

CHAPTER 42

Traffic was sparse leaving Baku, and Jet was letting out a sigh of relief when a sea of brake lights confronted them as they rounded a bend leading to the on-ramp for the M1 highway. Jet glanced at Itai, who adjusted a pair of laughably unstylish sunglasses and sat forward.

"Security checkpoint?" she asked.

"That's what it looks like."

Forty minutes later they pulled to a stop beside a pair of tanks flanked by a contingent of two dozen soldiers brandishing assault rifles and a handful of uniformed police, their squad cars parked near a van with bars across the rear windows. The officers were blocking traffic and questioning drivers. A cop strode toward them and looked the car over with a scowl and then peered inside at Itai and Jet.

"Where are you headed?" he demanded.

"Ashagioba. We want to get out of town until everything returns to normal."

"You're not Azerbaijani," the cop observed.

"No. I'm Israeli. My companion's Russian."

The officer's gaze lingered on Jet and he held out his hand. "Papers."

Itai fished his passport from his pocket, and Jet did the same. The officer took their documents and strode back to his car, where two other police waited. Jet leaned her head toward Itai.

"Seems pretty thorough, doesn't it?"

Itai nodded slowly. "Everyone's got to be on edge."

"I hope I was right that no cameras picked me up at the hall." She paused. "I should have changed my hair color."

"How? Nothing was open."

Jet watched the cops exchange some words, and then one of them leaned into the squad car and stretched a radio mic toward the officer with their docs. He opened Itai's passport and read the information from it and then did the same with Jet's. When he finished, he waited, making small talk with the others.

Five minutes later he was back at the car with their passports. "Open the trunk," he growled.

Itai shut off the engine and climbed from behind the wheel, and the cop accompanied him to the rear of the car. The station chief popped the trunk with the key and the officer shifted some items around before stepping away and grunting to Itai. "Okay. You can go."

Itai slid back into the car with a creak of his knee joints and twisted the ignition key. The starter ground and the chassis shook, but the motor failed to catch. He paused as the cops watched with annoyance, and then tried again, beads of sweat appearing on his forehead as he pumped the accelerator for all he was worth.

The engine coughed and backfired with a blast of black smoke from the exhaust, and then caught and hiccupped twice before settling into a rough idle. Itai slid the transmission lever into gear and they lurched off, Jet staring at him with thinly veiled disgust.

"Really, Itai? This is what we're betting the farm on getting us into the mountains?"

"I've been putting off a tune-up. The local mechanics are highway robbers. But don't worry. It'll make it. This beast is unstoppable."

She took her passport back from Itai and pocketed it. "What did they say?"

"Nothing much. Wanted to know why we were leaving the city, an exact address, that sort of thing. You heard my response."

"He didn't want to know anything more?"

"I got the impression they're just following orders. They were told to check everyone leaving the city, so they're doing it."

"I hope you're right."

"Me too."

They rolled up the on-ramp and increased their speed to a moderate pace as they left Baku's skyline behind them and skirted the

Jeyranbatan Reservoir on the way to the coast. After a dogleg north onto another highway, the deep sapphire of the Caspian Sea appeared on their right, the surface wrinkled by a gentle breeze, occasional wind waves glinting gold in the morning sun. A few children ran along the rocky beach by wooden fishing boats with peeling hull paint beached on the shore, a few gulls perched on the bows. Jet rolled down her window and let the smell of the sea wash over her, erasing some of the fatigue from sleep deprivation and stress.

"How far until this field where the drone's dropping the goods?" Jet asked.

Itai checked his watch. "Maybe another half hour or so. Depends."

"Is it going to land or just make a drop and fly off?"

"They said drop, so I'm assuming that's what will happen."

"And how will we find the package?"

"They'll send the exact coordinates to my phone."

She frowned. "If they can get a drone in under the radar, why don't they just have it shoot a couple of Hellfires or whatever at the hunting lodge and call it a day?"

Itai shook his head and snuck a glance at her. "As I said before, it's key that it appear accidental. A lone gunman who's never apprehended shoots the president with a homemade rifle, that's a tragedy that eventually becomes fodder for conspiracy theories. Take out others in the chain of command as well, and governments start getting involved and smelling a rat. We don't need the Russians coming in and complicating our lives – they already have far too much sway in the industries here. Give them a hint that Western interests might be trying to overthrow the government in their backyard, and it will get ugly. They demonstrated they won't back down in Ukraine. We want to avoid a replay."

"You don't think they'll figure that out anyway?"

"Not if you do your job correctly. The prime minister will have a heart attack from the sudden burden of the responsibility of running the country, and that will be that. Next in line is a gentleman we can do business with. Not ideal, and there's no guarantee he can win the election, but it's better than an evil we know and can't tolerate."

"Have you considered what you're asking me to do might be impossible?"

He nodded grimly. "I have. All of this is fluid. It's unfolding as we speak, and bigger brains than mine are working on it back home. I'm not going to waste energy on something nobody's consulting me about."

Jet nodded. "Very pragmatic."

"You get to be my age, you learn to be flexible."

She laughed. "That's exactly the word that springs to mind when I think of you."

"I'm glad you've retained your sense of humor. That's usually the first to go."

A bright glare shone from their left, nearly blinding her, and she shaded her eyes with her hand. "What's that?"

"Solar electric plant. Those are the panels. Hundreds of them."

"In an oil-producing country?"

"They export. This is the concession to the Green Party's incessant agitation for renewable energy. They also have wind farms up ahead."

"Surprising."

They continued along the shore in silence, the car stuttering occasionally. Every pothole was transmitted to the small of Jet's back with the force of rabbit punches. She shifted every few minutes, trying to get comfortable, but it was no good. She was sore from the Parkour the night before, and there was no position on the seat that relieved the aching.

Itai began checking his phone regularly and squinted at a road sign announcing an exit when the highway veered away from the sea.

"This is it," he said, and slowed to veer onto a two-lane road badly in need of maintenance. The landscape around them was beige, with few plants in the vicinity, a bleak contrast to the lush blue of the nearby water.

"Looks like desert," Jet commented.

"Yes. And up ahead are the mountains we're headed to. They're snowcapped in the winter."

She eyed the towering peaks, their slopes lushly verdant. "The brush should provide plenty of cover, at least."

He considered the terrain silently for a moment before responding, "We'll see."

The field was several bumpy miles off the highway, and by the time they arrived, Jet was ready to get out of the car and stretch her legs. Itai left the engine running by the side of the road, and she followed him to the far edge of the flat expanse, the tall grass brittle beneath their feet. Using the GPS monitor on his phone, less than ten meters from a crude wooden fence they found a package that weighed only a few ounces – an unmarked cardboard box eight inches square, barely dented from its descent from the drone.

"Doesn't look like much," Itai observed.

"It doesn't have to."

They retraced their steps to the car and Jet carefully unsealed the container. Inside were two pairs of latex gloves and a slim aluminum tube with a dispensing pump on one end, seated in a polystyrene protective casing. She inspected the tube for leaks, using one of the gloves to hold it, and then closed the case and slipped it into the glove compartment.

"Any handling instructions?" she asked.

Itai nodded and handed her his phone. "Read this. Describes everything you need to know."

Jet scanned the instructions as Itai cranked the wheel, executed a three-point turn, and headed back to the highway. She finished by the time they reached the road, and passed the phone back to him. "Simple enough. And they thoughtfully provided enough to kill a platoon."

He scowled, his expression stony. "Let's hope it doesn't come to that."

CHAPTER 43

Itai directed the old car off the highway onto a tributary that ran into the hills, the suspension creaking as it lumbered higher. The pavement eventually ran out at a small village that could have been frozen in time from centuries earlier, and they found themselves bouncing along a dirt road that twisted along the banks of a rushing stream. An occasional cow by the water raised its head as they drove by.

The few pedestrians and bicycle riders thinned as they climbed in altitude, and the green scrub was gradually replaced by conifers and dense vegetation. They reached a fork in the road and Itai consulted his cell again, muttering a complaint over the weak signal. The little device blinked and a download icon displayed, indicating that he had an incoming message, and he slowed to a crawl as he waited for it to finish, wary of losing reception at the worst possible time.

The phone chimed softly and he stopped the car to see what had arrived. He scrolled through several images and then turned to Jet, who was eyeing him expectantly.

"We got sat imagery of the lodge. Including thermal on a time lapse. The analysts at HQ have created a rough blueprint of the house's layout based on the roofline and the hot spots."

"How many guards?"

"We can review it once we're further along. Right now, I need to figure out where exactly we are and how to get to where the watcher is without drawing anyone's attention."

"You could try asking him."

"There's no cell coverage that far in the mountains."

"Ah."

He consulted the phone and pointed through the window at the split in the road. "The left is the continuation of this route. To the right is an old mining road. Not sure how bad it gets further up."

"So we take the main road?"

He shook his head. "Afraid not, much as I'd like to. If they've got any security in place, it would be on that approach. Better to chance the mining road and walk the final stretch if necessary."

"Anything would be better than the beating we're taking in this thing," she said.

"I won't take your slights about my car personally. I understand it's all in jest."

"How far are we from the lodge now?"

"Maybe...four, five kilometers."

"Won't we throw up a dust trail they'll see?"

"It's a concern. But my hunch is the road will peter out before we're in danger of doing so."

Itai twisted the wheel right, and the heavy old vehicle resumed its labor, the mining road barely passable in places where runoff had carved deep channels across it. They reached a wooden bridge that crossed the stream, and both got out of the car to inspect it.

"Think it'll support the weight?" Itai asked.

Jet moved to the edge of the bank and peered underneath the wood planks. "It should. Doesn't look like it's in too bad a condition. Only one way to know for sure."

"It's our way out, too. Don't forget that."

She shrugged. "Nothing ventured. You drive across and I'll wait on the other side. Less weight."

Itai gave her a dark look and trod back to the car. Jet picked her way across the bridge, noting that some of the planks appeared questionable up close, and then Itai was rolling slowly over the span. The structure creaked ominously and sagged near the middle. Jet was getting ready to call out a warning to him when he goosed the gas and the car accelerated the rest of the way. It bounced off the end near her and skidded to a stop where she stood.

"I was going to say might want to go faster," she said, climbing in.

"I'll remember that for the trip back."

They made it another kilometer and then the track narrowed to the point where it was impassible; the side had eroded away, the rocks that had supported it at one time washed down the side of a ravine. Itai turned the car around with Jet's guidance and parked it in a wider area, knee deep in grass. They retrieved their weapons and gear and set off on foot. The smooth soles of Itai's loafers slipped on the loose gravel as they walked, slowing their progress. The older man's breath sounded heavy as they followed the road higher, and they were forced to pause numerous times so he could catch his wind.

"How are you going to find the watcher?" she asked at one of their stops.

"He was under instructions to stay near the road. The map shows this one running fairly close to the property, so once we can see it, we'll seek him out."

"Who is he?"

"A grad student that I've used a few times to help on sensitive matters. As you've probably surmised, Baku isn't New York, so the resources at my disposal are limited. He's a good man, though, Israeli, named Harmon. Smart, discreet. A wannabe spy who thrives on these adventures."

"So an amateur with no training," Jet said, her tone indicating what she thought of that.

"He doesn't need much to watch a house and count guards, does he?"

"Assuming he didn't get captured on the road." She shrugged. "Hopefully he wore something dark or green, because otherwise we may be walking into an ambush."

"They have no reason to suspect anyone's got them under surveillance."

"Other than the president's execution by parties unknown while surrounded by his security team, you mean."

An hour passed, and then another. The sun was sinking into the mountains when they reached the lodge, the rich aroma of wood smoke drifting on the breeze from a gray curl floating from its stone chimney. They stayed low and made their way toward the main road, pushing branches from their path as they forged a trail.

They approached a rise near the road, and Jet grabbed Itai's arm to stop him, her pistol in hand.

"What?" he whispered.

She motioned with the gun. "I see a motorcycle."

"That would be Harmon."

Jet moved toward the bike, Itai trailing her. As they neared it, a tall, gangly young man with a hipster beard stepped from behind a tree, his expression alarmed until he spotted Itai behind Jet. His face broke into a smile and he took several steps toward them.

"Hey. You made it," he whispered.

"Yes," Itai said. "This is…Katya. Katya, Harmon."

Jet nodded, her eyes already scanning the road and the house. "Nice to meet you. How many guards, and what shift are they following?"

Harmon looked to Itai, who nodded reassurance.

"Um, I count eight, working, I think, eight-hour shifts."

"You think?" She glared at Itai. "Eight total, or eight each shift?"

"Oh, sorry. Eight at a time. Three walk the perimeter, and the others stay put." He extended his spyglasses to Jet. "You can see them through my binoculars."

She took the glasses from him. "Where's the security staying? In one of the outbuildings or the main house?"

"Appears to be evenly split. Some are over by that garage, in the bungalow, and the rest in the main lodge."

"Anyone come or go since you've been here?" Itai asked.

"One van came up the road and dropped off a few…women. Picked up three as well."

"How many is a few?" Jet asked.

"Four. Young, maybe…in their late teens."

Jet gave a contemptuous snort. "There's your entertainment committee. No point in being the most powerful man in the country if you can't have a little fun, right?"

Itai's face grew longer. "I wouldn't know."

She returned her attention to Harmon. "Anything else you can tell us?"

"Not really. Oh, they changed their shift this morning at eight, so if I'm right about the eight hours, they should be changing again at four."

Jet nodded and held the binoculars up. "Can I keep these?"

"Uh, sure…" Harmon said, appearing confused.

Itai approached the younger man and had a few words with him. Harmon nodded, but didn't look happy. He glanced at Jet and tried a smile. "Nice meeting you."

"Likewise. Might want to push your bike until you're a kilometer away so the engine doesn't alert anyone."

Harmon's expression shifted to annoyed. "I know that. I'm not stupid."

Jet didn't comment. How the young man felt about his duty being cut short was of no concern to her. She walked toward the rise while Itai spoke to Harmon in a low tone, and then the young man moved to the motorcycle and began pushing it toward the main road. Jet snapped her fingers and he looked back at her.

"You should go down the other way – there's a mining road in that direction that connects to the main one a few klicks away."

The station chief nodded agreement. Harmon sighed audibly, swung the bike around, and rolled it into the brush without another word.

Jet resumed studying the lodge with the binoculars. Itai joined her and sat down with a grimace.

"I'm too old for the field."

"Four o'clock's coming up soon. If Harmon was right, then the right time for me to make my attempt is around eleven."

Itai nodded. "Sure. Toward the end of the shift, when they're more likely to be tired or distracted."

Four o'clock arrived, and the guards were indeed replaced by a new crop. She followed them with the glasses until three disappeared into the bungalow and the other into the house.

She lowered the binoculars. "Let's see what HQ sent. It better be good, because right now that place is a black box."

Itai swiped the screen and opened the downloaded images, and then scanned through them as Jet looked on. "This is an aerial shot of the grounds, as you can see. There are the vehicles, the house, the bungalow and garage. Next, you can see the thermal image – where the heat signatures are gathered. Finally, this is a best-guess blueprint of the layout of the house based on the roof, the orientation, and so on."

Jet studied the final image for several long moments. "How do they know the bedrooms are upstairs?"

Itai shrugged. "That's the preferred way of building them here, I guess. And the thermals align with that. This was created using time lapse from last night, so you can see there are only a couple of rooms that only have a single signature. The target is in one of those. Likely this smaller suite," he said, tapping the screen gently and zooming in.

"More than one in that first set of frames," she observed.

"That was probably last night's company."

Jet nodded. "If that's correct, I need to circle around and get a look at the other side of the building. See what entry points there are."

Itai nodded. "You want me to go with you?"

She shook her head. "No. Less chance of being spotted with only one of us. I'll be back when I'm back." Jet looked overhead, where gathering clouds were turning the sky gray. "Hopefully those will stick around and block any moonlight." She sniffed at the air. "If we're really lucky, it'll rain."

"Great," Itai said without enthusiasm.

"Stay put," Jet whispered, and then took off at a fast pace toward the mining road, pistol in one hand and binoculars in the other, teeth clenched as she covered ground with the grace of a jungle cat.

CHAPTER 44

Amit Mendel swiped his security card through a scanner as he exited the Mossad's headquarters, and the steel and bulletproof glass doors slid open. The side entry he was using was one of three, and the guard watched him from behind the high counter without blinking, Amit's coming and going at odd hours unremarkable given the type of work that went on below ground.

Mendel strode to his car, a nondescript two-door coupe, and started the engine after placing his briefcase on the passenger seat. He backed out of his slot and drove to the main gate, the signage identifying the huge building behind him as a glass factory, and waited as another guard checked his license plate against those that had entered and then directed Mendel to swipe his card again to open the heavy iron plate that served as a barrier against inquisitive eyes.

Mendel was bone tired, having been working since the prior evening, and needed sleep – a luxury he'd trained himself to do without for long stretches if necessary. He turned onto the plant access road and drove toward his apartment in downtown Tel Aviv, where he lived alone. Family wasn't an option with the hours he kept and the juncture he was at in his professional career. Maybe when he was in his forties, he mused absently, knowing that the likelihood had just grown far less likely after the operation in Baku went sideways on him.

He forced himself to breathe deeply and remain calm, even as his mind replayed the events of the last twenty-four hours and the sudden upset in Azerbaijan. The director had been more guarded than usual in the last meetings, obviously suspicious of everyone on the committee that had appointed Leah to be Jet's control, and that didn't bode well for Mendel. Even though it had been structured as a group decision, if the agency dug deep enough, they'd eventually piece together the connection between Leah and him, and that would be sufficient to interrogate him until he cracked.

Mendel swore softly as a light turned red. It had seemed so simple: take a few million dollars in a Cayman account, switch the target from the president's double to the man himself, and terminate the hitter once the job was done. Easiest money he would ever make. A half million to Leah to do the heavy lifting, and two and a half for himself, added to the million he'd already amassed helping the Russians with information when they asked. It had seemed like a lock until the assassin had turned the tables on Leah. He hadn't foreseen that. Wouldn't have believed it possible, given her chops.

"What's done is done," he murmured. The light turned green and he gave the car gas, nobody on the road at that time in the desolate industrial area.

Twenty minutes later he arrived at his building and pulled into the underground garage. He parked and rushed to the elevator. The clock was working against him, and the less time he spent in his apartment, the better. He'd taken to keeping a bug-out bag filled with everything he would require to vanish since his field days, and the habit had stuck with him even now, when he piloted a desk. It would take him no time to grab it and his alternative IDs and head for a private airstrip where a prop plane was already waiting to spirit him to Port Said, Egypt, where he would drop off the face of the earth.

He'd debated staying in place and bluffing his way through any questioning, but his gut told him not to chance it. The risk of the director's people seeing through his story was high, and even if there was plausible deniability working for him, he didn't trust the director to give him the benefit of the doubt. No, the damage done by Leah failing to execute the assassin was terminal, and it was time to fold up his tent and head for greener pastures – maybe open a little bar in the Caribbean, someplace like Belize or Roatán, where he could grow his hair long and wear flip-flops and forget his past life. He certainly had enough to make that dream come true, if not to live large in a first world country indefinitely.

His second passport was top quality and would pass any scrutiny. Swiss, it identified him as Hans Gerber, a banker two years younger than his actual age, his hair color in the photo slightly darker than it was now, the goatee in the snap the most noteworthy element. That would get him to the Caymans, and from there, the sky was the limit. The Mossad wouldn't know where he'd gone, and if he kept his profile low, he'd be just another face in the crowd.

Mendel felt no guilt, either for his actions or abandoning his career. He didn't view his repurposing the assassin as anything but a smart business decision. The sociopathology that enabled him to make dispassionate decisions for his country's sake had come in handy in rationalizing his treason: if he hadn't agreed to go on the Russian payroll, someone else would have. He played in a dirty game where there were no rules, and he was under no illusions about how the world worked. When the opportunity to make real, serious money had arisen, he'd jumped at the chance, understanding that naïve ideals like patriotism or loyalty were for fools.

The elevator door slid wide at his floor and he stepped into the hall, his face outwardly at peace despite his churning thoughts. He moved to his door and unlocked it, and only a trace of regret assailed him at the sight of his furnishings when he turned the lights on. Those were possessions, of which he could get more. His life was another matter.

Twenty minutes later he emerged from his bathroom, his hair darker, his suit replaced by a short-sleeved navy blue resort shirt and a pair of crème linen slacks. A blue blazer over one shoulder completed his outfit – that of a privileged banker on vacation.

He took a final look around the apartment and walked to his laptop computer, switched it off and unplugged it from its thirty-two-inch monitor, and slipped it and the power cord into his bag. Satisfied that he'd gotten everything he needed, he moved to the door and switched off the lights, the habitual frugality ingrained.

The elevator ride to the basement garage seemed to take forever, and he heaved a sigh of relief when the conveyance slowed and the doors slipped open. His shoes clicked on the cement as he walked to his car, the gloom of the garage echoing with the sound. He was nearly to his slot when a familiar voice called out from the shadows.

"Going somewhere?" the director asked.

Mendel's shoulders slumped and he stopped, but he didn't turn around. There was no response he could offer. It was over.

Unless.

His hand slipped into his jacket, feeling for the small pistol there. Another voice spoke from near his car.

"Don't even think of it. Put the bag and jacket down and your hands behind your head," Avi said.

"What is this?" Mendel tried, forcing outrage as the blood drained from his face.

"We know about Leah. We know everything," the director said, his voice sad.

"What are you talking about? There's nothing to know," Mendel said, stalling for time as his fingers searched for the pistol stock.

"It took some looking, I'll give you that. Nothing obvious. No dating, clean phone records, no professional affiliation. But you can't hide everything, at least not forever. We know she grew up only a few blocks from you. From there, the elementary school records cinched it."

"That's it? She went to school where I did? So did half of Tel Aviv," Mendel spat derisively. "I've done nothing–"

Mendel spun, gun in hand, and Avi's weapon spit with a soft pop. The tranquilizer dart penetrated Mendel's shirt as he searched for the director's bulk in the shadows, but his vision quickly blurred and his limbs lost sensation. Mendel's knees buckled, and he dropped like a sack of rocks. Avi and two other men moved on him while the director stepped from the gloom, a frown in place, hands feeling for his cigarette pack as his men dealt with the traitor.

"You'll be interrogated. You will tell us everything, of course," the director said. "Whether it takes hours or days doesn't matter to me in the least. If you have any accomplices, we will learn everything. We both know that. My advice is to make it easy on yourself." The director raised a cigarette to his lips and stepped toward where

Mendel lay, his eyes wide, his breathing shallow. "I know you can hear me even though your body's betrayed you, so trust me when I say that this will be as unpleasant as you make it, no more. I have no interest in extending your suffering any longer than necessary. Be smart. Tell us what we wish to know, and it will be finished." He looked to Avi and nodded.

His men gathered up Mendel's gun and bag. Avi pulled the dart from Mendel's chest and dropped it into his pocket before dragging him to a dark SUV parked illegally at the end of the row of cars. The director lit his cigarette and blew a plume of smoke after them. His capacity for sorrow at one of his protégés betraying him was slim, his understanding of human nature such that little could surprise him. The director had seen too much to be anything but melancholy at losing a capable man. But there were more where Mendel had come from.

There always were.

His footsteps were ponderous as he walked to the SUV, trailing smoke like a dragon, as another in a long string of bitter days drew to a close. Avi opened the passenger door for him, Mendel wedged in the back like so much luggage, and the director nodded appreciation before climbing in without so much as a glance at the comatose man in the rear.

CHAPTER 45

Walnut-sized raindrops pelted Itai and Jet as the storm intensified; the tree cover offered scant protection against nature's fury. The cloudburst had begun at ten with a thunderclap, and then the heavens had opened and the deluge commenced with a fury that had taken Jet's breath away, the ground soaking up the water like a sponge. Itai huddled like a miserable wet dog beneath a pine tree as Jet paced nearby.

Jet had been gone for three hours and, when she'd returned to Itai's hiding place, had reported on what she'd seen and agreed to attempt the sanction. The lodge's perimeter wall was low enough for her to scale it, and the surface of the house offered sufficient handholds that she thought she had a better than even chance of success. Itai had been ecstatic to hear it and had acquiesced and called the director on the sat phone, but hadn't reached him. Jet had been annoyed but accepted the news without reaction – she'd have her chat with him upon her return.

She checked her watch for the tenth time and walked to where Itai crouched, dripping wet, the night black around him.

"I'm going to make my way there. If all goes well, I'll meet you back at the car," she said.

"Why not here?"

"No offense, but you should get a head start – I can move a lot faster than you can. And you'll catch your death if you stay out here much longer."

He looked doubtful. "You can find it no problem?"

"Worry about yourself," she said, checking the magazine of the suppressed pistol before slipping it into her waistband and testing the weight. She frowned, withdrew it, and unscrewed the suppressor and tried it again. Satisfied, she nodded and tossed Itai the silencer. "Too awkward for climbing. Hang onto it for me, would you?"

Itai caught it and nodded. "Good luck."

She cocked an eyebrow. "Luck won't have anything to do with it."

Jet vanished into the darkness like a phantom, leaving the station chief to stare at where she'd melted into the night. Itai searched the gloom for any trace of her but gave up after a minute and forced himself to his feet, sopping and miserable, the long way back to the car nothing he was looking forward to.

Jet raced along a game trail she'd discovered when looking over the grounds and followed it around to where she'd sat for hours, watching the guards as dusk's final light had faded. At the time, lights glowed inside the lodge and the generator purred from beneath the shelter of its sound-dampening enclosure, its steady thrumming reaching Jet a quarter mile away. Now, when she reached her vantage point, the house was largely dark. The downstairs had only a single lamp on, to judge by the faint illumination from the windows; but upstairs, three of the bedrooms were still lit.

She wiped the rain from her face, her hair hanging limp and running with water, and sat with her back to a tree trunk, resigned to waiting as long as it took for the party to wind down and the lights to go out.

Two and a half hours later, the entire house was dark save the downstairs, and the deluge had abated to a steady shower. Jet had mixed feelings about the easing of the rain – the inclement weather would increase the odds of her making it past the guards without being seen, but it would make scaling the outside of the house more difficult. Still, even a light rain was better than nothing; the guards would likely be worn down by the weather and not paying much attention to anything but remaining dry. She'd noted that the ones who had been patrolling the perimeter had reduced their rounds to once an hour and showed no interest in their job, hurrying through their paces in an effort to get back to the lodge's porch and out of the rain.

Jet stood and ran her fingers through her wet hair, combing it straight back and out of her eyes, and then made for the section of wall nearest the rear of the house. She paused ten yards away, listened intently, and then ran toward the sheer face and vaulted skyward. Jet was over the top in a blink and landed softly on the wet grass inside the grounds, grateful for the covering drone of the generator and the limited visibility from the drizzle.

The dark bulk of the house loomed ahead of her as she covered the ground in a sprint. When she reached the rear, Jet tried the back door, but wasn't surprised when it didn't budge. The easy way dispensed with, she eyed the rough exterior of the logs used to build the lodge, and reached out with wet hands to pull herself upward, using the windowsill beside the door to push herself higher with her feet.

Halfway up the side of the house, her left hand slipped and she fell backward. She kicked as she angled away from the wall and was able to twist as she dropped. She hit the ground, tucking and rolling, the wind knocked from her when she came to a stop, staring up at the sky with frustration. She regained her breath and moved back to the door to repeat her attempt, this time more slowly and with greater care.

Jet arrived at the second-story window she'd targeted and her fingers felt a small gap to one side; as she'd guessed, the window was unlocked, there being no reason to worry about security on a second-story bathroom – assuming the HQ architects were correct about the layout. She heaved and it opened, leaving just enough space for her to wriggle through, and she gripped the edge and hauled herself through it headfirst, arresting her drop with her hands on the tile of the bathroom floor.

She took a moment to get her bearings. A night light's glow from one of the electric outlets illuminated the space just enough so she could make out details. Jet rose and walked to the mirror, where a bedraggled version of herself that was almost unrecognizable stared back at her. She removed a towel from the rack and sopped up her wet footprints and the small puddle her body had left on the floor. Once it was dry, she stepped into the marble shower stall and wrung out her shirt and windbreaker, and then toweled the excess moisture from her pants, pausing occasionally to cock her head and listen for any sign of life on the other side of the door.

When she finished, she hung the towel back up with three others like it and regarded the scattering of objects on the vanity. A hygiene bag sat beside the sink, where a tube of half-used toothpaste lay next to a toothbrush. A stick of deodorant stood with a small bottle with a gold dome top. She eyed the collection and edged to the door to press her ear against it, the neurotoxin dispenser in her pocket ready for the main event.

~ ~ ~

Sanjar Nabiyev shifted on the four-poster bed, his upper torso standing out in stark relief against the white linen sheets. The girls had left him to get some badly needed rest an hour before, and he'd fallen into bed, exhausted; the demands of the evening had drained him in more ways than one. A bottle of expensive imported vodka sat half drunk on the table near the window, the three glasses by its side a reminder of his earlier excess.

He licked his lips, his mouth dry from the alcohol, his dreams vivid and disturbing as the rain hammered a tattoo against the roof, his sleep restless and unsatisfying. Metabolizing the vodka was proving more difficult with each night of the Russian's hospitality, and he'd reached the point where his body was protesting that it had reached saturation.

Nabiyev adjusted the pillow beneath his head and drifted in and out of slumber, the generator's muted hum masking the worst of the rain's pattering against the window. The air was heavy with humidity and somewhat uncomfortable in spite of the air conditioner that ran throughout the night.

A sound from the bathroom door startled him awake, and he flipped over, eyes searching in a darkness that was black as ink. He fumbled for the lamp on the night table beside his bed, still only half conscious, his head pounding like an anvil chorus from the drink.

The smell of the girls lingered on the sheets, but he pushed the thought aside as his fingers found the flat edge of the switch and twisted it on.

Light flooded the space, and he blinked as he stared around the room, his hair askew, his eyes bloodshot and wild.

"Guards! Come quick!" he yelled, his voice hoarse, and slid open the night table drawer and removed a semiautomatic pistol. He stood, the weapon pointed toward the bathroom, his hand trembling slightly from the sudden surge of adrenaline pumping through his body.

Footsteps pounded up the stairs, and the bedroom door burst open. Two gunmen with assault rifles swept the room with their weapons and froze at the sight of the prime minister, nude except for his underwear, his chest a dark mat of wiry black hair. The nearest of the men looked to Nabiyev with puzzlement, eyeing the gun in his hand with concern.

"What is it, sir?"

"I...I heard something. Someone was here."

"In here?" the guard repeated, his gaze flitting to the vodka before settling on the prime minister again. "Where?"

"In the bathroom." Nabiyev motioned with the pistol at the bathroom door. "In there."

The men exchanged a glance and nodded, their faces somber.

"Yes, sir. Would you mind pointing the gun away from us, please?"

Nabiyev seemed to just then notice the weapon in his hand and nodded. "Right. Of course."

"Thank you. We'll just take a quick look, then, sir."

Nabiyev sat back on the bed, the pistol by his side. The first guard walked toward the door, followed by his companion, and they stood on either side of it, AK-47s at the ready. The first reached for the knob and paused for a heartbeat, and then he twisted the knob and threw the door open, rifle pointed into the gloom.

A moment went by, and then another.

The men turned to Nabiyev.

"The window's open, sir. It was probably the storm. Wind. A gust caused the door to creak or something."

Nabiyev didn't look convinced and was preparing to protest when a particularly heavy sheet of rain lashed the window near the bed with a noise like the crack of a whip. The men suppressed smiles and nodded. "Or it could have been something like that," the gunman said.

Nabiyev's expression turned sheepish. "I…are the guards still patrolling the grounds?"

"Of course, sir. As we have since you arrived."

"You haven't noticed anything suspicious?" Nabiyev demanded.

"No, sir. In this weather, it's hard to see your hand in front of your face. Nobody's on the road. We'd have been alerted if anyone had come close to the grounds – we have motion detectors set up by the gate."

Nabiyev frowned, but had nothing to add, so he waved the men away and shook his head as though to clear it. "I could have sworn someone was in here."

The first guard returned to the bathroom and walked inside. "I'll close the window and lock it. That way the wind won't disturb you again." Out of sight of the prime minister, he rolled his eyes at his reflection in the mirror and moved to the window. Water was pooled on the floor beneath it, and he shook his head at Nabiyev's carelessness in a rainstorm. After peering out into the darkness, he slid the window closed and latched it.

The guard retraced his steps to the bedroom, and Nabiyev glared at them like they'd failed him. "I want you to search the property. Now. As a precaution."

The guards exchanged another look. The first pulled a small two-way from his jacket and held it to his lips. He relayed Nabiyev's order, listened as it was acknowledged, and then slipped the compact radio back into his pocket and nodded to the prime minister.

"Very well, sir. The men are going to do a sweep." He paused. "Would you feel better if we sat just outside the door?"

"I…no. There's no need. Carry on."

"Yes, sir. Call if you need anything, sir."

Once the men were gone, Nabiyev switched off the light and lay his head back on the pillow with a sigh. As of tomorrow, he would cut his alcohol consumption by half. Now that he was running the country, he needed to be sharp, and he was obviously imbibing too much if he was so easily spooked. His eyes adjusted to the gloom, and he took a final distrustful look at the bathroom door, slid the pistol under his pillow instead of back into the drawer, and stared into the darkness, heart thudding as anxiety slowly leached from his system and the last of the storm flogged itself against the roof.

CHAPTER 46

Jet hung by her fingers just below the bathroom window, teeth grinding at the effort of supporting herself with only a precarious handhold. Rain coursed down her face and she blinked it away, feeling for a toehold to relieve the strain on her arms. Light streamed from the window, and then it closed with a clunk, the snick of the lock engaging audible even above the sound of the storm.

Her right foot found a space between two logs and she tested it. Satisfied that it would support her, she brought one hand down to her waist level and felt for another promising spot, knowing there had to be one there from her trip up the sheer side of the lodge. She found it and eased her weight off her other hand, and then repeated the process of hanging while searching for another toehold, arms trembling from the exertion.

A gust of wind drove a wall of rain across her back, and Jet struggled to maintain her grip. After a few brutal seconds it eased, and she was resuming her descent when she heard voices from around the side of the lodge. She twisted her head to the side and glanced down at the ground, and then released her hold and dropped, tumbling in a roll when she landed. She recovered quickly and leapt to her feet and, when she heard the voices approaching, bolted toward the perimeter wall.

Flashlight beams jittered from the lodge as she drove herself faster, the rain gray in the beams, the lights playing along the ground at the base of the building. She ducked as she ran, willing herself smaller, hoping that her drop hadn't left an indentation in the ground to alarm the guards. She looked over her shoulder and noted the footprints already filling with water – if the guards were paying any kind of attention, the tracks would lead them straight to her.

Jet cursed at the luck that had her running from armed guards in the rain. Everything had been perfect, the toxin in her hand, the target snoring softly, the storm's sound sufficient to mask the sound of the door opening. She'd taken two steps toward Nabiyev's sleeping form, and her weight on one of the floorboards had caused it to creak – and the noise had awakened him. She'd barely made it back into the bathroom when the lights had come on and he'd cried out, signaling that her chance had eluded her.

She didn't have time to dwell on the failure. She took a quick look back at the lodge, and her stomach twisted. One of the flashlight beams lingered below the window where she'd landed, and the others moved toward it as the guards converged on the depression. A voice cried out and the lights swept the ground between her and the lodge as she poured on the steam, urging her legs to greater speed, seconds now the difference between life and death.

The downpour intensified and she zigzagged through a patch of tall grass, the soil firmer and less likely to show tracks. The only reason she hadn't been seen was the rain, but she knew she couldn't count on that for much longer. If they spotted her footprints, all uncertainty would be eliminated, and she could expect them to mount a full-court press to hunt her down, irrespective of the weather.

Jet reached the wall and threw herself at it, but her foot slipped as she was launching and she fell short. Instead of her hands finding the top, her torso slammed into it when her fingers missed their mark. She fell onto the wet ground and swore as pain radiated from her spine and the back of her ribcage. She fought for breath and waited for the agony to recede, more than aware that she was losing time she didn't have.

Moments later she sat up and tested her weight with her arms. She grimaced at the spike of pain that lanced from her ribs, but ignored it and forced herself to her feet. After a final look at the lodge, she took four steps back and ran at the wall again, this time her footing sure. Her hands locked on the top, but she froze, the pain blinding, and then heaved herself up, nearly blacking out from the effort.

More shouts from behind her sounded through the rain, and she rolled over the top of the wall and dropped on the far side. Her side throbbed and her breaths came ragged. After a moment to orient herself, she rose and took off at a trot. The ground here was rockier, the dense vegetation making it less likely the guards could easily follow.

Flashlight beams played across the top of the wall where she'd been only seconds before, and more shouts told her that the guards had discovered her tracks. She found a faint trail in the darkness and followed it toward the main road; and then stopped at the sound of an engine starting up at the lodge, joined almost instantly by another.

The exhaust tone told her everything she needed to know: the guards had ATVs.

Jet knelt and eyed the ground, trying to make out any trace of her footprints. Now that the soil composition had changed to a combination of dirt and shale, she couldn't see anything suspicious. And if the rain continued for any length of time, any footprints she'd left would be eradicated.

She stood and squinted at the darkness while her fingers probed her sore ribs. The ATVs revved and she sprang into action, pushing through the brush and doubling back toward the mining road. The guards would likely do a sweep of the exterior of the wall, but with no tracks to follow, they'd be wasting their time. It was possible that they'd ride to the mine road, but she suspected that given the conditions, they would stay close to the lodge in case the intruder who had breached their defenses was only the first onslaught from an unknown adversary.

Pain seared through her with every footfall, but she ignored it and powered on, jade eyes probing the gloom. The sound of the ATVs diminished as she battled her way through the brush, and then the foliage thinned and she was on the trail she and Itai had used for the final approach to their vantage point.

Jet picked up speed as the downpour eased. Her entire left side was now numb from her shoulder to her hip, her body providing temporary relief as shock set in. She was sure she'd broken a few ribs, or at least badly bruised them, but she couldn't do anything about it until she was clear of the threat on her tail.

The track veered to the left and she turned right, remembering that the mining road was down the slope, not up. Ten minutes passed, the ATVs now a distant buzz, and she emerged from the underbrush onto the road as the rain tapered to a drizzle. Visibility was still close to nil, but she could move with more assurance, the outline of the edge of the road clear even in the gloom.

She made her way down the mountain toward the bridge, pain returning as the adrenaline in her system bled away. By the time she made it to the wooden span, she was limping, favoring her right side and wincing at every step.

The stream surged beneath the bridge, swollen from the rain. She made her way across, noting that the wood had splintered in places from the weight of Itai's car. Her foot broke through one of the planks and she fell, catching herself with her hands only at the last minute, sending agony shrieking through her side again. She gasped from the intensity of the pain and stars danced behind her eyes as she fought the creeping darkness of unconsciousness, willing herself to stay focused long enough to make it to Itai. Her chest heaved with effort, and she slowly pulled her leg from the gap she'd opened in the wood with her boot, wincing with every movement.

A minute later she had recovered enough to stand, and she hobbled the rest of the way across the bridge. When Jet reached the far side, she looked around for the car, any tire tracks long ago erased by the water. Her eyes roved over the brush and followed the road, and she spotted the roof fifty yards down the slope. She picked her way slowly along the road; the ruts treacherous in the dark, and her ankle swelling in her boot reminded her that she'd exhausted any luck for the night. When she reached the vehicle, the windows were fogged over, and Itai jumped when she tapped on the driver's side glass.

He opened the door and regarded her. "Well?"

"I think I broke some ribs," she said, and limped around to the passenger-side door to let herself in.

Itai watched her in silence and then pulled his door shut and turned to her.

"So how did it go? Were you successful?"

She gave him a clipped report of her attempt, ending with a frown. Itai shook his head and reached for the ignition key. "Then it was a failure. This was all for nothing."

Jet fastened her seatbelt with a grimace and leaned her head back against the headrest. "Maybe not."

CHAPTER 47

Dust motes danced in the sunlight streaming through the lodge windows as Kazamov sipped a cup of coffee, a snifter of cognac beside it for fortification after a difficult night. The ATVs had awakened him and he'd been unable to sleep since then for more than minutes at a time, furious that anyone had made it past his security force and then managed to escape. He paid top dollar for his retinue of ex-Spetsnaz commandos, and the idea that an intruder could make it this close to his sanctum was disturbing, to say the least. The only good to come out of it was that Nabiyev hadn't been harmed, so as troubling as the night had been, in the end, it had been only that, nothing more.

Nabiyev had managed to sleep through the ATVs, and when Kazamov had checked on him that morning, he'd been groggy but otherwise unaffected by the night's excitement. He'd looked like he'd wrestled a bear, the vodka clearly unkind to him the following day, but he was alive and unharmed, ready to lead his country forward, if a little bleary-eyed and sluggish.

Sizzling echoed from the kitchen along with the clatter of crockery, and one of the servants appeared with a fine china plate heaped with sausage, baked bread, and eggs. Kazamov took an appreciative sniff.

"Will there be anything else, sir? More coffee?" the man asked.

"*Nyet*. This is fine," Kazamov said, his eyes on the screen across from him, where a news program was covering the latest from the capital. The coup had been put down, the looters and vandals arrested, the armed gangs contained. Earlier an unconfirmed report had stated that the assassination weapon had been discovered in the hall, but there was no further news about it, nor about the claims by the military officers who'd been taken into custody that the coup had been orchestrated by the president himself.

A woman with bouffant blonde hair read from a teleprompter with the bland sincerity of a bank teller, reciting the latest rumors masked as news. Most notable had been the statement from the Nationalist Party calling for restraint and calm, and of course Nabiyev's televised address, which had been well received by most.

Questions about the prime minister's whereabouts had been answered during the broadcast, and he was expected back in the capital by nightfall. There was still a curfew in effect during evening hours, but the civil unrest had passed and the city was largely calm. Outlying areas had reported no issues, but the military was continuing to advise that any lawlessness would be met with an immediate and unequivocal response.

Kazamov forked a mouthful of sausage and eggs into his mouth and chewed contentedly as he read the news feed at the bottom of the screen. He loved it when a plan came together, and his impromptu leveraging of the phony assassination attempt had been a masterstroke – and a bargain at the price. He was completely disconnected from the entire debacle, had total deniability, and best of all, the scheme had worked. An increasingly difficult parasite had been removed from office, and a more malleable one inserted. He was a kingmaker. It was a heady feeling.

A noise from the hallway drew his attention. A slender brunette beauty with heavy black Clark Kent glasses crossed the great room and beamed at him, her sweatpants and halter top bouncing as they struggled to contain her curves. "Good morning, Ygor," she purred.

"Morning, darling. May I offer you some breakfast and coffee? Or perhaps something stronger?"

She giggled and smiled again. "I'll have whatever you're having."

"Go into the kitchen and tell them to make you the Kazamov special, and to be quick about it."

"You're too good to us, Ygor."

"It is one of my curses – my generosity," he agreed, watching her walk to the kitchen with an appreciative eye.

The girl was one of many from a world-class selection he flew in from Moscow for special guests. The local talent was serviceable, but nothing like the Russian beauties to which he'd grown accustomed. This one was studying to be a doctor, or so she said. Whether it was true or not was unimportant to him.

A shout from upstairs interrupted his musing, and he frowned at the alarmed tone of the man's voice.

"What is it?" Kazamov called out.

"We need a doctor!"

"What? Why? What's happened?"

"It's the prime minister."

Kazamov leapt to his feet and hurried to the stairs, his bulk preventing him from moving very fast. He labored up the steps, sweat breaking out on his forehead from the effort. He paused at the upstairs landing when he spotted the two dancers he'd selected for Nabiyev's entertainment, their hands over their mouths, standing by the guest bedroom door and clad in only neon pink and green lingerie. Kazamov toddled past them and stopped at the sight of a guard inside Nabiyev's bedroom, pointing into the bathroom, his expression grim.

"Speak up, man. What is it?" the Russian demanded.

"He's...I think he's dead."

"Think? Does he have a pulse?" Kazamov snapped.

The guard didn't answer, his expression betraying that he hadn't checked.

"Get out of the way, you idiot," Kazamov barked, and pushed past the guard. There on the floor lay Nabiyev, mouth agape, eyes staring sightlessly at the ceiling. Kazamov retched at the overpowering smell from the pool of cologne the man was lying in. The precious nectar was evaporating from the shattered bottle on the floor, its gold dome cap resting against the base of the toilet. He stepped closer to Nabiyev and leaned down to touch his neck, but withdrew his hand at the feel of cool flesh.

"He's dead, all right," the Russian said. "What happened?"

"The girls found him. They called me." The guard hesitated. "I think he had a heart attack or something."

Kazamov shook his head and stormed from the bedroom, his face a mask of fury. All of his machinations had been in vain – the stupid bastard had overdone it with the booze and hookers, and his heart had given out.

His security chief met him at the base of the stairs, and Kazamov explained in a couple of sentences what had happened. "Get a doctor up here. Use the sat phone. I'm headed for the airport. I can't be delayed by the locals and their questions. Tell them I was here, but left before Nabiyev was found." Kazamov paused and turned his head. "Girls! Pack up. We're leaving in ten minutes."

The security man nodded. "So we found him?"

"Of course. He was alive the last time anyone saw him. In good spirits." Kazamov didn't wait for a response and instead returned to his seat at the table and downed the entire snifter of cognac at a gulp. The ebony-haired vixen sitting across from him was visibly scared by his mood and didn't utter a word. Kazamov speared a piece of sausage, took a bite, and spit it across the room in anger.

"Damn," he exclaimed, and yelled for the servant. "Pavel! Pavel, you dolt! My breakfast is cold."

CHAPTER 48

The mood at the Nationalist Party headquarters was festive on the evening of the election as Hovel's gutted administration conceded defeat to Yashar Bahador, who would become the new president of Azerbaijan by a slim majority of the vote. Bottles had been cracked and the hall was packed with triumphant supporters yelling, singing, and celebrating the win.

Bahador and Sergei stood in the administrative offices at a mirrored window overlooking the floor, a bottle of imported champagne open on a nearby desk, plastic cups in their hands. Bahador watched the revelry on the floor below with an amused smile.

"They seem overjoyed. That is good. Of course, now the real work begins," he said. "The entrenched powers will be lining up to corrupt anyone in my cabinet, and I fear that some may be able to resist anything but temptation."

"It is a huge victory. The first time the nation has had a real chance since we gained independence."

"Yes. But recall how quickly the parasites went to work then. Some things never change."

"It's a matter of selecting your staff carefully," Sergei said.

Bahador smiled. "Our staff, my friend. I didn't get here alone. Don't think I will forget that."

"I'm honored to serve in any capacity I can." Sergei shook his head as though bemused. "Nabiyev stroking out was timely, wasn't it?"

"Yes. Although we could have beaten him. He was no Hovel."

"There were rumors he was going to suspend the election."

"Rumors. This country is like a gaggle of geese, always squawking about a new conspiracy."

"I'm somewhat surprised they didn't stuff more ballot boxes."

"The observers made it impractical. After the loss of two members of the ruling party within a matter of days, they subjected the key stations to rigorous checks. Any significant variance from the exit polls would have thrown up a red flag."

Sergei took a long sip of his champagne. "I think they lost their will once Hovel was assassinated. He was always their backbone. Nabiyev was a weasel, but he didn't have what it takes to lead."

"Probably," Bahador agreed. "All water under the bridge now."

The lead-up to the elections had been chaotic, with voter intimidation, accusations of bribery and blackmail, and massive protests against any delays in the voters making their choice. When Nabiyev had died, his successor had proposed postponing the election for three months, but the popular response had been so pronounced that he'd quickly backpedaled and the vote had gone forward as planned.

An aide entered with a message slip and handed it to Bahador before hurrying off. Bahador read the contents and his face tightened. "There's rioting over at the coliseum. Cars burning. The police are sending over a squad to maintain order here."

"That's not reassuring. Who's rioting?"

"Doesn't say," Bahador said. "Might be staged by the administration. One of the things I've feared is that they'll try to create such upheaval that the people will demand they stay in power to protect them."

"That would be illegal."

Bahador nodded. "Yes, but it wouldn't be the first time something like that has happened, would it? There are no new ideas. Let's hope that it doesn't get out of hand."

Sergei checked his watch and eyed the camera crews below. "About time to make a statement, don't you think?"

Bahador sighed and set down his champagne. "I suppose. Something about peaceful transitions and a new tomorrow?"

Sergei smirked and felt in his jacket. "I have a little something written."

"Give me ten minutes to digest it in peace, and then it's showtime. Cue the dancing girls."

Sergei passed him the speech, two double-spaced pages, knowing that Bahador would memorize it quickly and only skim it during the broadcast or, even better, begin reading it and then toss it aside as though he was departing from the script. Cheap theater, but effective on the population, which had elected him based on a desire for meaningful change rather than a continuation of a corrupt and oppressive status quo.

"Thank you, young man," Bahador said, and turned from the window.

Sergei moved to the door and paused at the threshold. "I'll see that you aren't disturbed."

Bahador nodded again. "Ten minutes."

CHAPTER 49

Tel Aviv, Israel

Matt answered the knock on the door and his face broke into a grin at the sight of Jet, slightly worse for wear, standing in the hall with her emerald eyes gleaming in the halogen lights. He moved to hug her, but she stopped him and instead tiptoed and kissed him hard on the mouth.

When she pulled away, she was glowing, a small smirk twisting her lips.

"Sorry I couldn't call. They wouldn't let me," she said.

"That's one way to surprise me." He looked her over. "No hug?"

"Not for a while. I've got two fractured ribs and some pretty amazing colored bruises to show you."

His expression grew serious. "Aside from that, everything's okay?"

"Sure. Never better. Just going to need some recovery time." She looked behind Matt. "Where's Hannah?"

"In her room. Since she discovered my tablet and YouTube, I haven't been able to get her to put it down."

Jet stepped inside and took Matt's hand. He eased the door shut and called out, "Hannah! Mama's home!"

The little girl came tearing around the corner and Matt had to stop her before she threw herself at Jet. "Whoa. Mama has some boo-boos, so take it easy," he warned.

Hannah hesitated and Jet knelt to face her. "I can manage a real gentle hug. No squeezing, though."

Hannah's face lit up and she approached Jet with hands outstretched. Jet embraced her and decided it was worth the pain to feel her daughter in her arms. She kissed Hannah's cheeks and smoothed her hair, her eyes moistening.

"Have you been good?" Jet asked, holding her at arm's length.

"Yes."

"Of course she has," Matt chimed in. "Sweet as spun sugar."

"You didn't give Matt any trouble while I was gone?"

"It wasn't that long," Matt said.

"Felt like forever," Jet replied. "Thank God that's over."

"We were going to go to a little neighborhood spot for dinner in a couple of hours. You want to get cleaned up or anything? Or rest?" Matt asked. Jet had bathed at a clinic the Mossad used for its operatives after she'd been examined and X-rayed, and had donned the fresh clothes her escort provided, the fit of the elastic waist pants and stylistically baggy shirt loose but workable.

"Maybe before we go out."

The condo intercom buzzed, and Jet whirled around, having never heard the annoying screech before. Matt walked to it and depressed a black button. "Yes?"

The director's voice emanated from the speaker. "I need to have a word with the new arrival."

Jet eyed Matt, her expression conveying her annoyance. Matt pressed the button again. "Can it wait?"

"Ask her to come downstairs. I'm in a car out front. Shouldn't take more than a few minutes."

The speaker went dead, the director not one to wait. Jet swallowed her exasperation and placed a hand on Matt's chest. "I already got debriefed. This must be important."

Matt nodded wordlessly and Jet smiled at her daughter. "I'll be right back, honey. And then you can show me Matt's tablet."

"Mine too!" Hannah declared.

Jet rode the elevator down to the lobby level and walked out of the building into the late afternoon sunshine. A black SUV was waiting by the curb with all of the subtlety of a tiger tank. Jet strode over and the rear door opened as if by magic, revealing the director in the back, the vehicle smelling like an ashtray.

"Hop in," he said, and Jet did as instructed. The driver looked in the rearview mirror at the director, who nodded at him. "Take a walk. Get me another pack of cigarettes or something."

The driver exited the SUV, leaving them alone.

"I wanted to congratulate you personally," the director said. "That was nice work."

"Didn't go as planned, though."

The director nodded. "Things seldom do these days. But you pulled off a minor miracle, and for that you have my gratitude." He hesitated. "The National Party won the election, which was the second worst possible outcome for us – Nabiyev being the first. But we'll figure out a way to make things work. It looks like they're going to follow through with their plans to nationalize everything that already isn't, and open up a new round of bidding for the oil rights, but that's not your problem."

Jet returned his nod. "The station chief did a remarkable job. Above and beyond the call. Shame to waste a valuable resource like that in a backwater."

The director studied her. "Did he really? Well, I'll have to see what might be more suitable for him, then. Thank you for bringing it to my attention." He coughed, the sound wet and phlegmy. "Nice save on Nabiyev."

"I knew there was no way he'd have an expensive bottle of cologne and leave it behind. It was just a matter of time."

"Quick thinking," he agreed, studying her with interest. "I hear you're pretty beaten up."

She shrugged. "I'll live." She knew he would already have read her debriefing report, which would have a summary of her injuries, so wasn't surprised that he mentioned it. "But I'll never do anything like that again. It was completely upside down from the word go. From now on, you want me for something, I'm involved in the planning – and if I don't like the situation, I reserve the right to bow out."

"We can discuss all this some other time," he deflected. "For now, heal, and love up that gorgeous little daughter of yours as much as you can."

"I mean it. You stuck me into a bad situation, and you had to know the odds of me walking out of it were slim."

"I know you mean it. I did what I had to do on short notice. You did what you had to. It's over. We move on."

"Some with broken ribs."

"I won't call on you for anything that isn't absolutely top priority. I promise. In the meantime, enjoy your new life. It could be years before we have anything else requiring your skills."

"Just remember. I plan it or I walk."

His eyes hardened, but his voice stayed flat. "I heard you the first time." He coughed again. "Anyway, congratulations on a job well done."

"Thanks." She reached for the door handle. He stopped her. She met his gaze without flinching.

"We'll be keeping an eye on you," he said, his voice soft. "To ensure you're not bothered by anyone."

She nodded. "And you owe me a nice little house somewhere quiet. With a yard for my daughter."

"Of course I do. I'll see what we can come up with over the next few weeks. Meanwhile, heal."

She stepped from the car and pushed the door closed with her hip. The driver saw her from near the corner market and made his way back to the SUV. Jet turned her face up into the sun and let it warm her skin. She closed her eyes, the tension from the meeting fading, and a light breeze from the water stirred her hair as she breathed in the Mediterranean air.

The director's message, and the real purpose of the meeting, had been clear – Mossad would have them under surveillance, so she wasn't to try anything stupid, like disappearing again. In return, she'd get her house, and they'd leave her alone…for a time.

And if all went well, she, Matt, and Hannah would live happily ever after – or at least as long as *ever* lasted in Jet's world. It didn't seem like much after risking her neck twice in a week, but for now, reunited with her daughter and the love of her life in an oasis by the sea, a brief slice of ever would more than definitely do.

ABOUT THE AUTHOR

Featured in *The Wall Street Journal*, *The Times*, and *The Chicago Tribune*, Russell Blake is *The NY Times* and *USA Today* bestselling author of over forty novels.

Blake is co-author of *The Eye of Heaven* and *The Solomon Curse*, with legendary author Clive Cussler. Blake's novel *King of Swords* has been translated into German, *The Voynich Cypher* into Bulgarian, and his JET novels into Spanish, German, and Czech.

Blake writes under the moniker R.E. Blake in the NA/YA/Contemporary Romance genres. Novels include *Less Than Nothing, More Than Anything*, and *Best Of Everything*.

Having resided in Mexico for a dozen years, Blake enjoys his dogs, fishing, boating, tequila and writing, while battling world domination by clowns. His thoughts, such as they are, can be found at his blog: RussellBlake.com

Visit RussellBlake.com for updates

or subscribe to: RussellBlake.com/contact/mailing-list

BOOKS BY RUSSELL BLAKE

Co-authored with Clive Cussler
THE EYE OF HEAVEN
THE SOLOMON CURSE

Thrillers
FATAL EXCHANGE
FATAL DECEPTION
THE GERONIMO BREACH
ZERO SUM
THE DELPHI CHRONICLE TRILOGY
THE VOYNICH CYPHER
SILVER JUSTICE
UPON A PALE HORSE
DEADLY CALM
RAMSEY'S GOLD
EMERALD BUDDHA
THE GODDESS LEGACY

The Assassin Series
KING OF SWORDS
NIGHT OF THE ASSASSIN
RETURN OF THE ASSASSIN
REVENGE OF THE ASSASSIN
BLOOD OF THE ASSASSIN
REQUIEM FOR THE ASSASSIN
RAGE OF THE ASSASSIN

The Day After Never Series
THE DAY AFTER NEVER – BLOOD HONOR
THE DAY AFTER NEVER – PURGATORY ROAD
THE DAY AFTER NEVER – COVENANT
THE DAY AFTER NEVER – RETRIBUTION

Made in the USA
San Bernardino, CA
01 April 2020